P9-EDH-830

ECHOES

ECHOES

Jackie Hyman

WILLIAM MORROW AND COMPANY, INC.
NEW YORK

Recognizing the importance of preserving what has been written, it is the policy of William Morrow and Company, Inc., and its imprints and affiliates to have the books it publishes printed on acid-free paper, and we exert our best efforts to that end.

Library of Congress Cataloging-in-Publication Data

Hyman, Jackie, 1949-
Echoes/Jackie Hyman.
p. cm.
ISBN 0-688-09250-0
I. Title.
PS3558.Y467E24 1990
813'.54—dc20

90-5925
CIP

Printed in the United States of America

First Edition

1 2 3 4 5 6 7 8 9 10

For Kurt, Ari, and Hunter

ECHOES

PROLOGUE

March 1973
Nice, France

"What do you mean, we need tickets to get *off* the train? We showed them when we got on, in Paris."

"You must show them again." The uniformed man turned coldly away from Daddy to take the stubs of a well-dressed French couple who breezed by, indifferent to the bewildered Americans on the platform.

Laura stood motionless as her mother rummaged through her oversize purse. "Oh, James, what if we threw them out?"

Above them, the sign said NICE. That was an easy word; even Laura could read it. Except it didn't mean the same thing here that it did at home. Not at all.

"Then you will have to pay again," the man in the uniform said as he collected more slips of paper. A shadow moved behind him, not quite at the same time.

This place wasn't real. Laura could feel shadows all around, closing in. They should never have come here.

"We can't afford—"

"Daddy." Laura tugged at his sleeve. "I want to go home."

"Honey, please—"

"Could you have put them in your wallet?" Mommy said.

"I don't think—"

Couldn't they see that they had to leave before the shadows thickened and reached out for her? "Mommy, Daddy, let's get back on the train! I want to go home!"

"Laura, be quiet!"

She took a step backward, and then another. A stocky woman in a thick coat brushed by and muttered in annoyance.

Behind them, the train hissed.

"I have to go back!" Laura shouted, and ran.

She darted between people, ducked an outstretched hand, and

clambered up the steps into the train, biting her lip to keep from crying when she banged her knee. The hardest part was not losing her grip on Pooh Bear.

"James! James, catch her!" came Mommy's voice from behind. "The train's going to leave!"

Laura ran down the corridor. The door to one compartment opened, and someone thrust a case into the hall. It was a big black bag that looked as if it might have stethoscopes and needles and bottles of nasty medicine inside.

She jumped over it. At the end of the hall, the door stood open, and Laura ran through to the next car. From outside, close by, her mother called, "Baby! Please stop! You might get hurt!"

Behind her, Laura heard her father stumble over the bag and say one of those words she wasn't supposed to know about.

As she pelted through the second car, people called after her, but she couldn't understand them. A boy not much older than Laura tried to block her, but she plowed right into him, and he went over like a bowling pin.

A minute later, as she squeezed into the next car, she heard her father yell, "Laura! You cut this out!"

In the third car, she had a clear shot all the way—except that when she reached the far door, it wouldn't open. The train shook as Daddy ran toward her, and then he slammed to a halt as a bent-up old man with a cane stepped into his path.

Laura grabbed her teddy bear and plunged into an empty compartment. Standing on the seat, she could just reach the lowest luggage rack. Pooh Bear landed on the top one at her first throw, and Laura began to haul herself up, just like on the playground at home.

The train uttered a great wheeze. It was going to leave!

Only, without warning, something black came at her, something tall and black with great long arms that wrapped themselves around Laura's waist and pulled. She clung to the luggage rack and screamed.

"Honey! Oh, God, what are you doing up there?" It was Daddy, reaching past the tall man in black robes and catching Laura under the arms. "You look like a little monkey. Oh, Lord." As he lowered her against his chest, he was half laughing and half sobbing. Out the window, he shouted, "I got her, Kate! It's all right!" To the dark man, he said, "Thank you, Father."

Daddy carried Laura and Pooh Bear back down the corridor. She tried to struggle, but all her energy had left. "We have to go home," she whispered. "Please, Daddy."

"You silly thing," he said. "This train's going on to Monte Carlo. You wouldn't have gotten back, anyway."

When they reached the platform, Mommy hugged them both and said, "I found the tickets in my pocket."

"Let's get the hell out of here," Daddy said.

"Are you okay, baby?" Mommy asked as they walked back toward their luggage.

The little girl nodded. But she didn't stop trembling for a long, long time.

CHAPTER ONE

August 1992
San Paradiso, California

The house on Beatrice Lane looked exactly as he had left it that morning, except that the gardening crew had trimmed the seeding tips off the weeds in what had once been a lawn. A sprinkler lay rusting below the heat-singed skeleton of a bird-of-paradise plant, relic of one of Emma's long-ago landscaping binges. Still, the Spanish-style house retained a certain dignity, like an elegant lady fallen on hard times.

Joe Pickard, the mayor of San Paradiso, California, retrieved Monday's edition of the *Paradise Herald* on his way inside, then halted in the arched entranceway as a mass of close-held heat billowed against his face. Sweat trickled beneath his shirt collar as he crossed the fading rose-patterned carpet to switch on the window air conditioner.

It choked into life in the heavy fog of old cigarette smoke. A plume of cold air brushed across Joe's arm, and the staleness parted grudgingly, then closed in again as he moved toward the kitchen.

There was nothing out of place here, either.

It was all right then. Maybe. He dumped the newspaper on the table, shrugged out of his suit jacket, and jerked off the tie he'd already loosened in the car. The pack of cigarettes in his breast pocket was rumpled but nearly full. He lighted one and opened the newspaper.

A two-car fatal on the San Diego Freeway. Governor Armand Fisher once again denying that he'd pressured major corporations for campaign funds, and agreeing to appoint a nonpartisan panel "to clear my name." Joe had already heard about that this morning, from the governor's aide.

Senator Cruise Long was speaking tomorrow at the Orange County news editors' luncheon in San Paradiso. As mayor, Joe had been invited to sit at the head table, so he knew about that, too.

So far so good.

Joe Pickard crossed to the refrigerator and pulled out a cold beer. He stood there drinking it until the can was empty.

Emma used to carp at him about his beer drinking. Maybe she wouldn't have minded so goddamn much if it had been scotch. Or if he'd gotten elected state attorney general. Hell, it wasn't his fault politics weren't what they used to be, and the glitz boys were taking over. Used to be Sacramento was a private club, and the old boys ran things. He'd come along at the wrong time, that was all.

But you couldn't tell Emma that. She always knew just where to stick the needle. She noticed right away when his hair started to recede and his pants got a little tight. That's what beer does, she used to say. Beer and no guts, and gonads for brains.

She wasn't even impressed when he got elected mayor, because in San Paradiso it was the city manager who really ran things. The mayor was mostly a figurehead, chosen by his fellow city council members for a one-year term.

"They think you're somebody because you used to be in the state assembly," Emma had said during one of their arguments. "But you're a loser, Joe. Mom was right. Thank God we never had children, because they'd probably be losers like you."

She'd known just how to piss him off. Enough to grab that sagging throat of hers, enough to . . . No, not that much. Thank God, not quite that much.

Everybody wanted to pound some asshole into the pavement once in a while, didn't they? Last week, that was a coincidence.

The mayor of San Paradiso went into the bathroom to take a pee and came out a few minutes later stripped to his Jockey shorts and undershirt. In the refrigerator, he found a salami and a wedge of cheese.

Now where the hell was his knife?

Not in the nearly empty utensil drawer. Not in the cupboard with the plastic plates and cups he'd bought at Target after Emma got custody of the china. Finally, he gave up and hacked away at the meat with a steak knife.

He needed to remember, that was the thing. Put today's events all down exactly the way they'd happened, so he could say right off where he'd been at any given moment. If anyone should ask.

On the yellowing pad that used to be a grocery list, he wrote, *Eight-thirty to ten* A.M. *Blue Gull Café. Breakfast with governor's aide. Mel Kawasaki. No, Kawakami. Discussed using Orange County influence to help governor defend against accusations. Witnesses: Mel.*

He thought for a minute, and then added the name of the waitress. Gina Big-tits.

Joe piled the salami and cheese on a paper towel and carried it, along with the pad and pencil and another beer, into the living room. He switched on the news.

The international stuff came first. Scientists investigating the earthquake that had killed more than three hundred people last week in Paris had discovered a rift slashing across fifteen miles near Fontainebleau. And Ayatollah Al-Hadassi's revolutionary army had advanced to within twenty miles of the Saudi Arabian capital of Riyadh. But that was far, far away from San Paradiso, California.

"In Sacramento today, Governor Fisher announced that he will appoint a committee . . ."

Joe glared at the shined-up asshole posing as an anchorman, with his smug half-smile and hey-ain't-I-a-big-fuckin'-deal voice. Governor Fisher was a good man, a loyal man. He hadn't forgotten Joe. He was going to come through with something sooner or later for his Orange County campaign manager.

On the pad beside him, Joe wrote, *Ten A.M., give or take a few. San Paradiso Car Wash. Witnesses: Hell, who knows? Ten-thirty A.M. Dry cleaners.*

On-screen, Governor Fisher's patrician face was moving, and some words were coming out.

Joe wrote, *Eleven A.M. Conference re: amending a will, my office. Witnesses: client, Rhondie.* Rhondie, the secretary at his private law office, could account for his whereabouts the rest of the day. He'd even eaten a sandwich at his desk, reviewing a breach-of-contract suit due in court tomorrow.

On TV, two dogs raced toward a bowl of brown pebbles, slobbering as if it were T-bone steak. Cut. Flashing lights. A brunette with huge boobs was cooing something about her jeans. She looked a little like Gina Big-tits, only glossier.

One of these days, he ought to teach that slut some manners. Like not to call him "Mayorsy" in front of the governor's aide. Like not to get so damn busy flapping her mouth at the musclehead at the next table that she forgot to refill their coffee. Not to treat him like some jerk. He knew exactly how the sweat would shine on her face when he got her alone, when they had their little talk. . . .

They're just thoughts. Like I've always had. That's all.

On TV, the blow-dried asshole prattled on about a Mediterranean fruit fly captured in Gardena. Joe leaned forward to flick off the set.

"Police in San Paradiso"—Joe's hand hovered inches from the "on-off" button—"say a man walking a dog in Paradise Park this afternoon found the body of a woman stabbing victim. She has been identified as twenty-three-year-old Gina Lopez, a waitress at the Blue Gull Café in San Paradiso."

Joe stared at the screen. His throat didn't seem to be working right. *God, no.*

"Lopez, who got off work at ten A.M., was a student at Cypress College."

What time did Mel What's-his-face leave the restaurant? A few minutes before ten? Then I went to the car wash. Straight to the car wash. Then the dry cleaner.

"Police are exploring the possibility that today's murder is linked to the stabbing death last week of San Paradiso city employee Marla Rivers. Her purse has not been recovered, and robbery was suspected. However, Miss Lopez's purse was found only a few feet from the body with her paycheck inside."

That ugly cracked vinyl purse. How had it gotten into his car? He'd found it in the backseat and recognized Marla Rivers's name on the driver's license. That stuck-up typist in the planning department, the one who sniffed as if she smelled something bad when he offered her a ride. He'd wanted to . . . to . . . But he hadn't. All he'd done was bury her purse under a clot of smelly rags in a trash bin, before he even knew she'd been murdered.

How the hell had it gotten in his car? The windows were shut, the doors were locked.

He still had the list he'd drawn up for that afternoon. Straight from work to Colonel Sanders, home by the start of the six o'clock news. No time for a blackout, even if he believed in such things. No blood on his clothes. He couldn't have done it. No way.

Today, he'd had the same kind of vicious thoughts about Gina. Only they didn't mean anything. They never had, all these years. Except that once with Emma, when she pushed him too far and he held the knife to her throat. She begged and sobbed and it made him feel all-powerful, but he stopped. Somehow he stopped before the knife did more than nick the skin above her collarbone. That seemed like so long ago. Hushed up, in return for all his money, everything except this house, and even then he'd had to pay off her share. Shit, he'd had thoughts like this back in high school, and nobody had died then.

He'd even thought it was an advantage, in a way. Learning how to control his temper had taught him strategy, how to get on people's good side. How to brownnose his law professors, make friends with guys on the way up, like Armand Fisher. Only after things fell apart with Emma, somehow he'd lost the touch. Maybe it was her undisguised contempt. If your own wife didn't believe in you . . .

He looked down at the greasy paper towel. What he needed was more salami and cheese. Hell, he was just tired and hungry. So he'd had a few nasty ideas about Gina. Nothing the whore hadn't deserved. Besides, he hadn't found *her* purse in his car.

Joe went into the kitchen and glared at the steak knife. Where the hell was . . . ?

He walked into the spare bedroom. Nothing there but some dust. The laundry room. It smelled like something had begun to putrefy, but that was the way his laundry always smelled. Emma used to warn him about leaving wet towels around.

The bathroom.

He'd been in here already to pee. Nothing. Nothing peculiar about the john, the sink, the dusty venetian blinds. Joe let his breath out slowly.

Then he noticed the fleck of brown on the shower curtain, just above the moldy edge.

Joe ripped the curtain back. His knife lay in the tub, brown beads frozen on the long sharp blade.

It was happening again.

CHAPTER TWO

Heat. The earthy smell of sun on skin. Briny air, mewing gulls, the tinny hum of a transistor radio. The feather tickle of long, thickly curling hair on her neck and shoulders.

She turned onto her stomach, enjoying the sensation as her breasts pressed against the beach towel. Could the men see how high the red swimsuit rode on her hips? Did they feel as hot as she did? But she was safe from them, safe in her fantasy. She could hide forever behind the sunglasses, secret as the mysterious inlets of her body. No one would recognize her.

From where she lay on the Corona del Mar beach, Rita Crane Long had a close-up view of the volleyball game. College men—UC Irvine, judging by the T-shirt that clung to one sweaty torso—with young, strong bodies, unlined faces, shallow, hungry eyes. They'd become aware of her the moment she crossed the sand and spread her towel. It was no accident the ball had flown in her direction several times.

She was playing her own game, and it tasted delicious. She could smell her musky arousal. Tonight, Cruise would enjoy it. He would think it was for him. Only she would know that her passion belonged to that boy with the chopped-off blond hair, and then to the dark-skinned one who might be Middle Eastern, and then, one after another, to as many as it took to satisfy her imagination.

No one would ever know. Not even the men she used in her dreams.

A shadow cooled her, and she looked up. In front of her stood one of the college boys, a thick-chested specimen with dark hair. Hispanic, maybe, like Rita's mother.

"Listen," he said, tossing the ball from one hand to the other, "we're taking a break. You want me to get you a Coke or something?"

Rita drew her long legs into a peak as she sat up. "I'd love one, but I'm afraid I have to be going."

"Need a ride?" As she stood, the youth dropped his ball and helped her shake the sand out of the towel. "Maybe we could get something to eat?"

Up close, he was dismayingly artless. Too many words, such bony movements. Not even tempting. But then, she didn't want to be tempted, not in real life.

"I'm meeting my husband." Rita smiled behind her sunglasses. "Thanks, though."

"Win some, lose some," said the boy, and ambled away to join his friends.

"Barbie called." Cruise Long knotted his tie in front of the cheval glass.

"Broke again?" Rita stretched beneath the sheets, waking up slowly. Cruise's daughter, from his first marriage, rarely called unless she needed money. His son, Beau, rarely called at all.

"She's getting married," Cruise said. "In December. He's in computers."

"Don't tell me she wants you to give her away." Rita reached for her peignoir. "And pay for the wedding, I presume?"

"Both." Cruise sat on the edge of the bed. Despite his silvering hair, his face was remarkably unlined for a man of fifty-nine who had survived two failed marriages, two hard-fought races for the U.S. Senate, and a heart attack three years ago. "Do you mind?"

"Far be it from me to interfere." Rita stepped nude from the bed and slipped into the peignoir, letting it fall open suggestively. Her sexuality had been the lure that rescued her four years ago from a lukewarm career as an actress. She wasn't twenty-seven anymore, but Cruise seemed more than satisfied. "I am invited, aren't I?"

"Of course." Her husband reached out possessively to cup the curve of her hip. "Barbie has nothing against you."

Nothing, no. Except that there was only a few years' difference in their ages, and that in Barbara's eyes Rita was just another one of Cruise's playmates, like the ones he'd run around with while he was still married the first time.

There had been another wife in between, a mistake who lasted only a year and served as a useful buffer. Not even Cruise's children could blame Rita for their parents' divorce. But that didn't mean they had to like her.

"Busy schedule today?" She brushed her hair so it fell into dark seductive waves, and took a sideways glance out the window. The August sun was already baking the stately homes that stretched below them toward the ocean. She loved this house in the hills above Newport Beach. And the rented Georgian-style house in Washington, too, but it always felt so temporary.

"You haven't forgotten about lunch, I hope." Cruise moved away, already drawing into his statesman persona. Confident, well-briefed on current issues by a flotilla of aides, he was equipped by nature with invisible antennae that permitted him to negotiate the shark-infested waterways of politics. "I'll be expecting you about noon at the hotel."

"Of course." Rita was pleased that he included her in his public appearances, such as today's speech to Orange County newspaper editors. His first wife had stayed home with the children; his second had been an embarrassment. Rita was glad he considered her an asset outside the bedroom as well as in it. Any woman who took for granted her relationship with Cruise Long was a damn fool. "What else is on the agenda today?"

"Oh, I'm meeting a couple of the editors for a drink first." Cruise checked himself in the mirror and rearranged a strand of hair. "Until then, I'll be at my office."

Rita leaned forward for a kiss, careful not to rumple her husband's suit. "You were terrific last night."

Cruise squeezed her breast lightly. "I'm planning on a replay this evening. See you at lunch."

After he left, Rita sat at her dressing table, her body on fire. Yes, her stallions had been wonderful.

Downstairs, she could hear the door to the garage shut behind Cruise, and then his Mercedes purred away down the manicured street.

Her jeweled watch said a quarter to ten, but Rita felt no need to hurry and dress. The election was almost two years past, thank God, with its endless round of breakfasts, luncheons, teas, dinners. It would be another few years before she was called upon to hustle around the state reminding the minority groups that her mother came from one of the state's oldest Hispanic families, or cajoling groups of military wives with the fact that her father had been a sailor when he met her mother at the USO in San Diego. No need to pretend, just now, that their union had been a romantic fable instead of the disaster it really was, or that she had grown up loved and admired instead of as a half-breed who belonged nowhere, except perhaps in the backseats of her boyfriends' cars.

A tap at the door startled her. "Mrs. Long?" It was the

housekeeper, Ramona. "I have your breakfast, and the mail is here."

"Thank you." Rita waited as the woman entered with a tray and set it on a small table. "The senator and I will be lunching out."

Ramona nodded and departed. Her cooking was unexciting—scrambled eggs and toast for breakfast, usually a roast or chicken for dinner—but she'd come highly recommended for her reliability and her discretion. The last thing a senator needed was servants who gossiped.

Folding herself into a chair, Rita sipped her coffee and glanced over the mail. There were the usual bills and advertisements, a copy of *Vogue,* and a large manila envelope with no return address. The postmark read, SAN PARADISO.

Rita hesitated. She didn't know anyone in the town located a few miles northwest of Newport, yet the envelope was addressed to her. Well, no doubt it had to do with one of the charities on whose boards she served.

Her silver letter opener sliced through the paper, and she drew out a white folder. On the front, a label bore the typed words FOR YOUR EYES ONLY. It reminded her of a James Bond movie.

Rita flipped open the folder, pulled out an eight-by-ten black-and-white photograph and turned it sideways.

It was a photograph of her, naked, lying on her back on an unmade bed in what looked like a cheap hotel room, the far wall covered by blackout curtains. One man rode astride her while another watched in the background, nude from the waist down, smoking a cigarette.

She remembered their faces at once. Two of the college boys who'd been playing volleyball on the beach.

Dear God, was this someone's idea of a joke? She must have been recognized.

But . . . it looked so much like her. Where could they have found so perfect a model? Paste-up, that was possible, but she couldn't recall ever seeing a photograph of her own face tilted at that angle.

And by what bizarre chance had they replicated her fantasy?

Rita pawed through the folder and the envelope, searching for a note, but found none.

She stared at the photograph again, seeking some obvious discrepancy. But the knees were sharp, just like hers, and the toes long and slightly bony.

It had to be blackmail. The blackmailer would write again, or call, and threaten to show this to Cruise. He'd gone to a great deal of trouble to make it look like her. But she could prove him wrong.

Rita went to her rolltop desk and rummaged through the compartments until she found a magnifying glass. She switched on a lamp and examined the photograph closely, moving along the woman's breast.

No. Impossible. But there it was, the blue ink almost invisible: a tiny heart tattoo she always kept covered. He couldn't have known.

She'd seen the men only yesterday. Who could have set this up?

And how had he read her thoughts?

CHAPTER THREE

It was the Issue That Would Not Die, the one that always hovered between them, but until now it hadn't seemed all that urgent. This time, though, Lew brought up the subject while fixing breakfast, and when he started speaking in his deep judicial tones, Laura knew something had changed.

"One of these days somebody's going to find out about us." He flipped their pancakes over expertly, a skill he'd developed years ago while working as a short-order cook to pay his way through law school. "It isn't going to look good."

"I suppose not." Laura poured out two cups of coffee and added cream and sugar to them both. She liked small, orderly chores. "But it's not like we've done anything wrong."

"Being in the media, you ought to know how much appearances count for." Lew slid the pancakes onto plates and carried them to the table. The August sun was already scorching through the blinds of his condominium, stamping fade lines across the tan carpet. Despite the air-conditioning, a red rose drooped in its vase between the salt and pepper shakers.

"'Being in the media'? Uh-oh. This must be serious; I feel like I'm about to be sentenced." Laura smiled and fought to keep it from turning into a yawn. She'd been up late last night, attending a congressman's fund-raiser, and she had to write it up before she covered Senator Long's speech at lunchtime. It was almost seven-thirty, and she was going to have to hustle.

"Something odd happened to me yesterday." Lew poured a dollop of syrup over his pancakes. "Marcus Johns said he was going to be sorry to lose me. It seems he'd heard some rumor I plan to run for governor."

"Do you?" Laura grew very still. It was awkward for a political reporter to be sleeping with a judge of the Orange County Superior Court, but nothing like sleeping with a gubernatorial candidate. If

Lew ran for governor, they'd have to cool it for a while. A long while.

"If I were, I wouldn't let anyone know about it at this point. Certainly not my presiding judge." Lew finished off a large bite of pancake before continuing, "Armand Fisher and I are both Republicans, after all. Besides, I don't want people to think I'm going to spend the next two years politicking from the bench."

He hadn't denied it. "You didn't answer my question." Laura didn't want her neat, predictable life to change. The stability left her mind clear to focus on ferreting out facts, filling in the holes in real-life puzzles. Reporting, she sometimes felt, meant bringing at least a semblance of order out of chaos.

Well, maybe she didn't want life *too* simple. Not so simple she didn't have Lew to complicate it.

Six months ago, she'd been helping out with an overload of trials and had tried to interview Judge Lewis Tarkenton about a libel suit. They'd both stood there in the corridor staring at each other the way they were doing now. Pulling at each other, resisting, and yet knowing that they were going to succumb.

She'd swapped cases with Jane Lomax, the regular courts reporter, removing the immediate conflict of interest, and two nights later she and Lew went to bed together.

It was more than a physical attraction, she'd known from the beginning. Laura wouldn't waste time and energy on a man whom she couldn't respect, who wouldn't challenge her mind and her spirit. She'd broken up months earlier with a radio reporter, because, in spite of his wit and playfulness, she kept sensing a central fuzziness where his integrity ought to be.

Not Lew. Lew was so honest he didn't even cheat on his taxes.

Now, he reached across the table to stroke the back of her hand. That he did it absentmindedly endeared him to Laura all the more. Being taken a little for granted made her feel so permanent.

"I haven't decided," Lew said finally. "It's about time we had a governor in this state with some vision, and I'm egotistic enough to think that might be me. But I don't have to decide for another year."

"Any idea how the rumor got started?" The reporter in Laura wouldn't let the matter drop.

"None at all. This is the first time I've mentioned it to anyone."

"What about the kids?"

"That's another reason for not jumping into any decisions." Lew had been battling his ex-brother-in-law for the two months since his sister, Sarah, collapsed with an aneurysm, a small organic time bomb that in the course of one sunny afternoon had changed two children's lives forever.

There was a custody hearing coming up in two weeks. "Do you really think any judge would pick that drunk over you? I mean, he abandoned them years ago."

"He's putting on a great act for the social workers." Lew shook his head. "Hell, I'm a judge, and I don't know what *I'd* do about Kyle and Terri. A father is a father, after all. How can a stranger ever really know what goes on in a family?"

"You're always so damn fair," Laura said. "The guy's a bastard."

"And you're always so damn feisty." Lew grinned. "Which is why I'm a judge and you're a reporter." Reluctantly, he glanced up at the plant-draped oak clock in the kitchen. "I hate to bring it up, but don't you have to go?"

It was quarter to eight. "Oh, God, why couldn't I have been born rich?" Laura dashed into the bedroom for her overnight bag. They'd both agreed it would be too awkward to live together. Once the gossip started, Lew would be blamed for every anonymous bit of information leaked by prosecutors, defense attorneys, or police captains. And her objectivity might come under question.

"Take care," Lew said. "Don't worry. We don't have to make any decisions for a long while yet."

"Thank God," Laura said.

They kissed, and she was off in her aging red Honda Civic, scooting along Paradise Avenue toward San Paradiso.

Damn it, Lew *would* make a good governor. He'd been a prosecutor, an assemblyman, and now a judge; more than that, he blended the old sixties ideals with hardheaded practicality. A good choice for a state known for its curious blend of radical voices and conservative governors.

And me, a politician's wife?

She was too forthright. She'd only get herself and Lew into trouble. Laura shook her head and sighed.

The two-story stucco box that housed the *Herald* squatted like a bulldog in the sunlight. Laura parked her Honda in the lot and entered the rear door, bypassing the backshop and heading upstairs.

There was a timeless quality to the newsroom, she noted as she entered, as if it were suspended in a kind of technological Neverland. The same flat lights illuminated the same blond desks, day or night; identical computer terminals flashed their waiting cursors; the air smelled faintly of photographic chemicals. Along the walls, blowup color photos froze forever the Sunday pictorial smiles of frolicking children and the dramatic moods of sky and ocean.

Laura tossed her purse under her desk, which was near the center of the large room. Other reporters trickled in; a lone woman sat typing at her terminal in the Features department at the back, while a couple of bleary-eyed men drank coffee in Sports, which maintained its rumpled identity behind a row of file cabinets.

Next to Laura's desk, amid a pile of files and reference books, Steve Orkney, the police reporter, pecked away at his keyboard. He didn't even look up, just said, "Hi, gorgeous. Break up with the mystery man yet?"

"Not yet. Don't clear your calendar." She tried to keep her tone light, but for once their mock flirtation didn't seem funny.

Laura retrieved her tape recorder and began transcribing the congressman's speech onto the computer screen, skipping the half that was bullshit. Lost in the process of shaping the story, she didn't come up for air until two or three hours later, when the editor, Greg Evans, stopped by her desk.

"You on deadline? Can I see you in my office?" It sounded like a request, but it was a summons.

Laura forwarded her story through the computer to the metro editor. "I'm up."

Greg led the way. His office was opposite Photo, with a picture-window view of the newsroom. He left the door open and gestured her into a plush chair.

"You're covering Cruise Long today?" The editor sat on the edge of the desk, facing her. His hair was blond, slightly shaggy, the way a lot of men wore it who grew up during the sixties.

She nodded. "I'm due at the luncheon in about an hour."

"What's your focus?"

"There's his proposal for immigration reform." Although Greg ruled with a velvet touch, Laura always felt slightly nervous in his presence. She was only five years out of journalism school, after all, while Greg had covered some of the most important stories of the past few decades before settling into the role of editor. "I was going to ask him about the remark that was quoted in *Newsweek*, about restructuring the INS."

Greg shook his head. "You'll be lucky to get in one or two questions, and there are better ones."

Laura wished she'd spent more time preparing instead of thinking about Lew. "I usually come up with my best questions about thirty seconds ahead of time," she admitted.

"Like asking a certain assemblyman why he's lying about his voting record?"

They both smiled. Laura had popped that question out of the blue at a Republican fund-raising dinner, dispelling the hail-fellow-well-met atmosphere and provoking a string of denials so complex they bordered on the nonsensical.

It had been considered an act of sheer madness when Greg tapped her to fill the seat of the paper's departing political reporter three years before. Laura wasn't devious enough, had been the general sentiment in the newsroom.

But that was exactly why Greg had picked her, he told Laura privately. Her direct approach, her intolerance for dishonesty, were exactly what Greg was looking for to shake up the area's complacent politicians. At the same time, Laura had worked hard to brush up her background knowledge and sharpen her technique.

Still, her editor was usually way ahead of her. She had almost, but not quite, grown used to it.

"The Senate has a vote due on aid to China," Greg said. "Long's been making sympathetic noises, but a lot of the Republican leadership don't believe in giving wheat to communists, especially since they've wiped out enough dissidents to fill a couple of football stadiums."

"I'm sure the starving babies are all hard-line followers of Marx." Laura tried to follow Greg's thinking, to figure out what Long's vote on the issue would reveal. "Cruise likes to promote himself as the champion of innocent victims. But maybe right now he cares more about keeping in the good graces of his party."

"Exactly. The question behind the question is whether he plans to run for president." Greg propped his feet up on an empty chair.

"So we're trying to figure out the senator's ambitions from his vote on China?" she said. "I'll do my best."

"A couple of other editors and I are having drinks with him before lunch. If he lets anything drop, I'll fill you in," Greg said. "Oh, and I think you should try to line up an interview with his wife."

"Rita the Bimbo?"

"Rita the maybe future first lady. Besides, I thought you two hit it off. It sounded like it, that article you wrote during the election."

"She's an actress. She gave me charming quotes, and I used them," Laura said.

"Rita may be our best bet," Greg added as she rose to leave. "She's not nearly as cagey as her husband."

Laura went to the ladies' room and gave herself a quick once-over with pressed powder and a hairbrush. She finished touching up her lipstick and went out of the ladies' room humming the old Beatles' song "Lovely Rita."

On her way to the hotel, Laura stopped for a red light at Paradise Avenue when a flash of color caught her eye from the corner of the sidewalk.

A birdlike old woman stepped down from the curb. The dyed red hair, heavily rouged cheeks, and pale, knowing eyes seemed to belong to a long-ago time, a distant place.

I know her from somewhere. The part I've forgotten.

Mist gathered at the edges of Laura's sight. She closed her eyes and opened them again, but it didn't go away. It swirled around the old woman, giving the impression that she was swathed in a hooded robe.

Clammy air riffled along Laura's arms. She felt as if she were looking at a surrealist 3-D painting, one that appeared normal when turned a certain way. But at a different angle, you glimpsed another reality entirely.

A horn blasted, and in a blink the murky strangeness vanished. The old woman had crossed the road and turned a corner of the sidewalk, and the light was green.

Disoriented by her hallucination, Laura had to force herself to operate the car. Shifting gears with intense concentration, she swung onto Campanile Way.

What she'd seen felt like some kind of . . . echo. Maybe it meant she was beginning to remember things from her early childhood.

Into Laura's mind popped Aunt Ellen's face, warm and reassuring. Most children didn't remember much from before they were seven, Ellen said. Besides, losing both your parents in one year would knock anyone for a loop.

Laura knew, because she'd been told, that she'd been born in Providence, Rhode Island, where her father was an art-history student at Brown; that her parents had moved to France the year she turned seven so he could research his dissertation. It had been, Uncle Fred once said, a comparison of how Spain's civil wars had affected the art of Goya and Picasso.

Only he'd never written it, as far as Laura knew. He'd become obsessed with strange ideas to the point of madness. Aunt Ellen had mentioned the subject reluctantly, after much prodding, and quickly dropped it again.

He'd come home after Laura's mother died in a car accident, and left the little girl with her aunt and uncle in Cincinnati. A year later, he died of a heart attack in a Washington, D.C., hotel room.

Not much to go by, a few bare facts, when you grew older and tried to piece together your identity. Laura felt sometimes as if she'd stepped out of a void when she was seven.

She shook her head. That hallucination—Lew would probably say it meant Laura hadn't got enough sleep last night.

Trust him to come up with a rational explanation for anything. He and Aunt Ellen would get along great.

Laura turned onto Beach Boulevard and headed for the Hotel Paradise.

There was something so sterile about the seven-story steel-and-glass structure with its plush lobby and broad reception desk that it dispelled the last of Laura's lingering anxiety.

She strode to the ballroom. At a little before noon, the room was just starting to fill up. Rita Long stood at the foot of the dais, chatting idly with Mayor Pickard.

Readjusting the heavy strap of her purse, Laura took an assessing look at the senator's wife. They'd talked when Laura covered her speech to the San Paradiso Republican Women's Club, but that had been two years ago, when Long was running for reelection.

Since then, Rita had let her dark hair grow into long, sleek curls. And she'd lost that gaunt, fashion-model look, along with the air of defensiveness. The senator's wife was maturing into her role.

Still, there was something about her that Laura found vaguely disturbing. A sensual air that recalled the half-remembered image of a woman lying on a couch, wearing white gauzy pajamas, her arms drawn back behind her head. A painting, perhaps, in one of her father's art books.

The mayor moved away. Laura crossed the room. "Mrs. Long? I don't know if you remember me; I'm Laura Bennett from the *Paradise Herald*. My paper would like to interview you, if it's convenient."

"Why?"

"You're always of interest to the public," Laura said, which was putting things diplomatically. "Let's face it, you bring a certain . . . glamour to the political scene."

A flicker of uncertainty softened the other woman's tense features, and it occurred to Laura that Rita was only a few years her senior. *I could be in her position someday, if Lew runs for office.*

"You did a nice job with that interview," Rita said. "It's unusual to be quoted accurately. But I'll have to ask my husband."

"Sure." Laura pulled out her notebook. "Could we set something up? You can always cancel if necessary."

The tall woman hesitated only a moment before retrieving a small calendar from her purse. "Thursday afternoon looks clear. Two o'clock, at my house."

"Okay if I bring a photographer?"

"Can't they take my picture today?" She indicated the knot of photographers checking out lighting on the dais. "Then I won't have to have my hair done."

"Good idea." Laura waved over the *Herald* photographer and set him to work taking mug shots of Rita. After excusing herself, Laura worked her way around the room, renewing acquaintances with city council members and the sprinkling of other political figures in attendance. Most of the guests were editors or broadcast-news directors.

Over the years, Laura had trained herself to make small talk, to probe lightly for information. Confrontation might make good television, but you antagonized your sources. Still, it wasn't always easy to tone down her instinctive bluntness.

Finally, Laura located the press table and sat down, exchanging greetings with reporters from the *Register* and the *Times*. She turned to watch Rita join her husband as he strode into the room.

There was something undeniably charismatic about Cruise Long that went beyond his appearance, although he was handsome enough. Like many leading lights in politics, he wasn't noteworthy for his ideals, his depth of knowledge, or his long-range view of the needs of the country. He was, on the other hand, reasonably but not excessively rich, deft at compromise, a resonant speaker, quick to see where the main chance lay, and boundlessly self-confident.

He and Rita made a striking couple. A lot of dumb jokes had gone around the newsroom when Senator Long married the sometime actress known for her roles as set decoration in teen-exploitation films. *Why did the senator give his wife a diamond necklace for a wedding present? He knew she'd like it because it's Long and hard.*

Then, gazing at the dais, Laura took a good look at Mayor Pickard for the first time that day. He was pulling at a thin strand of hair, and his jowly face had the pale cast of a newfound mushroom.

The city council traditionally selected a new mayor from among its ranks after Labor Day, and Pickard couldn't be too happy about the prospect of losing his title. He was the kind of guy who adored politics even though the affection was clearly one-sided. He'd served two terms in the assembly and one term as a state senator, but he'd lost in the primary when he made a bid for state attorney general. The San Paradiso City Council had been meant as a way station, but it was beginning to look as if it would be permanent.

The food arrived. As she ate, Laura listened idly to the gossip of the reporters around her, and wondered whether Greg had finessed any interesting tidbits out of Long.

As the sherbet was served, the president of the editors' association launched into introductions. Finally, Cruise Long rose to speak, nodding to acknowledge the applause. "On my way here today," he began, and then stopped. He frowned and shook his head dazedly. In the shocked hush, Laura felt embarrassed for the man. What was wrong with him? She watched Rita reach up to touch her husband's sleeve, and then, with a low moan, the senator collapsed over the podium.

He hung there for a moment, his eyes wide. He was looking straight at Laura. As if he were pleading for something, or trying to warn her.

The senator's face vanished, and Laura was staring into a hotel room, a big formal place decorated in colonial style. Only she wasn't really there; she was eight years old, and her father had collapsed at the foot of a bed, and he was staring at her desperately across the distance.

She remembered now, that flash of vision that she'd rejected as soon as she saw it. Too horrible for a child to accept, so awful she'd thrust it out of her consciousness for nearly twenty years.

Because the next morning, Aunt Ellen told Laura her father had died of a heart attack at the age of twenty-seven.

Now, the same thing was happening to Cruise Long, right in front of her.

CHAPTER FOUR

A half-dozen reporters arrived at the same time as Laura outside the emergency room at Fountain Valley Regional Hospital, where a sympathetic but firm policeman kept them at bay. They stood around, notebooks dangling, leaning against parked cars and trading speculation.

Laura could still hear the echoing thud of Senator Long's body hitting the floor, followed by Rita Long's scream.

Only when the paramedics raced in had Laura remembered that she was a reporter and that this was a story. She'd called in a bulletin to Bill White, her metro editor, and rushed over to the hospital. Greg remained at the hotel, interviewing witnesses.

Around her, the reporters' gossip hushed suddenly as Long's chief aide, Bob Fillipone, walked stiff-legged through the emergency entrance and faced them.

"Senator Long died at twelve forty-five this afternoon," he said. "He has a previous history of heart disease, but the coroner will be performing an autopsy." In answer to a question, he said, "There'll probably be an official cause of death by this afternoon, but you'll have to call the Coroner's Office."

Laura hurried to get the news desk on the phone. When she returned, Rita Long was coming out, guarded by Fillipone and the policeman. Some of the reporters called out questions, but she ignored them.

As the aide helped the senator's widow into a car, her eyes met Laura's.

"I'm sorry," Laura said. Unexpectedly, she felt tears pricking. What if it were Lew?

The door closed, breaking the contact. She waited a while longer, but the doctors wouldn't say anything, and the policeman wouldn't let them inside. The other reporters drifted away, and Laura drove back to the paper.

She couldn't shake the sense that there was more to Cruise Long's death than a simple heart attack. The look in his eyes at that final moment reminded her of that childhood vision of her father's death and the impression that he'd come to some horrifying realization. The oddest part was the feeling that both of them had been trying to communicate with Laura, as if she were the one person who could understand.

Steve Orkney raised an eyebrow as Laura sat down at her desk, but didn't speak. She must look as stunned as she felt.

The senator hardly knew Laura, probably didn't even remember her name. And he certainly didn't know her father. Other than the fact that both men had died of heart attacks, there was nothing to link them.

Forcing her attention on work, Laura put in a call to the Coroner's Office and was told there wouldn't be any autopsy results until morning. She picked up the interview notes Greg had left for her in the computer, and was about to write the obituary when he signaled from his office.

"Quite a shock," Greg said as she stepped inside. "You okay?"

"I'm fine." She was a professional, after all. "What's going on?"

The editor sat back in his chair. "The next story," he said, "is who's going to replace him."

Once again, Greg had beaten her to the punch. Whoever was appointed would serve two years and have an edge in the next general election. Hard-hearted as it might seem, this was an important subject.

"The traditional choice would be the senator's widow," Laura said.

A flicker of respect touched Greg's usually unreadable eyes. "You set up an interview with her yet?"

"Well, yes, but I figured it was off, after what happened."

"At her house?" A nod. "Then be there."

Laura didn't like the idea of barging in on a widow two days after her husband's death. But that was one of the things a reporter got paid to do. "All right."

"Who else?" Greg said.

They discussed a few names, then concentrated on Orange County. It was, as Greg pointed out, their circulation area, and also where a lot of Fisher's backers came from.

"We're back to Rita Long," Greg said. "Or . . . ?" He paused for her to fill in the blanks.

"Joe Pickard was his Orange County campaign manager," Laura said. "But he's a has-been. Or a never-was."

"The governor has a reputation for rewarding loyalty. And Pickard would do his bidding." Laura named a few other old faithfuls in the party, but Greg dismissed them. "What about potential rivals for the governor's own job? He's pretty vulnerable right now."

"You think he'd give somebody a plum appointment just to get rid of him?" Laura could see that the answer was yes.

"I heard a rumor"—Greg leaned against the edge of his desk—"about a certain judge named Lewis Tarkenton. You ever run into him?"

Laura nodded wordlessly.

"Check him out," Greg said. "Those are the top three in my book right now. If I think of any more, I'll let you know."

Laura walked numbly out of his office. Things seemed to be closing in on her much too fast. "Coincidence," she said out loud, and caught Steve's answering grin.

"Talking to yourself?" he said. "Take Dr. Orkney's prescription and dip into that whiskey bottle they hide in Sports."

"Are you kidding? Those guys drool in there when they pass it around." She tried to smile but gave it up as a lost cause.

Although her work involved constantly shifting her focus and adjusting to change, Laura counted on order in her own life. Greg's dragging Lew into the story upset her sense of balance, and it took half an hour of drinking coffee and rereading notes before Laura could settle down.

She spent the rest of the day working on the senator's obituary and calling his acquaintances around the country for laudatory comments. Everyone was shocked to learn of his death, but no one seemed unduly broken up about it.

During their ritual midafternoon coffee-break-at-the-desk, Laura related Greg's comments about a replacement. Steve, peeling back the wrapping from a gooey bearclaw he'd bought out of a vending machine, didn't seem impressed by the short list of possibilities she and Greg had drawn up.

"Who says the governor's going to pick someone from Orange County just because Long lives here?"

"Greg wouldn't go off half-cocked."

Steve licked sugar off his fingers. "I didn't say he would. Greg never takes a piss unless he's figured out precisely what he has to gain from it." His cynicism reminded Laura of how much more suitable Steve would have been for the political beat than she was. Still, he never seemed to resent her for lucking into it.

"You think Greg has some special reason for picking those three?" Laura frowned. "The only way he could know what the governor's thinking is if the governor told him, which is ridiculous."

Steve sighed. "You're forgetting. What put Fisher over the edge in a race as tight as a virgin's . . . jaw?"

Now that he pointed it out, Laura could see what he meant. "That editorial Greg wrote supporting him."

"Which was, you'll recall, immediately picked up in Fisher's campaign material and blown out of all proportion to the measly size of this newspaper." Steve tapped his fingers against his desk. "Greg has a remarkable 'instinct' for news out of Sacramento."

"But Long only died a couple of hours ago. The governor wouldn't have had time to draw up a list, let alone go calling anybody."

Steve finished his coffee and tossed the Styrofoam cup into the wastebasket. "Hell, I don't know. Who am I, anyway? Just a lonely, sex-starved bachelor."

"I'll keep that in mind." Laura went back to her story.

It just made things worse if Governor Fisher really might pick Lew. She closed her eyes, and his face leaped into her mind, smiling, the day they took his niece and nephew to Disneyland. After lunch, he'd surprised Terri and Kyle by buying them each an oversize stuffed animal.

The delight on Lew's face as he watched their reactions had, if anything, exceeded theirs.

They needed more days like that. Lots more. And it was beginning to look as though there might not be any.

CHAPTER FIVE

It was after six by the time Laura parked in front of the beige stucco fourplex where she lived, a few blocks from the paper. As she climbed the stairs to her second-floor unit, she noticed that the Vacancy sign was gone from the window of the apartment below hers.

Laura hoped whoever it was didn't have a loud stereo or a dog.

She dumped the mail on the living-room sofa before going to the phone. Lew answered on the third ring. "Hi," she said. "I've got to talk to you."

"I heard about Long. I'm sorry," he said. "Are you all right?"

Laura wilted onto a chair. "I'm . . . okay."

"The hell you are," Lew said. "You sound shaky."

"That isn't why I called." She took a deep breath. "My editor thinks you might get the appointment. He heard you may run against Fisher, and he thinks the governor might want to boost you out of his way."

"How in blazes did that get around?" Lew snapped. "I wish I knew how this thing started." Then he paused. "In any case, I presume he told you to write about me. And your journalistic integrity would be compromised if we were still sleeping together. Right?"

"Something like that." Laura clung to the sound of his voice. She didn't want to deal with this issue, not yet. "Lew, I know this is going to sound strange, but right before he died, the senator looked straight at me as if he were trying to tell me something."

"Honey, you've had a shock, seeing a man die right in front of you. Don't start reading things into it." Lew sounded so assured, it made her feel a little better. "As for your journalistic integrity, I'll be right over to compromise it some more."

"No. I need to think." Laura couldn't face him now. "Lew—would you take the appointment if it was offered?"

"I don't see how I could turn it down."

So there it was. Push had come to shove long before she was ready for it. "I'll call you in a day or two."

"Don't keep it all inside, Laura," he said. "I love you."

"I love you, too."

She jerked a frozen dinner out of its nest of ice and stuck it in the microwave, then prowled around the apartment, throwing open windows to let in some air.

Idly, Laura pawed through the mail. There was a bill, an ad for carpet cleaning, a department-store catalog, and a thick brown envelope from Aunt Ellen.

The timer dinged on the microwave, and she carried the envelope to the table. As she started in on her rubbery seafood Newburg, she pulled out the contents.

There was a letter on top, postmarked Cincinnati and written on Aunt Ellen's familiar flower-bordered stationery. Underneath lay a packet of thin envelopes with foreign stamps on them.

Dear Laura, the note read, *I know I said I was going to stay in this house forever, but I've changed my mind. It's too big for me, with Fred gone. I've opened escrow on a condo and put the house up for sale. Of course, I'll always have a spare room ready anytime you can visit.*

The letter even smelled like Aunt Ellen, lily-of-the-valley and coffee. Or maybe that was Laura's imagination; you couldn't really capture the smell of coffee, could you? Any more than you could save the past, those comfortable years with her dear, stodgy aunt and uncle.

Laura speared a soggy green bean and returned to the letter.

This is by way of explaining the enclosures. I've barely made a dent in the attic, but I did come across these letters your father wrote from Europe. They stopped when your mother died, and I'd forgotten I even saved them. If I find anything else of his, I'll send it along. Love, Ellen.

Laura stared down at the top envelope. A voice long silenced lay waiting within these yellowed rectangles.

Suddenly, she wanted intensely to read them, to find the answers to questions she'd never thought to ask until now. What had obsessed her father, how had the accident happened that killed her mother? What had he been doing in Washington before he died?

Laura slit open the first envelope. The ink had faded over the past two decades, but she could still make out the precise handwriting:

April 22, 1973
Easter Sunday
Madrid

Dear Ellen,

Got in Friday night, anxious to catch my first glimpse of Goya's paintings at the Prado. Kate still in Nice, playing on the beach with little Laura. I arrived as I always do, in an academic fog, rattling through train stations with my nose buried in a book. A good thing my destination was the last stop. . . .

James Bennett walked out of the train station with his bag slung over one shoulder and his mind still lost in the book he'd been reading about Goya and the Spanish civil war.

After a brief consultation with a more practical volume, *Europe on $10 a Day,* he managed to find the subway. When the car came, it was crowded with people and stank of peppers and body odor. It thumped along, and riders breathed and paper crinkled, and he couldn't quite see anything, just smell and hear and feel them.

James rarely connected with his environment except when he was with his daughter. At seven, Laura's unexpected ways of seeing things made him take notice, too. The rest of the time, history existed more vividly for him than the twentieth century.

It was only when he exited the subway, following the guidebook's directions to a hotel, that James noticed something was wrong.

For one thing, it had been full daylight when he went down, and it was deep night now. For another, he couldn't see the buildings clearly, or the street, although he sensed they were there. All he could see were masses of people, hundreds and hundreds of them, shouting and waving and pressing past without ever quite touching him.

Panic squeezed his lungs. James stood motionless on the sidewalk, trying to unfreeze his mind. He knew he ought to take some sensible action.

Kate. It took a moment to call up his wife's face, that firm, no-nonsense mouth. When he had it sharply in mind, his heartbeat slowed.

What would Kate do?

James gestured to a bulky passing figure, a man blurred by the darkness. "*Por favor, ¿dónde está—?*"

The man hurried by him and vanished.

Spotting an open restaurant across the street, James stepped down from the curb. Instantly, a policeman rushed at him, shouting in incomprehensible, sibilant Spanish, and he retreated in haste.

Had he arrived in the middle of a revolution? That would be just like him, not to have heard the news, James reflected. The best thing, he supposed, would be to return to the train station, since he didn't expect he could find the American embassy in all this chaos.

With only a few wrong turns, he managed to retrace his path, but when he got to the train station, he found it shuttered and the walkway outside nearly empty.

"Please!" He abandoned his high school Spanish. Surely, someone here spoke English. "Please, I have no place to stay—I have to get out—"

The few men lingering on the sidewalk turned away.

James forced himself to stand still, to breathe normally. He felt terribly hot, despite a cool April breeze sifting past his cheeks. Perhaps he was coming down with something.

If only it weren't so misty tonight. The air had a thick smokiness that veiled the outlines of things. Oddly, as he stood there gazing into the night, his anxiety melted away.

James shifted the bag against his shoulder and waited.

Only a faint swish announced the car, and then it was there, a big, old-fashioned black thing high off the ground. A door creaked, and someone got out.

James closed his eyes for a moment against a wave of heat. When he opened them, he could see the driver quite plainly, a wizened, humped creature, with a nose like a beak. Folded lids hid the eyes.

It sighed to him in some language that sounded like French filtered through a glass of champagne. A place to stay, that's what it was offering.

"Okay," James said. "I can't pay much." His voice came out flat.

The air inside the car was hot and moist. Tendrils of mold furred the armrests, and the seat squished beneath him as if the stuffing had gone rotten.

To his surprise, James felt quite safe there.

They drove for a long time, but he didn't mind. His muscles ached from standing and walking, and his mind nodded fuzzily toward sleep.

They were passing through a city, but he couldn't be sure it was Madrid. He'd read about wide modern streets, the royal palace, the cathedral, but all he saw was one twisting lane after another, all the buildings shuttered with iron gates across the doorways.

Now and then, the driver would hop out of the car and clap his hands, and some beast-man would shuffle up from a hole in the ground, jangling his keys, and they would hiss together, and then the beaked man would climb back in, and on they went. Around and around, downward and downward. James was so dizzy he had to close his eyes. He knew time was passing much too rapidly, but he couldn't seem to get a grip on it.

Finally, the door beside him opened, and the shriveled face of his driver poked in. "Here," he said, quite recognizably. Even up close, James couldn't see any eyes behind the thin folds of flesh.

"How much?" Tentatively, he held out a dollar. The driver snatched it greedily and shuffled off.

A door stood open in a building, and James climbed the steps. At the top was a desk, and some vague shapes took another dollar from him and led him to a small, bare room with a thin bed. It was even hotter than the car had been, and he lacked the energy to open a window. There was nothing outside, anyway, but humid darkness.

He must have slept and awakened several times in the night, hearing high-pitched cries and grunts from the other rooms, slithers and rattlings and dry, shifting noises. He wondered what sort of things prostitutes did in Madrid, to create such sounds.

> *I'm quite safe here at this hotel, even if it is on the seedy side. I've been feverish for two days and haven't gone out yet, although I'm anxious to get to the museum.*
>
> *So you see, Ellen, it was all a hallucination, but it seemed so real at the time. I wanted to write you because I always lose diaries when I try to keep them, and I know you save my letters. For some reason, I find myself wanting to keep a record of my experiences. Perhaps I'll use them in a paper someday.*
>
> *By the way, all those crowds Friday night, it was because of a parade. I foolishly arrived on Good Friday without a hotel reservation.*
>
> *Please don't tell Kate. She worries about my absentmindedness enough as it is.*
>
> *Love,*
> *James.*

James Bennett. James Lawrence Bennett, candidate for a doctorate in art history at Brown University. Daddy. A tall man with a clipped beard and dark eyes looking out from a black-and-white photograph. What did Laura really remember about him? A tweed coat that smelled of tobacco, a puppy he'd brought her at Aunt Ellen's. Bear hugs, and then a sudden withdrawing.

She stepped out onto the small balcony that opened off the living room. To the west, the sun was setting bloodily amid the smog. The air felt thick and still. From Beach Boulevard a block away, the smell of exhaust choked toward her.

Maybe she was a little feverish, too. Or just off-center from everything that had happened today.

A shift of movement on the ground level caught Laura's eye. Someone was coming out of the newly rented first-floor apartment. Leaning over the railing, she glimpsed a bright Gypsy-print blouse and a fluff of red hair.

Black-rimmed eyes turned up toward her. It was the old woman she'd seen crossing the street. For an instant, Laura felt herself falling, being sucked down, her ears filled with jangling. . . .

The old woman went back into the apartment. Laura shook her head to clear it, then snatched her purse off the couch and fled. She went where she always went when she got tired of being home, to the South Coast Plaza mall, shopping for color and light and the comforting ordinariness of strangers.

CHAPTER SIX

"The United States today proposed an emergency summit of world leaders to assess the unprecedented impact of natural disasters on France and China. A White House spokesman said the purpose is for East and West to coordinate aid and to allay mutual suspicions by signing a nonintervention pact.

"In France today, thousands of people are fleeing Paris in the wake of a series of aftershocks. The latest tremor to hit the capital city this morning registered five-point-three on the Richter scale. . . ."

Sergeant Daryl Wilkinson reached over and flicked off the radio on Detective Hertz's desk. Norm Hertz, the phone wedged between his shoulder and his ear, shrugged to show it wasn't his fault the eight-in-a-row Barry Manilow retrospective had been cut short by news bulletins.

Daryl checked his watch. Mickey's little hand was edging past the seven, and through the window on the far side of the large, square room, summer twilight was muting into darkness. The days were getting shorter already, damn it. And he was missing those evenings and weekends at the beach, all those swelling female bodies with swimsuits curving down to there and up to here. All because of some maniac.

Even Lieutenant Grover had gone home already. You couldn't blame the guy. His wife was losing a battle with cancer, and their kids were falling apart under the strain. He was needed there.

Hertz hung up. "No make on the license plate."

Daryl hadn't really expected one, but they had to check out every tip, every report of a car seen near the Blue Gull Café Monday morning. "Let's go over it again," he said wearily.

The detective lighted a cigarette and plopped into the chair next to Daryl's desk. "Okay. She gets off work ten A.M.—"

"No, let's look for parallels." Daryl leaned back wearily. "Other than the obvious fact that they were both young, attractive, and female." Shit, why would anybody want to go around knocking off girls, anyway? A few compliments, a couple of drinks, and they'd fall into bed. What more could a man want?

"Neither one had a car that day," Hertz said promptly. "Which of course brings us back to hitchhiking." That was a possibility they hadn't ruled out, but it seemed unlikely. Women were cautious these days.

"Or someone they both knew and might have accepted a ride with. Someone who was at both places, probably knew both of them, and would be considered trustworthy," Daryl said.

"You really hate the guy, don't you?" Hertz looked around for an ashtray and, not finding one, dumped his ashes into his cupped hand.

"You mean because the arrogant son of a bitch was the swing vote in cutting our benefits last year? Why the hell would you think that?" *And if he's the reason I'm sitting here dying of terminal horniness while the beach bunnies are giving it away to the college boys, I'll kick his ass all the way to jail.*

"It's purely circumstantial," the detective pointed out. "Besides, where's the motive? Where's the history of violence or mental illness? It doesn't figure."

Daryl had to admit that was true. But he would have given 10-to-1 odds that Joe Pickard was their man. "Maybe I'll drop by and ask him a few more questions. Just to shake him up."

"Hey, don't forget, he's the chief's boss." Hertz's hand was getting full of ashes, and the cigarette was burning low. "Think we can call it a night?"

"Go home," Daryl agreed. "I'll take care of Hizzoner."

He pulled on his suit jacket and picked up his briefcase. This was one hell of a case to land only two months after his promotion to sergeant. Now if he could just get one piece of hard physical evidence against that bastard Pickard, he'd nail the guy.

He only hoped it happened while there was still a bit of the summer left to enjoy.

Kiki Bellaga was behind the front desk checking out a stack of *Parents* magazines when she saw Mayor Pickard come into the library and stop in front of the videotape display, the way he did a lot of times. The way a lot of people did. The tapes were free, and you could keep them out for two days.

She finished sweeping the scanner over the magazines and

handed them to a harried mother who barely had time to say thanks before dashing after a fleeing toddler.

Kiki peered across to the reference desk and met the gaze of her friend Elaine. The other woman nodded toward the stocky figure of the mayor, and they both giggled.

It was the first time she'd seen the mayor since last Friday, when she'd run into him at Widget, a trendy new nightclub in Buena Park. Joe Pickard, already tanked up and feeling no pain, had asked Kiki to dance, an experience that she'd discovered involved a lot of feeling and clutching. Well, all right, as her ex-husband used to say, she was built like a brick shithouse, and nobody could believe she was a day over twenty-five, let alone ten years. You couldn't blame the guy, maybe, even if he ought to know better than to mess with a city employee. He wasn't too bad-looking either, if you didn't mind thinning hair and a paunch.

Then the band had segued into a slow number, and she'd found herself pulled close enough to feel how hard he was, and he'd reached up right under her sweater, and she'd let out a shriek. Right there in the middle of the dance floor. He'd stumbled backward and knocked over another couple, and Kiki had started laughing hysterically. So had Elaine, when she heard about it. His Hard-on the Mayor, she'd called him.

Suddenly, Kiki realized Joe had noticed her, and she felt herself flush. He looked furious, as if he'd caught her exchange of giggles with Elaine and guessed the cause. Well, he'd brought it on himself, hadn't he?

But it didn't seem funny anymore, not when she noticed how red his face was getting and the way he was clenching his fists. Jeez, he looked kind of scary when he was mad, and stronger than she would have thought. Only . . . the anger was fading into something else. As though he was afraid of his own rage.

A thump to one side drew Kiki's attention. It was that redheaded girl again, the little brat who came in here at least once a week, pulling books off the shelf. "Hey!" Kiki flew around the counter.

The girl tossed a handful of books onto the linoleum and shot toward the exit. Kiki's futile attempt to block her was rewarded with a sharp kick in the leg. As if in slow motion, Kiki felt herself collapse onto the floor as the little monster escaped. A sharp pain twisted through her ankle.

Joe Pickard bent over her, his face a mask of concern. "Looks like you hurt your ankle."

"I think it's sprained," Kiki admitted, wiggling her toes and wincing.

"Kiki?" It was Elaine. "You'd better go home and soak that." The library would be open for another hour and a half, but the staff could manage without her, Kiki knew. Besides, if she couldn't stand up, she wouldn't be good for much.

"Call me a cab, would ya?" She let the mayor help her up, and then found she had to lean on him. "I won't be able to drive with this."

"I'll give you a lift," he said.

She hesitated. After his performance last Friday, she wasn't sure she wanted to be alone with him. On the other hand, cabs were expensive.

"A ride," Joe Pickard said. "Just to be sure you get home safe."

"Okay," Kiki said. Hell, she didn't have anything against the mayor, not really. He wasn't drunk now, after all.

The mayor's house on Beatrice Lane was a disgrace, Daryl Wilkinson reflected as he parked a half-block away. The guy had really let it run to seed since his divorce. On the other hand, at least he wasn't some smug rich bastard.

As he walked toward the door, Daryl checked out the windows but saw no sign of lights. Still, he stood to one side while he rapped on the door. You never wanted to take chances, even with what looked like an empty house, even with your own mayor.

No answer.

I just wanted to go over Monday morning's events with you again, sir. Sometimes people remember things, things that didn't seem important at the time. Things I might think were important. Like, why doesn't anyone remember seeing you at the car wash you say you went to? Of course, he wouldn't really dare ask it that way.

Daryl walked around to the back door and knocked again. Nothing stirred in the house. The garage was closed, but the door hung at an angle that suggested it didn't roll up and down easily. The mayor probably parked on the street, when he was home.

There was a rickety potting shed in the backyard. Daryl cracked open the door, and the smell of old chemicals and musty soil rolled over him. Didn't look like anybody'd potted a plant in there for years.

He checked his watch and found he could barely make out the time, seven-thirty, in the fading light.

Well, he'd just have to catch the mayor some other time, Daryl concluded reluctantly, and headed back to his car, not looking forward to having dinner at a hamburger joint and going home alone.

Joe Pickard gripped the steering wheel with clammy hands. It had nearly happened again. This time, it would have been her.

He pulled into the left-turn lane at Granada. "This way, right? I mean, correct?"

Kiki giggled beside him. Her ankle couldn't hurt all that much. "Yeah. Correct. It's two blocks down on the left."

He didn't like being made fun of, especially not by some cocktease of a library assistant who wore her sweaters too tight and liked to snuggle up to men on the dance floor, then push them away. When he saw her and her friend laughing at him, he'd felt the fury pound through him. He'd known, suddenly, that if he didn't protect her, she would turn up dead tomorrow morning.

It was crazy. Was somebody watching him? Even if they were, how could they know what he was thinking?

Well, this was one little tootsie who was going to be just fine, even if she did deserve to be taught a lesson.

The apartment complex turned out to be large, with remote parking, which meant Joe had to support Kiki as she limped toward her unit. He didn't really mind, though. She smelled like a whole bouquet of overblown flowers, and she kept bumping against him suggestively and then apologizing.

When they got to her building, she pointed up to the second floor. "Got a hoist?"

"Right here." Joe scooped her up, one arm around her back and the other beneath her fanny. Kiki giggled.

The only problem was, she weighed more than she looked like. And he wasn't as young as he used to be. By the time they got to the top, Joe was panting, and his pants felt as if they were about to split.

"You look like you could use something to drink." Kiki opened the door—it was the first unit, thank God—and led the way inside. The place looked like a motel room to which someone had added a bunch of thrift-store doilies and lots of little china shepherdesses. There was an A-frame dollhouse on the coffee table, full of tiny dressed-up teddy bears and cutesy-poo furniture. "How about some vodka?"

"Got any beer?"

"Yeah, I think so." She dug through the refrigerator and pulled out a can of plain-wrap lite. Horse piss, but Joe took it anyway and chugged half of it before he came up for air.

"It was sure nice of you to give me a ride." Kiki sat on a chintz-covered chair and took off her spike-heeled shoes.

"How's your ankle?" He ought to get out of here, he really should. But he was tired of watching television.

"I think it's swollen." Kiki leaned over, giving him a nice view of her boobs through the V-neck of her blouse. "But I'll live."

You sure will. "Anything else you need?"

"What've you got in mind?" She tilted her head flirtatiously and then giggled again. "Sorry. I guess I am kind of a tease. I didn't mean to embarrass you the other night. But you caught me off-guard, you know?"

"I was drunk." Joe felt his muscles start to relax. "I got a little grabby."

They looked at each other. "I guess we might as well," Kiki said.

"Your ankle doesn't hurt too much?"

"It feels a lot better now that I've got my shoes off."

Somewhat awkwardly, they made their way into the bedroom. Kiki giggled a couple of times while she was taking her clothes off, and she nearly changed her mind when she discovered Joe didn't have a condom, but then she found one in her bedside table. Having sex with her felt good, even though it went too fast. She came, too, grunting and hollering.

"You want me to stay tonight?" Joe asked when his breathing had returned to normal.

"Yeah—I mean no." Kiki made a face. "Elaine'll be stopping by in the morning to give me a ride. She's kind of a gossip."

Joe was surprised how disappointed he felt. "Maybe we could do something Friday night."

"Yeah. I'd like that."

He washed up, kissed her good night, and went home.

As he opened the door, he thought, *I'm going to hire a cleaning crew for this place.* And maybe a decorator from one of those department stores. Get the house fixed up again.

Kiki didn't bother to put on a nightgown after she washed up in the bathroom. Her body still tingled at the slightest touch, and she thought she might want to masturbate later.

She definitely needed a lot more of what Joe was handing out, and a lot more often. It was funny how, lying down in the dim light, things like a paunch and thinning hair didn't make any difference.

In fact, she kind of preferred a man like him, a guy who wasn't twenty-five and muscular and full of himself. A guy who appreciated what he got.

Elaine wouldn't understand. Well, she wouldn't have to know. Not for a while.

Someone tapped on the door.

Oh, damn. Not that woman from downstairs who was always borrowing something as an excuse to snoop around. She must have heard the bed creaking.

Kiki went to the door stark naked. Let the old biddy get a shock if she wanted to poke her nose into other people's business.

She looked out the peephole. Joe!

"Hey!" Kiki threw the door open. "Forget something?"

"Miss me?" he asked.

"You bet." Maybe she'd let him stay all night after all. "You hard again?"

"Damn right."

It was kind of funny, though. He sounded as if he were mouthing the words, as if he weren't quite sure what they meant. Maybe he'd been drinking some more, only he didn't smell like it.

That was another funny part—he didn't smell like himself. Joe had this nice raw scent, sex and beer and a little end-of-the-day sweat. This guy didn't smell like anything.

Only it was Joe. It had to be.

"Well, come on in." Kiki stepped back and let him close the door. "You can see I'm all ready."

Joe woke up the next morning feeling as if spring and his birthday had arrived on the same day. He felt great until he turned on the radio and heard that a friend had found the slashed body of library assistant Kiki Bellaga sprawled on the floor of her bloodstained apartment.

CHAPTER SEVEN

The TV set was turned on in the newsroom when Laura arrived Wednesday morning. On her way in, she glanced at it and saw men in long robes clambering atop overturned cars, waving torches as they pressed through city streets. Fires spurted as they passed, and the air filled with screams.

"What the hell is that?" Laura stopped by Bill White's desk.

"Riyadh," he said. "Saudi Arabia has fallen. What little stability there was in the Middle East just went down the tubes."

The camera cut to a close-up of a bearded, thin-faced man, his eyes shining with the light of fanaticism. "This is only the first step in our jihad!" he cried in heavily accented but grammatically perfect English. "We have won our battle against the Saudis. Now, Arabia will lead the way in the greater war, the holy war against the devils of the United States!"

"The least he could do is come up with an original line." Laura stalked across the newsroom. Why should it matter so much that a city halfway around the globe had fallen into chaos? They had enough trouble right here in San Paradiso. You couldn't even turn on your car radio without hearing about another murder.

On TV, a news analyst was describing Al-Hadassi's abrupt shift a few years ago from a moderate Iranian leader to a bloodthirsty revolutionary. In spite of numerous references to Islamic fundamentalism, the commentator had no real explanation for what had turned the gentle shepherd into an attack dog.

Someone turned off the set. The clicking of computer keys and ringing of phones sounded like silence.

Laura sat down, fiddled restlessly with her tape recorder, and watched Steve shuffle back from the cafeteria with a cup of coffee.

"Listen." He positioned the cup atop a file on his desk. "Could you help me out? I've got a press conference this afternoon about the new murder, and there's an angle I need some help with."

"Sure." During an off-year for elections, Laura helped out on other beats. "Name it."

"Sergeant Wilkinson suspects Joe Pickard. I thought maybe you could chat him up."

"Pickard?" Laura said. "A murderer? That's ridiculous."

"He gave Kiki Bellaga a ride home last night after she sprained her ankle at the library." Steve hit the "save" button on his terminal. "That's according to Kiki's girlfriend, the one who found the body."

"He'd have to be pretty damn stupid to kill someone he was just seen with." Laura flipped her Rolodex to the coroner's number. "But sure; I need to talk to him anyway, about the appointment. I've just got to wrap up the autopsy on Senator Long first."

"*Muchas gracias,*" Steve said. "Oh, and by the way, just in case, watch out for him, will you? No late-night meetings in secluded areas or anything."

"I'm not stupid." Laura grinned. "Honestly, Steve."

The line was ringing at the Coroner's Office. She pulled out her notepad as the deputy coroner came on.

He read a statement. "The autopsy on the body of Senator Cruise Long was inconclusive. Toxicological tests should be complete within two weeks."

"What does that mean, 'inconclusive'?" Laura asked. "Have you definitely ruled out a heart attack?"

"I'm not authorized to give out any further information," the deputy coroner said. "Try us again the end of next week. Excuse me, I've got another call waiting." He clicked off.

Inconclusive. Not a heart attack?

A puzzle. Part of a news story, part of the game of tracking down facts and opening up Chinese nesting boxes to see what lay inside. Firmly, Laura clamped down on the quiver of anxiety. The coroner was talking about Cruise Long, not her father; there was no connection.

She spent the morning writing the story. She also got authorization from Bill to work overtime at the funeral Saturday.

Then she called the secretary at Joe Pickard's law office and made an appointment to see him at one o'clock.

Behind his desk, the mayor oozed sweat despite the spasmodic air-conditioning. He kept mopping his forehead with a handkerchief and losing his train of thought.

"I'm afraid I'm not being very helpful," he said finally. "I haven't talked with anyone from the Governor's Office. Frankly, uh, I suppose you heard about the murder. I drove that young woman home last night—you see, she couldn't drive with that ankle, and—well, what with all the murders, I wanted to be sure she got home safe. And she did. And now they say there's no sign of breaking and entering. She must have opened the door. But why would she?"

The pleading tone contrasted oddly with his large-boned, puffy features, as if a little boy were whining out of a grown man's mouth.

"I guess the police must be giving you a hard time." On the desk, the voice-activated tape recorder started up as Laura spoke. She didn't want to take notes. She needed to concentrate.

"Just doing their job." Pickard pulled a cigarette from his pocket, said he hoped she didn't mind, and lighted it. "I know how it must look, but frankly—I—" He seemed to recall whom he was talking to. "Well, it's a terrible thing, that's all. I hope they catch the son of a bitch, and fast."

"It does look curious," she said.

He paused. "My . . . driving Kiki home? Yes, yes, I know." He squirmed like a bug in a tight corner.

Let's see if we can fit a few more pieces into the picture. "Did you go inside with her?"

Beads of sweat blistered his skin. "I had to—her ankle, you know."

"How long did you stay?"

"A few minutes—I had to carry her up the steps, and I was tired."

She grilled him a while longer, until she felt she could visualize the scene. Joe Pickard, lusting after a teasing library assistant. They'd probably gone to bed together, although he didn't say so.

Nothing in his tone struck Laura as menacing, so she changed the topic back to politics, but she wasn't getting anything usable there, either. Joe was too much of an emotional wreck.

Finally, she stood up. "If you do hear anything from the governor, I'd appreciate your letting me know. Even if it has to be off-the-record."

"Of course." Pickard leaned against the desk as he shook hands. His grip felt clammy. "And . . . be careful. Lock your doors."

The waiting room was empty as Laura left, except for the secretary brushing polish onto her nails.

Although the sun bristled overhead, it felt cooler outside. Laura remembered a serial murderer she'd seen in court once, at sentencing.

He could have been a garage mechanic or a gardener, someone you wouldn't have noticed in the street.

After letting out the stifling air, Laura rolled the passenger window most of the way back up before she started the car.

About three blocks from the Mayor's Office, she felt the steering wheel pull. As the car began to list, she veered into a supermarket parking lot and got out to check on the problem.

The left front tire was almost completely flat.

Standing by the car, her energy seeping away in the heat, Laura gazed around for a public telephone. There might be one inside the store, but whom would she call? She'd dropped her auto-club membership six months ago because she never used it.

Grumbling at her own stupidity, she opened the hatchback and unsnapped the carpeting that covered the spare tire. When she'd decided not to renew her membership, she recalled thinking that she knew how to change a spare. What she hadn't taken into account was the likely effect of grease on her dress.

A white car glided toward her between the parked rows, a sleek Olds Regency like the one Lew drove. Laura waited for it to turn aside, but instead it stopped nearby.

Lew! Laura stared in relief as he waved and got out. What was he doing out of court in the middle of the afternoon?

"Hi." He strolled over and inspected her tire. "Good thing I spotted you."

"Why aren't you—"

"A juror fell ill. I had to recess early." He reached around her and closed the hatchback with a snap.

"What are you doing?"

"Neither one of us is dressed for changing tires." For some reason, Lew wasn't meeting her eyes. "Come on. I'll give you a lift to my place so I can change."

The heat reflecting off the blacktop twisted up around him in long wavy lines. Laura had never realized before that you could actually see the air sizzling. It threw Lew into an odd perspective, as if she were viewing him through a layer of gauze. As if he wore a net draped over him, pressing down like a stocking mask over a robber, distorting his features, making his eyes longer and narrower and his nose flatter. As if he weren't Lew at all, but some stranger. Trying to lure her into his car.

She couldn't even see Lew anymore, just a dark figure against a faint redness that deepened and flickered as she watched.

"Laura?"

"No, thanks." The words seemed to come from far away. "I'll wait here."

"Don't be ridiculous." Impatience strained his voice. "It must be over ninety degrees today. What's the matter with you?"

"Have you got a business card?"

"A what?"

It was crazy, but she needed some proof that he was really Lew. "A business card. Or your driver's license."

He felt in his pockets. "I must have left my wallet in my desk. That's embarrassing. What if I'd run into a cop?" He grinned, but it wasn't Lew's grin.

In front of the supermarket, two women were exiting with carts full of groceries, and a man knelt to retie a little girl's shoe. Everything looked so normal.

"I have to make a phone call." It was the best excuse she could think of.

"Fine. You can use the one at my—"

"Right now." Knowing she was making a fool of herself but unable to stop, Laura half ran to the store.

Inside, she peered through the window, between two large pasteboard signs advertising the week's specials. Lew got into his car and drove away. Maybe he'd gone to change his clothes. Maybe he was ticked off.

And maybe it wasn't Lew.

Laura found a telephone outside the manager's office and dialed Lew's chambers. The bailiff answered. Yes, he said, court had recessed early, but he didn't believe the judge had left for the day, just stepped out of his office for a few minutes. If she'd like to leave a number, he would have Judge Tarkenton return the call.

"No, thanks. I'll call back."

Well, there, she *had* made a fool of herself. But the feeling lingered, that she'd been in danger. That there was a side to Lew she'd never seen before.

It couldn't be him, could it, who killed those women? There was no reason to connect him with the murders, no reason at all, but Laura tried to remember as much as she could of the victims' disappearances. The second one had got off work at ten o'clock in the morning. Lew would have been in court.

This was crazy. Lew wouldn't hurt anybody. Besides, if he'd wanted to kill her, he'd had plenty of opportunities before this. It would be foolish to risk being seen right here in a public parking lot.

And what about those kids? She'd seen the love on Lew's face the day they'd spent with Kyle and Terri. That was when she'd realized he wasn't acting out of a sense of duty, that somewhere along the line he'd bonded to his niece and nephew with a ferocity she'd thought was reserved for her.

Lew was a good man. She'd simply been spooked after the interview with Pickard, that was all.

He didn't come back, even though it took her half an hour to change the tire. The exercise left Laura drenched in sweat beneath the heavy garbage bag she'd transformed into an impromptu apron.

Back at the paper, she dialed Lew's chambers again, and he answered on the second ring.

"Was I imagining things, or did I see you in front of the Alpha Beta on Beach Boulevard an hour ago?" Laura said.

"I've been in the courthouse all afternoon," he muttered distractedly. "Somebody's been spreading the word I want to be the next senator or governor. I had to swear up and down to Marcus Johns that I hadn't spread the damn rumors myself."

"I hope you managed to convince him." *And me,* Laura thought. *I want to be convinced, too.*

"Apparently so," Lew said. "He assigned me the Draper Dagmar case."

Draper Dagmar was a major Orange County land developer and political donor, one of Governor Fisher's key backers. He'd been indicted by the grand jury for allegedly bribing county planning officials to get one of his projects approved.

The trial was expected to be a media circus. It was rumored that Fisher had used his influence to help Dagmar clear away governmental red tape and that his name would get dragged into the proceedings. In light of the scandal over how the governor raised his campaign funds, it should be quite a show.

Laura could just imagine how some of her colleagues would react if they heard that Fisher might appoint the judge hearing Dagmar's case to the U.S. Senate.

It would be even more uncomfortable if people found out about the judge's love affair with the *Herald*'s political reporter. "It would be better if we didn't see each other for a while, wouldn't it?" She glanced around to make sure she wasn't being overheard.

"I'm afraid I have to agree with you."

"You didn't—you're sure you didn't go out for a drive?" she asked. "That man looked exactly like you, Lew."

"I ought to know whether I was in the courthouse all day, shouldn't I?" he snapped.

"Okay, okay."

"I'm sorry," he said. "I'm just in a bad mood. It's a rotten way to break up. Only temporarily. You understand that?"

"I do. I'll . . . talk to you soon." Laura replaced the phone in its cradle. She felt dried out, as if all the moisture had evaporated from her skin.

Could there be someone else who looked exactly like Lew and drove the same kind of car? She even had the impression that it had been Lew's license plate or a number very close, but at the time she hadn't thought to check.

God, what if she'd got into the car?

She shook her head. The heat must be making her hallucinate.

Laura thought of her father and the months before he died. He had insisted that war was about to erupt as the result of some mysterious evil, Aunt Ellen had said, and believed it was in his power to stop it. At the time, Laura couldn't understand how someone as sensible as her father could become obsessed with such crazy ideas.

Now, she was beginning to understand.

CHAPTER EIGHT

Madeleine lined up the yogurt cartons on the refrigerator shelf, five of them, orange and lemon, vanilla, blueberry, and strawberry. They looked much like what she bought at the dairy in Nice. But the brick of cheese she placed beside them, encased in thick plastic, had an artificial brightness that troubled her.

Most things about San Paradiso troubled her. The landscape was too flat, its straight roads lined with boxy gas stations and prefabricated hamburger restaurants every few hundred kilometers. They made her soul ache.

Madeleine reached up and arranged a few boxes and jars in the cheap wooden cabinets. The joints in her fingers protested, but she would not listen. Her own body, at least, must be her ally in this foreign place.

Retiring to her bedroom, she avoided the window. There was no point in gazing out at bland regular angles and endless unclouded sunlight. Bad enough the way the light streamed across the wall, transfiguring her antique brass crucifix into a small, primitive decoration.

Nothing looked familiar here, including herself. Madeleine turned to the cruelly clear California mirror and saw that it framed a face that had become a battlefield against time. Not her face, surely, with that heavy rouge and those impossibly dark lines around the eyes. Red dye clung outrageously to her thinning, brittle hair. It hadn't looked so outrageous in Nice.

Her hand slipped into the drawer of the dressing table, onto the jeweled haft of the knife. The blessed knife, carried to the Vatican itself for the ultimate benediction.

In the sunlight washing through the window, the imitation jewels glinted dully. At home they had glittered like rubies and emeralds.

What else had changed in transition?

Madeleine stared at the knife. Perhaps her purpose was as deceptive as these jewels. The best thing, the right thing, might be to pack up her pitifully few belongings and go home.

Was it really madness, James, after all?

She saw him again, the ghost of him, sprawled across the bed smoking a Gauloise, his thin, gentle face dark with sweat from a Nice summer nearly twenty years ago.

"Did I ever tell you, Madeleine, about my great-grandmother?"

She turned sharply. Had someone really spoken? No, of course not. But she had heard him so clearly.

"Please," she said aloud. "Tell me if I'm wrong. Tell me if I'm about to do something terrible."

But he was gone, damn him. Damn him to hell for turning to her in his grief, becoming her lover and then leaving. Going back to America, never knowing that in all her years, he was the only man she'd loved.

It was a silly story he'd told about his great-grandmother, who had gone crazy after her husband's death and tried to conjure him back. When she became pregnant, she claimed a demon had appeared in the guise of her dead spouse, but everyone else thought it was the iceman, James said, because she got pregnant in the summer.

Madeleine smiled, remembering what she'd said, that she had slept with one or two demons herself.

And he'd chuckled, not sure he believed her stories about working for the Resistance, and told her, "You're either a terribly brave woman or a terrible liar, Madeleine."

A little of both, yes, James.

But then he had said the part that frightened her. About his great-aunt, his grandmother's twin sister, who at the age of thirty-five murdered her three children, to stop, so she said, a curse. And his mother, hospitalized for paranoid schizophrenia, raving that monsters were out to get her.

Had he, too, been mad? But then, Madeleine must be mad as well, for she had seen things only God could account for. She had seen James in front of his strange painting once, seen him change into something not human. That was why she believed he really could have gone through the painting, in his desperation, and brought back something not of this earth. Something she must now kill.

The earthquakes had made her realize the need to take action. It was all as James had feared, biblical catastrophes and turmoil among nations. The coming of chaos.

A breath caught in Madeleine's lungs and rattled softly. Oh, she was getting much older than she'd ever intended. In the white California sunlight, she stared down at the thick blue veins on the backs of her hands. Were these the hands of a righteous woman, or of a deranged slayer?

It wasn't too late to go back. How bizarre, to believe one old woman could save the world. Better to turn this knife against herself before she took an innocent life.

Still wavering, Madeleine tucked the dagger into her skirt pocket and emerged into the living room. She dialed the TV to one of those foolish game shows that served only to break the silence.

But the game show had lost its turn to a news bulletin. A woman with jaw-length straight hair faced Madeleine and said, "Refugees fleeing Riyadh claim troops loyal to the Saudi family are making a last stand in a fortified residence just outside the city."

And then the anchorwoman did something odd. Glassy-eyed, with no inflection, she said, "They've come through."

For a minute, Madeleine thought she'd imagined it. Then the announcer rattled some papers and said, "Excuse me. We've just learned that the rebels have broken through the last pocket of resistance. It is believed several members of the Saudi family have been executed. We'll bring you the information as we receive it. This is Grace Saunders for CBS News."

Madeleine turned off the set.

They've come through. Through the painting, in the wake of the demon.

Grace. The woman's name was Grace.

Reaching into her pocket, Madeleine touched the blessed knife. *Thank you, God, for showing me the way.*

All that remained was to find the right moment to kill the monster.

CHAPTER NINE

Once upon a time, when Rita was a little girl, there had been a song called "What a Difference a Day Makes." She remembered her mother singing it, along with another one: "*Que Será, Será*—Whatever Will Be, Will Be."

One song had been about heartbreak, the other about hope. But neither one told you how to get through the pain.

It hurt so much that Rita gladly took the sleeping pills the doctor had prescribed, and didn't get up until four o'clock Wednesday afternoon. Then she couldn't seem to do anything. When she stepped into the closet to choose something to wear, the scent of Cruise overwhelmed her. A blue shirt, tossed carelessly across the doorknob for Ramona to pick up, bore a small grease spot near the collar from the fettuccine they'd eaten Monday night. His bathrobe rustled slightly when she brushed it; he always carried cellophane-wrapped mints in the pocket. There must be enough of him here, little fibers and cells clinging to the clothes and the shoes, to re-create the whole man.

Rita managed to make it to the shower before giving way to sobs. Her whole body shook; it frightened her. She pressed her forehead against the tile and felt her chest throb.

What was going to happen to her without Cruise?

He hadn't left her penniless. She'd seen the will when he drew it up; this house and a third of his other property went to her. The rest was divided between his children.

But what about everything else? The friends they had, who were really his friends; the parties in Washington, the banquets, the golf tournament in Palm Springs where people kept coming up to shake his hand? The way she felt when she was with him, proud and special. The way he'd taken over her life, the power he radiated. She felt like a wild creature that had been tamed, and then was thrust into the forest again.

There was so much to do. She had to meet with the funeral director tomorrow morning. The best of everything; that would simplify the decisions. But she knew there must be condolence cards piling up downstairs and at his office that would have to be answered. Maybe Cruise's staff would help. And she'd need a dress for the funeral, navy blue. Black on widows was melodramatic, he'd once said. She had to do everything right. She wanted Cruise to approve.

Letting her hair hang wet around her shoulders, Rita pulled on slacks and a short-sleeved sweater and went down the hall to the bedroom they'd turned into an office.

The answering machine showed a red light, so she rewound the tape and played it. There was a message from Bob Fillipone: The autopsy had been inconclusive. What the hell did that mean?

The next voice on the tape made Rita sit up straighter. It was President Harkness himself, calling to express his condolences. The president!

That was all. Neither of Cruise's children had called, not that she'd expected them to. Nor were there any messages from Rita's relatives. She hadn't expected that, either. Her mother was dead, her father long gone, and she'd never been close to the others.

Well, she'd been alone before, hadn't she? But it had been different. Now, she was in the spotlight. Now, anything she did would be reported on and gossiped about. If she went back to acting, she would have to choose her roles carefully. She'd have to be very, very discreet about men, too. Not that, right now, she could imagine ever feeling sexy again.

Rita smacked her hand down on the desk. Damn Cruise anyway! Why had he lifted her up, only to leave her? Why did the bastard have to go and die?

Her eyes were filling up again when she noticed the stack of mail. Sympathy cards, half a dozen of them. They must have been posted the minute people heard the news. Mixed in with them she found a few household bills, and the *Pennysaver* with its endless ads for yard sales and baby-sitters.

At the bottom of the stack was a legal-sized white envelope with no return address, postmarked San Paradiso.

The photograph that had shocked her so much yesterday had vanished from her thoughts completely. It seemed, now, that it had been weeks ago that it arrived.

It hardly mattered anymore, Rita realized. She'd been so afraid of how Cruise would react. Now, he would never see it.

Still, her breath felt fluttery as she slit open the envelope and pulled out the single sheet of typewriter paper. It said, *You will be offered the appointment to complete your husband's term. You will turn it down.*

The hell she would! Rita crumpled the sheet and threw it into the wastebasket. Not that she really expected to get such an offer, but if she did, it would establish her as a person of importance in her own right. Senator Rita Crane Long. Someone distinguished. Not just a leftover from someone else's life.

Could the photograph really be used against her? Wouldn't any objective person see that it had been faked? Cruise might have been taken in; he was a proud and possessive man, after all. On the other hand, the press loved a scandal. They'd particularly love one about Rita.

She'd have to talk it over with Bob Fillipone. They might be able to undercut the blackmailer by telling the press about the picture first. An injunction against printing it might help, too.

Rita pressed the intercom and asked Ramona to bring her something to eat. Yes, scrambled eggs would be fine.

Something was nagging at the back of her mind. Something about the photograph and the note.

Who could have sent it? Someone else in the Republican party who wanted the seat for himself? Someone from her own past who harbored a grudge? Some extremist on the right or left?

Whoever it was, he had sent the photograph while Cruise was still alive.

The significance took a moment to sink in. Maybe, she thought, the blackmailer had changed signals in midstream. But it was also possible he'd known all along that Cruise was going to die.

Quickly, Rita dug into the wastebasket for the envelope. The postmark bore Monday's date. She read it twice, and then checked the calendar, to make sure. It didn't seem possible.

So that was why the autopsy hadn't pointed to a heart attack. Whether the coroner could detect it or not, her husband had been murdered.

Whoever the blackmailer was, he'd got close to Cruise without arousing alarm, and killed him silently in front of all those people. Now, his focus had turned to Rita.

When the eggs came, she found she'd lost her appetite.

CHAPTER TEN

On Wednesday evening, Laura carted her clothes basket down the steps to the ground level and around to the back of the fourplex. The door to the laundry room stood ajar, and she approached it cautiously. All the tenants had keys, and the room was supposed to be kept locked.

It wasn't quite eight o'clock, but already the last wisps of daylight had faded. The August twilight warned of early darknesses to come.

She thought of the murderer, at large somewhere in San Paradiso. Had they known him and been stunned at the last minute, those three women he killed? Or had he been a stranger?

"Hello?" Laura called from outside, holding the basket in front of her like a shield. She felt foolish, pretending a pile of dirty laundry was any kind of defense.

"'Allo, I am almost finished," replied a woman's voice with a French accent.

It had to be the new tenant. Laura thought about coming back later, but she couldn't avoid meeting the woman forever.

"Don't hurry. I've got plenty of time." She wedged the door open with her body and hauled the heavy basket inside. "My name's Laura."

"Madeleine," said the woman.

She was shorter than Laura, and busy at the moment folding linen underclothes with bent, arthritic fingers. Then she set the lingerie aside and looked up. In the flat, thin light of an overhead bulb, her eyes seemed to be sunk in inky pools, and her hair looked more orange than red.

The point of her chin, the twitch of those thin lips—like someone Laura had once known but couldn't quite place.

"You're the new tenant." Laura felt her way into the conversation. "Did you move in today?"

"Yesterday." Madeleine watched her as if seeking some elusive detail. "I saw you going upstairs."

"I'm afraid I wasn't in any shape to be neighborly yesterday." Laura sorted her laundry. "Something happened that was kind of . . . traumatic."

"In what way?"

Laura brushed aside a twinge of resentment. She didn't like the sense of being interrogated, but perhaps she was overreacting. "I suppose you heard about Senator Long dying. I saw it happen."

"You've never seen anyone die before?" Madeleine began arranging ruffled blouses on fat, crocheted hangers.

"You ask such strange questions."

The woman continued working. "I suppose it sounds that way. I grew up during the war. It amazes me that you young people are so sheltered from death."

"Actually," Laura said, "I was riding in the backseat when my mother died in a car accident, when I was seven."

"You remember this?"

"No," she said. "I've been told about it. The funny thing is that I feel as if I saw my father die, less than a year later. I had this—I guess you'd call it a psychic flash. I'm sorry. I don't know why I'm telling you this. It isn't something I usually talk about."

The newcomer stopped buttoning a blouse, and Laura could have sworn the vein-ravaged hands were quivering. "You look like him."

"What?"

"I didn't expect it, that you would look like him. It's the mouth and, what do you call it, the eyebrows," Madeleine said.

"You knew him?" Laura let the detergent box fall to the floor. "Madame Marin! We lived with you. What are you doing here?"

As she spoke, Laura realized that since she'd seen the woman in the street yesterday, memories had prickled through her consciousness. The past was coming back to her, and it wasn't merely by chance.

"Ah." Madeleine smoothed out the wrinkles in a narrow black skirt. "I suppose I should have written. I had your address several years ago from your aunt."

"You came all the way from Nice to see me?"

"Not really," Madeleine said. "Although I thought it would be nice to see you again. I've come because of my memoir. It was published last year in Paris, a small success. I was a kind of Mata Hari for the Resistance. It was suggested to me that certain persons in

Hollywood might find this interesting. *Eh bien,* I look at a map, and I see that San Paradiso is not so far from Los Angeles." The old woman shrugged.

"And here you are." Laura added soap to her laundry and pushed in the coin tray. The quarters dropped, and the machine churned into life.

Used to pursuing puzzles in her work, Laura could see the pieces to this one didn't fit. It was beginning to seem as if all these strange occurrences were linked, and yet they couldn't be. Senator Long staring as if trying to warn her, the letters from her father turning up, Madeleine Marin moving into her building, that inexplicable episode with Lew in the parking lot.

She didn't believe Madame Marin had come here to hawk the film rights to her memoirs. That was a job for an agent. And why hadn't the Frenchwoman knocked on Laura's door first thing?

But this wasn't a news story, and Laura wasn't reporting on it. No sense asking questions until she knew which ones were the right ones.

The older woman finished folding her laundry. "*Bonne nuit,*" she said, and vanished out the laundry-room door.

As she climbed the steps to her own apartment a few minutes later, Laura wondered what could have brought the woman such a long distance after so many years. And why she didn't seem particularly eager to renew Laura's acquaintance.

April 24, 1973
Madrid

Dear Ellen,

You may be surprised to receive this letter so soon after my last one. You see, I simply can't write these things to Kate, and I need to tell someone. You won't take them too seriously, I'm sure.

I've had the strangest experience, and this time I don't think it was fever. . . .

James stood for a long time, staring at the painting, unmindful of the tourists shifting around him as they dutifully checked off the Prado museum on their list of Things Seen.

"The Witches' Sabbath" was one of Goya's "black paintings," dark depictions of supernatural subjects done in a style that prefigured Impressionism. The long, horizontal canvas had nothing to do with his Ph.D. subject, with the impact of Spain's wars on Goya's works. But it fascinated and compelled him.

Dark, nightmarish peasants, the whites of their eyes gleaming unnaturally, stared transfixed at the silhouetted figure of a goat. Seated and robed, the goat-devil appeared to preach to them.

They were here around him, those dark faces. He could feel their fetid breath on his neck.

This wasn't simply a painting, he knew instinctively. The canvas had pulled something out of Goya's soul. A piece of the artist lived on here, not figuratively but literally.

The canvas throbbed as James stared at it. He could swear that it moved.

He swallowed and tried to bring himself back to reality, but the other people and paintings in the room were mere shadows. Only he and "The Witches' Sabbath" had edges.

He wondered if there were some rational explanation for this experience. His fever; that was possible, even though he no longer felt hot. Or perhaps it could be understood as the excitement of an art historian finally come face-to-face with the work of a genius he had previously admired only from afar.

Perhaps other scholars felt this same way on viewing the subjects they had studied so intensely.

But that didn't explain the easel in front of him, the canvas and paints and brushes he'd sought out this morning after he first encountered the painting.

James had a slight facility for sketching, yes, he would give himself that, but he certainly hadn't distinguished himself as a copyist in his oil-painting classes. He was an analyst of art, not a creator or even imitator of it. Right now, he didn't even know where to begin.

Nevertheless, his paintbrush seemed to know.

It felt its way through the eerie light flickering over blurred faces and whited eyes. He realized that he had neglected to block out his work in advance, to estimate the spatial relationships. It didn't matter. The creatures sprang up beneath his brush, so that the picture seemed to be emerging from his canvas rather than being laid on top of it.

A current flowed into the brush. Looking down, trying to be objective about it, James could see the flesh ripple along his arm. He felt a mild tingling, nothing more.

Something was passing from him into the canvas.

His detachment surprised him. The mere act of copying this

Goya work was drawing out some previously unsuspected essence, leaving a small dark space in—did he just imagine that it was his chest? Surely, such a thing as one's soul didn't dwell in any particular part of the body.

His soul?

James had never been a religious man. Vaguely, he did believe in the existence of a God, but not in the towering old-man figure of Michelangelo's Sistine Chapel. If he had been asked, he supposed he would have said that God was the supreme life force.

As for the Devil, James had never given much thought to it, either. The Devil, for him, had always been a useful pivot in certain plays and operas, imaginary like fauns and faeries.

Standing here in this clean, well-lighted gallery of the Prado, he felt one of these great forces envelop him. As if it had always owned a share of his soul and was claiming it now.

And transferring it to his painting.

He knew the energy from the original had pulled him to Madrid and lulled him into this trancelike state. He was standing before an immense source of power that had been stolen in the same manner from Goya nearly two centuries before.

The scholar in him wondered what use he was expected to make of this copy and why he had been chosen. Whether it had anything to do with his family's peculiar history.

The man in him shivered before a great inescapable will that might be wondrously good or terrifyingly evil.

After an unmeasured time, James stepped back and saw that his painting was finished.

Behind him, a man and a woman paused. "Incredible," the man said loudly, perhaps thinking James unable to comprehend English. "It looks exactly like, don't you think?"

"Except for those little lines over the goat," the woman said. "His hand must have slipped."

"Still, he's very good."

"So is a copy machine."

They moved away. They hadn't felt it, whatever was radiating from the paintings. It held James motionless for several more minutes.

Only his eyes shifted, checking above the goat's head. The woman was right; those little lines didn't belong there.

And yet they did. If you connected them cleanly, he saw, you'd have an upright rectangle. It looked, he supposed, somewhat like a door.

Don't worry about these moods of mine, dear good Ellen. Tend to your roses in Cincinnati, pray for the Reds to win the pennant, and give Fred a hug for me. These strange impressions will pass sooner or later. Someday we will all come home and be as we were.

Your loving brother,
James

But they hadn't all come home, after all.

Laura set the letter aside and checked her watch. Nine-fifteen, almost time for the last load of laundry to be done.

She had nearly finished reading the stack of letters. There were a lot of references she didn't understand, to people and places and events in art history. Some letters were concise and coherent, others rambling and near madness.

If only she knew what had happened to her father's painting. Not that it mattered, most likely, and yet . . .

In these past few days, she had begun imagining layers of impossible reality, seeing connections where surely there were only coincidences.

Yet James had written with calm certainty that a part of his soul had passed into a painting.

Laura wanted to see it. To wipe away this nagging fear at the back of her awareness that once, long ago, she *had* seen it and been changed forever.

Folding the letter aside, she scrawled a note asking her aunt if there might be a copy of a Goya painting somewhere in the attic.

Then she went down to get the laundry.

CHAPTER ELEVEN

"Lew Tarkenton won't give you an interview?" Greg Evans glanced across his desk for confirmation. "I don't blame him. From what I hear, he's shot his mouth off about wanting the appointment, and Long isn't even buried yet."

For once, Laura wished her editor weren't so intensely involved with the actual news-gathering. She knew so many things about Lew that she couldn't tell him, and not much that she could. She hated to look as if she hadn't done a thorough job.

"I've been doing some research into his background." Greg flipped open a steno pad. "An antiwar activist during the early seventies. Arrested twice, but charges were dropped both times. He cooled it after he entered Stanford Law. Married at twenty-five, wife a radical feminist who divorced him and entered a commune—that's a trip, isn't it?"

"She's an executive with Arco now," Laura said.

Greg made a note. "Good work. So I suppose you know the rest." He snapped the pad shut. "I think he's the hottest contender."

Laura was startled. "What about Mrs. Long?"

"What did you call her? Rita the Bimbo? I think the public sees her the same way." Greg swiveled back in his chair and put his feet up on the desk. "You're interviewing her this afternoon, right?"

"If she'll let me. And don't forget Joe Pickard."

Greg waved his hand. "From what Steve says, he's got more serious problems to deal with. Keep me informed on how it goes with the widow. But keep chipping away at Tarkenton."

"Sure." A sense of unease trailed out with Laura. Why did Greg have to fasten on Lew? She sure as hell hoped the editor didn't really have an inside track to the governor.

It was past noon, time to head for Newport Beach. Laura ate a hamburger in her car, sitting in the Burger King parking lot and listening to the news on the radio. A terrorist bomb had ripped through a Paris railroad station packed with people fleeing the latest aftershock, leaving at least fifty dead and hundreds injured. A group claiming responsibility for the attack was believed to be linked to Ayatollah Al-Hadassi. The incident was to be discussed at the emergency summit, which had been scheduled for Sunday.

It comforted her a little, that the world's leaders would be gathering. True, all they hoped to accomplish was to coordinate aid and agree not to turn nature's tragedies to their own political ends. Yet she felt like a child on learning that her parents now acknowledged there really were monsters under the bed. Someone with real power had taken charge.

Through the windshield, Laura noticed that the sun had gone behind a cloud. The air shifting through her rolled-down windows turned clammy and dense.

Dark mist closed in, defying Laura's attempts to blink it away. Beneath it, like a faint tracing, she could still see the cars lined up at the drive-thru, but she couldn't make them out clearly.

Overhead, clouds bulged in striated piles. Like muscles. Like some huge malevolent shape blotting out the heavens. For one vertiginous instant, it became more real than the steering wheel gripped beneath her hands or the palm tree towering over the restaurant.

Real. Like the figures her father had painted, springing up from the canvas. A projection from within, that's what James had written. Part of himself, pouring onto the canvas.

If she let herself go, would the titan in the sky shrink down and take solid shape in front of her? Maybe she should let it. Maybe she should stop running away.

Or maybe this was insanity, Laura thought. She'd read that schizophrenics sometimes stood back from themselves, watching with a sliver of sanity while the rest of the self went mad.

It frightened her, this chaos inside her own mind. She wouldn't give in to it. Not now, not ever.

She closed her eyes for a moment. When she opened them again, she saw only a white, cloudless sky, the sparkle of sunlight on restaurant windows, and cars waiting in line for their allotment of burgers and fries.

A song Laura hadn't noticed ended on the radio. "Time for our one-thirty traffic update . . ." Time to pull herself together and head south.

The area of Newport Beach where Rita Long lived lay a few miles uphill from the heavily developed coast, on a large lot with a view down across the ocean and all the way to Catalina Island. The architecture was more pompous than distinguished, Southern Gothic with a touch of Pompeii.

Laura checked her makeup in the rearview mirror and applied lipstick, then picked up her purse, notepad, and tape recorder. Her breath squeezing in anticipation of having the door slammed in her face, she marched up the walk and rang the bell.

It chimed and echoed. A minute later, the door was opened by a Hispanic woman with salt-and-pepper hair. "Yes?"

"I'm Laura Bennett from the *Paradise Herald.* I have an appointment with Mrs. Long."

The woman regarded her dubiously. "Just a minute." The door clicked shut.

Laura stretched her shoulders, grateful for the small shaded porch. There was nothing else welcoming about the house, with its clipped square lawn and boxy shrubs.

Finally, the door opened again. To her surprise, the housekeeper said, "You can come in now."

Laura followed her through a marble-floored hallway and into a vast sunken living room, where the housekeeper left her. Blue and white everywhere, blue curtains draping oversize windows, white couches atop a blue carpet, two huge blue-and-white Chinese vases by the fireplace. There was a faint smell of mustiness in the air that seemed out of place.

"Miss Bennett." Rita Long descended two steps and came toward Laura. She wore a dark gray dress with a white yoke and her hair was pulled back with a banana clip. "I'm sorry. I'd forgotten about our interview. I was at the funeral home all morning."

"I wasn't sure whether we were still on." Laura sat down, relieved when her hostess did the same. "I'm terribly sorry about your husband."

"Yes." Heavy makeup under Rita's eyes did a poor job of concealing the dark circles. "Yes, it was—it was a shock."

Laura opened her notepad and set the tape recorder on the coffee table. "Why don't we start. . . ."

"Miss Bennett." Long red fingernails tapped against the oversize mahogany coffee table. "There's really no point in our doing an interview. I am no longer a senator's wife. There is no reason for the public to be interested in me now."

"I'm not so sure," Laura said. "There's been some speculation that the governor may decide to appoint you to fill your husband's position until the next general election."

Rita's face went white, and she seemed to have trouble swallowing.

"Are you all right?"

The widow exhaled deeply. "I'm sorry. It's just . . . there are so many things . . . unsettled. Unknown. Even—even exactly how my husband died. No, I haven't heard from the governor, if that's what you're asking. As for anything else, I just don't know. You're not going to write this up, are you? I thought I could trust you—last time you were very fair."

"No, I won't write anything, not at this point," Laura said. "I'm just doing some background interviews with people who might be considered for the position. It may seem indelicate to think about it right now, but your husband held a very important post."

"Yes, yes. I know." Rita looked around for something. "You don't have a cigarette, do you? I stopped smoking a while back, but I could use one now."

"I'm afraid not." It surprised Laura to realize she felt an affinity for Rita. "Do you ever get the feeling," she heard herself say, "that there's something strange going on here?"

"Strange?" Rita's nervous movements stopped abruptly.

"The autopsy not showing anything, for instance. I'm sorry if I sound tactless. But"—Laura felt as if she were speaking into the wind, straining to making herself heard—"I was looking right at your husband when he collapsed, and I felt as if he were trying to communicate something."

"Is this how reporters go about gatherings stories these days?" Rita stood up and paced toward an end table. She pulled open the drawer and found a cigarette. "A fishing expedition, is that what you'd call it?"

"No. I was asking for myself, not for the paper." Laura turned off the tape recorder and folded away her notebook. "I'm sorry. That was a very inappropriate thing for me to say. Seeing him die upset me, but I have no right to inflict my feelings on you."

"You're an unusual sort of reporter." Rita ignited the cigarette with a gold-colored lighter. She seemed calmer now.

"I'm finding that I tend to get a little too involved with my stories," Laura said. "Can we talk again sometime?"

"If—if I see any point to it." Rita reached for a small bell, and almost instantly the housekeeper appeared.

"Thanks for your time," Laura said before following the woman. She was surprised how fresh the air smelled when she stepped outside.

There is something, she thought as she drove away. Something Rita can't tell me.

CHAPTER TWELVE

"We've gone over this before." The mayor was trying to sound impatient, but to Daryl Wilkinson he sounded scared. Even the big oak desk on which the city council had seen fit to lavish its funds failed to make the man behind it look confident.

"Yes, but, sir, you're our key witness. You might have seen something without even realizing it." And maybe if they ran over this story often enough, he'd slip. "Yesterday, you couldn't recall exactly what time you left her house. By my calculations, you must have arrived at her place about, oh, seven-fifteen."

"I told you, I don't remember. I guess I got home about eight."

"Mr. Pickard, Kiki only lived a few minutes from your house. Unless you were there for a while . . ." Daryl had hammered on this point yesterday, but Pickard kept shifting around. If he would just agree on a time, a time that Daryl could prove was a lie . . .

"Okay, then I must have gotten home about seven-thirty."

"Must have, or did?"

Pickard reached for a tissue and mopped his forehead. "Seven-thirty, eight, what's the difference?"

"Because I dropped by your house to ask you a few questions, Mr. Pickard. And I was there at seven-thirty." Daryl clamped his lips together. Damn it, he'd tipped his hand too soon.

But the mayor shut his eyes in weary resignation. "Okay, she invited me in. We talked for a few minutes. That's all."

Daryl pressed the point. "One of the details we haven't released to the press is that the victim had had intercourse that night." He tapped his pen against his notebook but didn't take his eyes from Pickard's face.

"Oh, Jesus." The fat man took a deep, shuddering breath. "Look, as I'm sure that friend of hers told you, I'd run into Kiki before. We had a—a kind of flirtation. Well, when I took her home, she invited me in."

"You had sex?" This was getting interesting.

The mayor nodded reluctantly. "Yes. I offered to stay over, but she said her girlfriend would be coming by in the morning, and she didn't want any gossip."

I don't blame her. "What time did you say you left?"

"Eight-thirty, nine, something like that. Look, I"— Pickard made a vague gesture with his hands— "I really liked Kiki. I took her home because—because I wanted to protect her. Because women keep getting killed after being around me, and I wanted to make sure she was safe. As God is my witness, I didn't do it." Shit, it looked like the guy was going to start blubbering. "I *liked* Kiki. I wanted to see her again. Sergeant, I don't know who's doing this or why, but I think they're trying to frame me."

"People don't go around murdering women to frame somebody," Daryl said. But the idea pricked at him. Joe the Slow wasn't exactly a nobody. He probably had enemies. Maybe ambitions, too, that might threaten somebody. Hell, Daryl didn't know anything about politics. Maybe if something big enough was at stake . . . "Whoever killed Kiki Bellaga apparently just walked in the door. Why would she have let him in?"

"I don't know." Pickard fumbled with a pack of Marlboros. "I made sure the door was locked before I left. I even looked around the parking lot. Sergeant, I sure as hell didn't want her to die."

This was getting them nowhere. "Let me know if you think of anything else," Daryl said, snapping his notebook shut.

He walked out to his car thinking about the victim's friend, Elaine. She'd been extremely upset, but coherent. "It was that creep. He was getting back at Kiki."

Why had Pickard been so quick to confess? As a lawyer, he ought to know he was putting himself under even more suspicion, not to mention how this would look if it came out in the press. And why had he insisted her door was locked when he left? There were no signs of forced entry, and why would Kiki open the door for a stranger?

The plain fact was that Joe Pickard wasn't very smart, and he didn't think fast in a pinch. Whoever was murdering these women had been slick enough not to leave any evidence and clever enough to trick them into letting him get close.

Daryl didn't want to think what he was thinking. But there it was. His gut instinct was changing. He began to suspect that someone was framing Joe Pickard, or at least using the guy as a convenient, bumbling foil.

Daryl didn't like the way Lieutenant Grover and Captain DeWitt were looking at him. They were sitting in DeWitt's office, a glassed-in cubicle slightly bigger than Grover's, which was next to it. From where he sat, Daryl had a good view of his own desk and of the other detectives coming and going, talking on the phone and making notations on their reports. He wished he were out there with them. He wished he hadn't requested this meeting. What the hell had come over him, anyway?

"Other than the mayor's word, what makes you think someone would try to frame him?" DeWitt was saying.

Looking at it after a night's reflection, Daryl had to admit that Pickard's stupidity wasn't much of an argument.

"He had to see that we'd connect him to the victims," Daryl said instead. "Driving Bellaga home was a dead giveaway."

To his relief, the lieutenant nodded slowly. "It's always possible he really wants to be caught, but you've got a point there."

"Have we got a tail on the mayor?" DeWitt asked.

"As of two days ago." Grover rubbed the heel of his hand over his forehead. His wife was back in the hospital, Daryl had heard that morning.

"And have there been any signs that somebody else is following Pickard?"

"No, but then, we weren't looking for that," the lieutenant said.

"Well, tell them to look for it." The captain's tone was a dismissal, and the other two men took their leave.

"You really think he's being set up?" Grover asked as soon as they were outside the captain's office.

That was the question Daryl had been putting to himself all night. "I'm not sure. It's just a possibility."

"And a damn scary one." Grover paused outside his own office door. "Because it means that if we arrest Pickard and the murders stop, we still don't know if we got the right guy."

"Yeah. Damn it." As he walked to his desk, it occurred to Daryl that it might be worth it to lock up Pickard, just so nobody else got killed. Only whoever was doing this obviously liked his work. Which meant that, sooner or later, he'd find an excuse to start up again.

Daryl had an uneasy feeling for the rest of the morning, as if he'd missed something important. He went over his notes from yesterday again and again, but nothing clicked.

Steve Orkney, the cop reporter from the *Herald*, always came by the station about eight-thirty in the morning and hung around until after briefing. Today, he turned up again at noon. The desk officer, who was near retirement and a soft touch for Orkney's dirty jokes, let him back to Detectives.

"Something I can do for you?" Daryl never entirely trusted a reporter, but Orkney had been on the job a long time and knew enough not to go poking around reports he wasn't supposed to see or to print anything he overheard in passing. Which was about as much as you could ask.

"How about if I take you to lunch?"

"You asking me out on a date?" Daryl snorted. "Should I get my hair done?"

Orkney chuckled. He was a heavyset guy, but not a slob. Shrewd. He'd helped the police out a time or two, running stories that they were looking for witnesses, that kind of thing. "Well, I've heard a few things that might or might not be helpful. And since I've got an expense account I hardly ever use, why don't we blow it on lunch?"

So Orkney had been snooping around on his own. Well, Daryl had learned a long time ago that people who clammed up around the police would yak their brains out to a reporter. Made them feel important. "Okay. What've you got in mind?"

"How about the Beefmaster on Beach Boulevard?"

"Sure. Why not?"

They went out to Daryl's car. On the radio, the announcer was talking about the summit meeting President Harkness had called for Sunday. Great Britain, France, and Canada had already agreed to participate, and Britain had offered to provide security in the city of Perth.

"Where the hell is Perth?" Daryl muttered. "Isn't that in Australia?"

"I think they mean Scotland."

The Beefmaster was crowded, but they had to wait only a few minutes. They ordered, and then Daryl got to the point. "What have you heard?"

"I've been hanging out at the high school. Doing color, you know, how scared everybody is and what precautions they're taking." Orkney looked around the room as he spoke, but apparently he didn't spot anybody significant.

"And?"

"One of the guys acted kind of uncomfortable. Like he knew something he didn't want to talk about. So I shined him up, and he finally let slip that his girlfriend found a purse in a trash bin last week—she's into recycling cans or something."

A purse. Marla Rivers's purse? "What did she do with it?"

"Took it home, found some money inside, and spent it on pot. He didn't know what happened to the purse after that."

Daryl took a pad out of his pocket, ignoring the waitress's arrival with their food. "What's her name?"

Orkney waited until the woman left. "Juliet Noonan. You'll let me know what you find out, right?"

The bacon burger smelled great. Daryl wolfed it down, along with the cottage fries. "Gotta go."

"I knew I shoulda waited," Orkney sighed, collecting the remainder of his meal into his napkin. He paid the bill, and they left.

The high school provided the girl's address and phone number. When Daryl went by, the girl wasn't home yet, but her mother, who seemed surprised by the whole thing, let him in when he showed his badge and explained about the purse.

"She isn't in any trouble, is she?" Mrs. Noonan asked as she led the way through the tract house.

"Not if she cooperates," Daryl said.

"She's really not a bad girl. Just kind of wild sometimes, but I guess all teenagers are. Oh, her room's in there."

It looked like the Great Earthquake had struck and left devastation in its wake. The bed was unmade, clothes lay strewn across the floor, and the vanity table was heaped with open jars and tubes of makeup.

"She keeps her purses in the closet," the mother said.

Carefully, Daryl slid open one of the doors, not wanting to brush against anything. He had to step aside to let some light onto the jumbled mass of purses. Most of them were clearly designed for teenagers, funky bags made of denim or little moccasin-leather jobs.

"That must be it." Mrs. Noonan, standing just behind his shoulder, pointed at an oversize red handbag. "It doesn't look like hers."

The cracked, once-shiny vinyl surface was smeared with fingerprints. Most probably belonged to Juliet Noonan.

But maybe, if he got lucky, one of them would lead to the killer.

CHAPTER THIRTEEN

"We aren't talking about my father's will, we're talking about common decency." Rita, holding the phone several inches from her ear, could still hear her stepdaughter's strident voice. "You know men don't think about sentimental value. Those things belonged to my grandmother. He left you plenty of money to buy anything you want."

Barbara Long had an uncanny ability to infuriate. She knew just where to twist the knife.

"If you'd like to draw up a list of items, I'm certainly willing to consider it." Rita traced curlicues along the edge of her calendar with a gold-plated pen. Around her, the house felt curiously still and tense. She wished Ramona didn't take Friday evenings off to visit her son in Los Angeles. She didn't like being alone.

"You can hardly expect me to remember everything," Barbara whined. "I'll have to look through the house. I can come over right after the funeral tomorrow."

"There will be people here," Rita said, although she wasn't sure it was true. "You can come over next week, if you like."

"Well, that certainly gives you time to dispose of things." The bitchy edge to Barbara's voice belied a face that, as Rita recalled it, was china-doll sweet, framed in expensively cut and dyed honey-blond curls.

"I don't think you're quite in control of yourself." Rita was pleased with the diplomacy of her answer. Cruise would have approved. "Furthermore, I have no need to dispose of what belongs to me. If I choose to give you anything, Barbara, it is for the sake of goodwill, not because I owe it to you."

"Well, I don't suppose there's any more to say then, is there?" The telephone line crackled with outrage.

"That's up to you."

The phone crashed down. Rita replaced her receiver quietly and rubbed the back of her neck, trying to banish her stepdaughter's words along with the tension. She had enough to worry about without Barbara.

Restless, Rita flicked on the radio while she turned to the stack of condolence cards on the desk. She'd been relieved to find no anonymous messages in today's mail.

The music faded into news. "The leaders of Egypt and Israel have both agreed to participate in Sunday's summit on aid to destabilized nations. Meanwhile, in China today, Beijing has been surrounded by a mass of peasants seeking food stored in the capital city. The rebels are reported to be heavily armed with assault rifles and rocket launchers. . . ."

Somehow the world's disasters made Cruise's death seem a little less overwhelming. Other people had lost family members, and more. At least Rita had a comfortable home, and she lived in a country at peace.

She reread one of the condolence cards. It was from an assemblywoman whom Rita vaguely recalled as having bluish hair and a taste for snakeskin shoes. On a black-bordered card, Rita wrote, *Your expression of sympathy is a great comfort. Thank you for thinking of me at this difficult time,* and signed her name, *Mrs. Cruise Long.* It was correct; she had checked her book of etiquette. Only divorcées had to go back to using their own first name.

On the radio, the announcer's tone grew excited. "This just in. Joseph Pickard, the mayor of San Paradiso, has been arrested in connection with the murder of Marla Rivers, one of three women slain in San Paradiso during the past two weeks."

Rita stopped writing.

Amid static hum, another male voice said, "Mayor Pickard's arrest results from the discovery of certain physical evidence which I am not at liberty to disclose."

"That was Lieutenant John Grover of the San Paradiso Police Department," the announcer said. "He declined to say whether Pickard would also be charged with the other two murders."

A commercial for radial tires came on. Rita turned off the radio and closed her eyes.

She could see the banquet room where Cruise had collapsed, the long head table stretched out in front of her. The only people who had got close to Cruise, besides Rita and Bob Fillipone, were some of the editors. And Joe Pickard.

He could have put something in Cruise's glass.

Pickard had been Governor Fisher's Orange County campaign

manager. He might have considered himself in the running to fill Cruise's position.

But how could he have known about the boys at the beach? How could he have staged the photograph?

Well, someone had managed to do it, and it might have been Joe Pickard.

She would have to wait for the autopsy results before she made any accusations. After all, there was still a slight possibility Cruise had died of natural causes. She didn't want to make hysterical accusations.

Besides, Joe Pickard was already in jail.

Which meant she was safe. Safe from the man who might have murdered her husband, safe as long as he remained behind bars.

Suddenly, Rita felt like celebrating. It meant she was free to accept her husband's post, if it were offered to her. Senator Rita Long. She would be strong enough then to withstand people like Barbara and all the others who looked at her with contemptuous eyes. Surrounded by her aides, she would sponsor bills, make speeches, fly back from Washington to meet with her constituents. Her constituents. She liked the sound of that.

Downstairs, she heard a sharp noise, like a single knock on a table.

Rita's heart jerked. "Ramona?" But she wouldn't be back this early.

The ice-maker? Sometimes it let a cube fall through the server window onto the floor. Rita kept silent for a moment, listening. The house seemed to hold its breath, too.

From downstairs came a faint rustling noise. Should she call the police?

Then Rita remembered that Barbara had a key to the house. She could have driven over from her hotel in five, ten minutes.

That little bitch, trying to frighten me.

She found the small gun that Cruise kept in the desk drawer. Rita wasn't sure how to use it; she wasn't even sure if the safety was off. But it would probably scare the hell out of Barbara to be confronted with it.

She stood up and moved down the hall. Her bedroom slippers hardly made any noise on the carpet. At the top of the stairs, she waited and listened again.

A draft of hot air soughed against her cheeks. It smelled foul, like trash burning at a landfill. Instinctively, she took a step backward.

Where had that come from?

It was hot outside but cool in the house, and they kept the

windows sealed. Tentatively, Rita inhaled again, and was relieved to find both the heat and smell were gone.

She wondered if she'd imagined the noises, or if they weren't just the house's natural creakings that she'd never noticed before. Maybe she was having some kind of hormone surge. Maybe even . . . no, not pregnant. Her period had just ended Sunday.

"Barbara?" She tried to make her voice firm. "If that's you, you'd better say so. I've got a gun."

Another gust of hot air hissed by her, like someone whispering behind her back. Like people talking about her, making plans for her, unseen people steering her as she walked slowly down the stairs. *Rita, Rita, who do you think you are? Rita, Rita, you don't belong here. Don't belong.*

At the foot of the steps, she hesitated. To her right, the living room opened off the hallway. Directly to her left was the powder room; further down, she would come to the dining room and, through it, the kitchen.

"Ramona? Barbara?" She would give anything to see her stepdaughter now.

Here, this way. The heat blew toward her through the dining room, thick and foul.

Rita broke into a sweat. There was a telephone on the wall to her left, but she couldn't seem to reach for it. Her body felt heavy, like that of a woman in labor. Her feet shuffled forward, one slow step at a time; the trigger on the gun cut into her finger. There was no carpet in the hallway, and her rubber-soled slippers made faint sucking noises on the polished wood.

Rita, Rita, we've been waiting for you.

The hallway lengthened ahead of her, so that the dining-room door was a faint speck of light in the distance. Her breath rattled, and her heartbeat thundered like a storm breaking in the damp heat. Faces in the clouds, faces on the wall. Boys' faces, men's faces. Faces she'd long forgotten. Hungry, leering faces. Mouths that wanted to take what she had and then spit her out. The men before Cruise, the casting directors and assistant producers and the boys from high school. *Rita, Rita, we know what you're good for.*

"Get out of my house!" The words burst out and went nowhere in the dead air.

She found herself at the door to the dining room. Choking, stifling hot, rancid. The room was swollen with fumes, near bursting. She could hardly move in the thickness, but something dragged her through the white burning light to a portal.

In the kitchen, everything was red. The stove was red, the walls were red, the counter was red. So hot she couldn't bear to enter. Water poured out of the window in the refrigerator, steaming and evaporating on its way to the scarlet floor. The sink was red, the cabinets were red. Rita's face began to scorch; she could feel the skin cracking and peeling.

Rita, Rita, you'll like it here. Nice and hot. Lie down for us, Rita. We know what you're good for.

She knew she must be dreaming. She knew that if she could just take some kind of action, this hallucination would disappear.

Something moved, off to her left, and she swiveled. The door to the pantry was spinning around and around, as if it were hinged in the middle. A mirrored door, flashing and grimacing back with her own distorted face.

Only it wasn't quite her face. There was something solid revolving inside the door, another Rita. A Rita dressed in a tight scarlet dress cut all the way up her thigh and down so low that her breasts hung out. An obscene Rita spreading her legs and laughing.

You can be replaced, you know.

Rita tried to fire the gun, but it clicked emptily. She tossed it aside and jerked open a drawer, scrabbling wildly until she found Ramona's butcher knife.

The thing in the door was still going round and round, but not laughing anymore. Its painted mouth twisted as it stepped into the kitchen.

Oh, God, it was real, as real as she was.

Rita held up the knife. Her whole body felt stiff and alien, but she had to keep functioning. She tried to speak, but the only thing that came out was a vague raspy noise.

The Rita-thing smiled cruelly. *I'm not strong enough yet.* Its voice had a hollow ring. *Soon. Keep your damn knife. We'll teach you a few lessons yet, Rita Rita Rita.*

It stripped off the dress, undulating crudely as the fabric peeled away from the flesh, thrusting out its breasts and pelvis as if posing for some porno film. Naked, it taunted her with pouting lips and curling narrow tongue. A forked tongue, coming out of a metamorphosing body. Not a body at all but a transparent body-shape, and inside something writhed, thick and serpentine, a lizardlike creature with little yellow eyes, spinning, spinning into haze. . . .

A blistering wave of red rolled toward Rita. She was going to be incinerated. Red dust, red flames, red world. Red in her mind, red behind her eyes, red in her throat. Red air, impossible to breathe . . .

She sagged onto the linoleum.

When Rita woke up, the house was dark and quiet. Her body had stiffened from lying on the floor, and her head felt cottony, but there was no pain except for a slight soreness in her throat. No sensation of heat, no burned patches of skin, just this hoarse sandpaper feeling.

Pushing herself into a sitting position, Rita checked the luminous clock on the wall and saw that the hands were edging past seven. She couldn't have been unconscious more than a few minutes.

Awkwardly, she climbed to her feet and switched on the light.

Then she felt it, the breath of warm air from the oven. The dial was set at 400 degrees. Ramona had said she would bake a meat pie for Rita's dinner. She must have forgotten to switch it off.

After checking that the meat pie was safely in the refrigerator, Rita turned to pick up the gun from the floor. That was when she spotted the butcher knife stuck into the table.

It made an ugly gash in the thick oak. Pinned beneath it was a folded sheet of typewriter paper. After three tries to free the knife, Rita pushed rather than pulled it loose.

Inside the paper were typed five words: *You will turn it down.*

It couldn't have come from Joe Pickard.

Whoever it was, he must have drugged her. And he didn't just want Cruise's job. He wanted to strip away Rita's dignity, to push her back into the mire, to make her crawl and fuck her over.

She wasn't going to let him. Not if she could help it, whatever the cost.

CHAPTER FOURTEEN

On Friday night, Laura watched a videotaped comedy and thought about Lew. She missed having him to snuggle against, and without him, nothing seemed very funny.

The phone call from her aunt was a welcome interruption.

"I wasn't sure I'd catch you home on a Friday night," Ellen said.

"Just watching TV." Although Laura had mentioned Lew a few times, she never felt comfortable discussing the relationship with her aunt. There was a quality about Ellen that she didn't know how to deal with. A comfortable certainty that things worked themselves out, that life was as neat as the crewel embroidery on the pillows Ellen made. Laura didn't want easy reassurances about getting back together with Lew.

"I was calling about the letter I got from you today." As her aunt spoke, Anne Murray sang softly in the background. "I've been looking through the attic. You know, now that you mention it, I do recall seeing a painting that your father brought back from Europe. It was rather strange; I can't say I liked it, but I don't know much about these things."

"What did it look like?" Laura asked. "Did you recognize it?"

"No, but James said it was a copy of a Goya. There was some kind of animal in it, a horse or a goat or something. Anyway, it's not here. It was rolled up inside some brown paper; I remember he repackaged it that way after he showed it to me. Well, there's nothing like that in the attic."

"Did Dad have an apartment of his own after we got back from Europe?"

"Not that I know of. He kept everything here, except what he could pack in a suitcase."

He'd been on a business trip to Washington when he died. Why would he have taken the painting with him?

"Do you remember the letter he wrote about it?" Laura said. "How he copied it, and it seemed as if part of himself was transferred onto the canvas?"

There was a brief, uncharacteristic pause. Finally, Ellen said, "I don't think you should dwell on what he wrote. The only reason I sent you those letters was for, well, sentimental reasons, I suppose. And because you're so levelheaded, I didn't think they'd affect you."

"But they *are* disturbing," Laura said. "And my grandmother. Your mom. If she was crazy, and it's hereditary . . ."

"I don't believe my brother was mad," Ellen said. "But he may have had a—what is that term?—psychotic episode while he was in Europe. After I got those letters, I discussed them with a family doctor. He said such things can happen, a sudden breakdown and then, poof, it's gone. Never to return."

"I'd feel better if I could find the painting," Laura said.

"I hope to God he burned it. Don't dwell on this, Laura. You could bring something on."

After they hung up, Laura wondered if her aunt was right. And if it was already too late.

She must have fallen asleep in front of the TV, because when she woke up, the tape was rewinding, and Laura realized she'd been dreaming about—what? A car, something about her father and a car.

She'd read through the rest of his letters last night. They became odder and odder, with bizarre reflections sandwiched between the most mundane details. There had been only a few references to his family; in one, he said he and Kate quarreled over his insistence that the painting rolled up in the closet was a focal point for something of great urgency.

Laura leaned her head back. Maybe it was an echo of her dream, but suddenly she had the sensation of riding in a car. The smell, that was the strongest thing, leftover cheese and sausage and the dusty fur of her teddy bear. Pooh Bear. God, she'd forgotten him entirely until this moment. Pooh Bear. And her mother's voice . . .

"I think we should go home. Really home, to America." Kate's tone was dry with weariness.

The light faded to a trickle of gray light, and the couch felt sticky. The walls arched close, shrinking the room. Laura, too, had shrunk, to child size.

"For once in my life, I have to take a stand." Her father's anxious tenor came from the front seat.

"A stand? What sort of stand?" Kate demanded. "You say you

aren't even sure if the painting is good or evil. A copy you painted yourself! Honestly, James! In your rational moments, can't you see how screwy this whole thing is?"

"It's the door." All she could see of her parents was two silhouettes. "The door is opening, Kate. It wants me to pass through it."

"James, I'm going to take Laura and go home. I don't feel safe here."

"No, please. Look, I don't know why I've been chosen. I don't even know what I've been chosen for. I'm not very brave. I need you with me." Headlights flashed by on the road, briefly highlighting her father. Her mother remained in semidarkness.

"I've looked at the painting," Kate said. "When you weren't home. I didn't see any door. It's a good-enough copy, I suppose, but there's nothing special about it. This whole business . . ."

"I'm not crazy, Kate." His voice trembled. "I keep evaluating myself, trying to be objective. Really, my mind functions perfectly. I understand your point of view. But I'm . . . *bonded* to that painting. It's got my blood in it, in a sense. It needs me. I don't know what for, yet. . . ."

It was hot back here. Something watched as they drove through the void.

"We're leaving," her mother said. "You can come with us, but you're not taking that damn painting."

Please stop. Can't you see we're in danger?

"We can't. You can't. Kate, you have to stay here with me, you and Laura."

"I'll do as I damn please!" The road turned scarlet ahead of them, but Laura couldn't make out any buildings, street signs, nothing but a great enveloping glare. Headlights, aimed straight at them.

"Damn it—"

"James! Look out—the truck!"

A fireball burst around Laura. *Mommy! Mommy!* Something breathed hoarsely, its raspy breath searing her arms and legs. The monster from her nightmares had caught them, and it was eating her mother. *Daddy!* Where was Daddy? She screamed, screamed until the sound shattered into needles of glass.

Footsteps thudded. Someone pounded on the door. "Laura?"

The room squeezed her, sucking the air away. Her legs hurt.

And then she was back, here and now in her apartment. Not in a car in the south of France twenty years ago.

"Laura? What has happened?"

Shakily, she opened the door to Madeleine, taking a moment to remember who the Frenchwoman was. "It came back to me, the accident that killed my mother."

"It came back to you?" Madeleine repeated.

"They were arguing in the car." Laura moved aside.

Madeleine stepped in cautiously, pausing to survey the room. Her eyes were a pale, pale blue, as if they'd been washed too many times. "You remember all this?"

"I know I was only seven, but . . . Oh, who knows, maybe it's my subconscious, making it up." Feeling the need to do something, Laura walked over to the VCR and ejected the cassette. "Would you like some coffee?"

"Yes, thank you."

In the kitchen, Laura poured out two cups. She didn't like confiding in Madeleine until she knew more about why the woman had really come to America, but there was no one else who remembered that period of her childhood. "Why would my father say he'd been chosen for something?"

"Your father said peculiar things sometimes." Madeleine took the cup of coffee carefully from Laura's hand, as if it were an offering.

"Was he crazy?"

The other woman watched her steadily. "I used to think so. At times."

Laura waited for her to finish, but she didn't. "Why did you really come here, Madeleine?"

"I can't tell you until I'm sure." The woman sipped her coffee in tiny slurps.

"Sure of what?"

"Of you," Madeleine said. "If you really don't know what I'm talking about, that's good. Except that of course I can't trust what you say you know or don't know. As you can't trust me. Really, I must go, now that I see nothing has actually happened." She set her almost-full cup on the coffee table, slopping a little of it onto the scarred wood.

Laura had learned that the direct approach was sometimes best, even with the most devious subject. "Why were you surprised the other day, that I look like my father?"

"You think of such clever questions." Madeleine opened the door. The air that drifted in was warm for so late in the evening. "I respect your intellect. Perhaps you got it from your father. Perhaps not."

It wasn't fair, that Madeleine held a key to at least some of the secrets and refused to share it. Accompanying her to the door, Laura felt a sudden urge to grab the old woman's arms and force her to stay. Force her to talk.

As if she understood, the Frenchwoman paused and studied Laura. Studied her like some kind of specimen, like a monkey in a cage. Her condescension was irritating, infuriating.

Through Laura's anger, Madeleine looked entirely different. Not like a frail old woman but like an insect with bulging, watchful eyes. An ugly little pest to be crushed. To be squeezed until that wrinkled throat contracted and the eyes went dull . . .

Laura stepped back, shocked. Had she actually contemplated choking Madeleine? The thoughts hadn't seemed to be hers at all.

"I knew it was still there." Madeleine's eyes held a triumphant light edged with fear. "That little . . . warp. Not quite Laura today, are we?"

"I . . . don't know what you mean."

"We will talk more later." Madeleine brushed past her out the door. "At my convenience, Laura. You will remember that." She walked a trace unsteadily down the steps.

Laura leaned against the doorframe. She wished Madeleine had never come. That Madeleine had died a long time ago, taking her secrets with her.

Except that they were coming back of their own accord.

Her parents' last argument—why was she remembering it now? Had she blocked it out for so long because they were arguing about her and she felt responsible for the accident? Or was it because of something far more terrible, something even her adult self couldn't face?

As she bent to pick up Madeleine's cup from the coffee table, Laura noticed a sheet of paper lying on the rug, half hidden beneath the sofa. It must have fallen out of the stack, she thought, but when she lifted it she saw that it was addressed to her mother, not her aunt, and that she hadn't read it before. Madeleine must have slipped it there.

August 15, 1973
Madrid

Dear Kate,

I know you didn't want me to come back here, that you've been worried about me since April. I've been distracted, I know. Inconsiderate of you, and impatient with Laura. But please believe me, I had to come. . . .

He had to see about the painting.

Only the week before, he'd taken it out of the closet, hoping to find it was merely a crude copy after all.

That was when he noticed the change.

The dark faces, the white eyes no longer fixed on the goat. They turned toward the back of the painting, toward the faint lines he'd inadvertently added above the goat-devil's head.

Only they weren't just faint lines anymore. It was very plainly a door.

James had sat for a long time in the room, staring at the picture. Maybe it was his imagination. Maybe it was because the canvas had been rolled; could oil paints shift?

He didn't see how.

Kate and Laura had gone to the beach. From outside came the clatter of traffic and the rattle of French voices at a café.

The world he knew wasn't real anymore. Nothing was except his family, and this growing certainty that he must, absolutely must, open the door.

James looked back at the painting. The faces were still turned; the door was still there.

He tried to think clearly.

It seemed to him that even if he were insane, even if his perceptions were not trustworthy, he could force them into accuracy for a few minutes at a time. If he stared very hard at something, he could see it as it really was.

Which meant that what he needed to do was to take the copy back to Madrid and set it up next to the original. Then he could tell whether the faces and the door had truly altered. At least, he thought he was still capable of that much.

But he had to do it now, before he lost his resolve or let Kate talk him out of going. And so he went alone, without telling her.

He couldn't find the hotel where he'd stayed before, but this time he didn't need to. There were plenty of rooms for rent in Madrid in August.

The guard at the Prado glanced briefly at the canvas and let him in. As he walked through the corridor, James could see easels set up here and there, with students hard at work. He stopped behind a youth laboring to copy "The Naked Maja," one of two paintings Goya had made of the duchess of Alba, reputed to be his mistress. In the companion picture, the dark-haired woman reclined on a couch in the identical position, but wore gauzy clothes.

In the original, the naked duchess stared boldly out at him, unselfconscious at the tumbled freedom of her breasts, the lush curve of her belly, the hint of dark hair between her smooth thighs. She knew she could inspire lust even after the passage of nearly two centuries.

He glanced again at the copy. No passion throbbed beneath the skin, no wantonness gazed out from the dark eyes. His discernment had not slipped, not enough to confuse an amateur replica with the real thing.

James walked on through the rooms, to the paintings Goya had created two decades after the Majas.

He stopped before "The Witches' Sabbath" and unrolled his copy.

There was no question. His picture had changed.

It had mutated even further since he'd last examined it. The door was no longer tightly delineated; there was a funny blur on the right side of it. The kind of blur you might get in a photograph if something moved while you were shooting it.

The door was opening.

James stared at it, unable at first to think what this might mean.

A door to where?

He rolled up the canvas and hurried out of the museum.

Outside, he walked for a long time, trying to sort out his thoughts. It seemed that when he had first stepped into Madrid, he had put himself into the hands of some power he didn't yet understand.

It was Goya's work that had drawn him. Across the centuries, they shared some undisclosed bond. Perhaps Goya, too, had a mysterious ancestor, some alien strain within. Perhaps once there had been a door in his original, too. But for what purpose?

On a modern street, in front of a glassed-in shop window filled with stylish manikins, James sank onto a bench.

Someone was watching him.

He studied the shoppers striding by, the elegant black-haired women always in pairs, the men with their pants cut a little too tight. Not them.

The sense of being watched came from inside the rolled-up canvas. Shivers prickled along James's arms.

Bad, a bad thing, that painting.

Or was it? He was, after all, notoriously timid, a pale student who had been more at home in libraries than at mixers on Saturday night.

A fellow who hardly even dated. He wouldn't have met Kate if she hadn't come boldly up to him in the college cafeteria and asked for his help with some homework.

Help she hadn't really needed, he'd discovered. But by then, he'd already fallen in love. Otherwise, he might have run away, as he wanted to run now from this new demand on him.

To open a door. No, to open it *wider;* it had already begun to swing toward him a little. An invitation, perhaps, from whatever lay within.

Or had it opened to let something out?

The shivers returned, harder. He would write to Kate, ask her to help. Only . . . help with what?

James wanted to believe that stepping through the door would reveal marvelous truths to him. That it would finally enable him to soar above the constraints of character that kept his research mired in mediocrity. This painting had, after all, been inspired by Goya's own masterpiece.

Surely, Kate would help him master his cowardice.

I'll be back soon. Then we can discuss this calmly together. You are my greatest strength, you know. I'm counting on you to pull me through.

Love,
James

But her mother hadn't helped him open the door; she'd fought with all her strength against it.

And died.

A coincidence, surely. An automobile accident.

And her father's heart attack, had that been an accident, too?

He'd taken the painting to Washington. Laura wondered whom he'd gone to see there. And whether, after his death, whoever it was had stolen the canvas.

The possibility frightened her. It would mean the painting really did have power, and that someone else wanted it. Enough, maybe, to have killed her father.

Checking her watch, Laura found that it was almost nine. The library closed at five on Fridays. She'd go tomorrow, before the funeral, to find a book on Goya. Seeing a reproduction of "The

Witches' Sabbath" wouldn't be the same as viewing her father's copy, but maybe it would bring back some incident she'd forgotten.

Laura didn't really want to look at the Goya, but she would do it anyway. Because all the years she'd prided herself on digging out journalistic truths, she knew now that she'd been avoiding whatever truth lay buried inside her own memory.

CHAPTER FIFTEEN

The funeral of Senator Cruise Long was held at the First Universal Church of Newport Beach, sometimes known as Our Lady of the Cadillacs. Arriving at the last minute, Laura had to inch her car through the congealing traffic. On the sidewalk in front of the church, two television minicams targeted the arriving celebrities, and half a dozen photographers flashed through the crowd.

The World of Goya: 1746–1828 sat on the backseat of Laura's car, unopened. She knew she shouldn't have taken the time to stop at the library. It could have waited until Monday. But once she committed herself to a course of action, she wanted to get on with it.

The parking lot was full, and it took another ten minutes to angle into a tight space two blocks away. The temperature hovered around 90 degrees, although it was still fifteen minutes shy of eleven. Fighting her way toward the church through drifts of gawking sightseers, Laura could feel the curl wilting out of her hair.

She paused half a block from the church to unpeel the notebook from beneath her arm and note the presence of one aging movie star, two senators, a couple of congressmen, and several watchful men who talked into their sleeves. Secret Service. So the rumor that Vice President Harlan Whiting might attend was true.

As she finished jotting down the names, Laura saw a familiar figure stride toward her. Greg, of course, wouldn't miss a scene like this.

"I've been looking for you," he said. "The vice president just pulled up."

"Oh, Jesus. Thanks." Laura shouldered her way through the throng to the front of the church, standing on tiptoe to see over the other reporters' shoulders.

The vice president was getting out of a limousine, looking solemn for the cameras. Someone shouted a question about tomorrow's summit meeting.

"I've just received word that Soviet leader Aleksei Karponov has agreed to attend the Perth summit," Whiting said. The vice president held up his hand to silence a flurry of questions. "We also have acceptances from Japan, Jordan, and India. This is going to be a real world summit. We hope that in working together to help China and France, we can also begin to forge new and stronger ties among the participating nations." He smiled for the cameras, and the Secret Service agents cleared a way into the church.

Following, Laura paused in the doorway, nearly overwhelmed by the thick fumes of hair spray and sweat. Someone said the air-conditioning would be fixed any minute. Not in time to do any good, she reflected.

Greg had saved her a seat along the center aisle. As soon as she slid into place, he pointed to the front row. "Those are Long's children from his first marriage."

A young man turned his head, and Laura glimpsed a weak chin and a thin face overpowered by his father's strong nose. The woman beside him had thick blond curls, but Laura couldn't see her face.

"Barbara Long is getting married in a few months," Greg murmured. "She was named the outstanding debutante a couple of years ago. Graduated USC; lives in San Francisco now, plays at public relations."

Ahead of them, a side door opened, and Rita Long's slender figure emerged, dressed in dark blue. Bob Fillipone escorted her to a seat on the opposite side from Long's children. The vice president had been placed beside her, an honorary member of the family.

Fillipone sat on Rita's right. Her right-hand man, Laura thought. Was he simply being kind, or was he gambling that the widow would be the next senator?

Before working for Long, the aide had served as assistant to a Tennessee representative. Then, as Long's chief aide, he had drawn up several important pieces of legislation. An ambitious man, she supposed, but one without the strong geographic ties, the fame, or the wealth required to become a major candidate. She wondered if it bothered him, being stuck behind the scenes.

Several people tried to get Laura and Greg to shift toward the center of the row, but they forced the latecomers to move by them. The church was filling up, the heat of hundreds of bodies making Laura feel as if she'd been locked in a car in the hot sun.

"You'd think the senator would have more influence with the

powers that be." Greg studied the back of Rita Long's head. "How would you say she's holding up?"

"She's strong," Laura said.

"Once the funeral's over, the governor won't waste any time appointing someone." Greg was nothing if not single-minded.

Laura observed Rita and the vice president nodding politely to each other. There ought to be more to funerals, she thought. People should cry and tear their clothing.

A minister in a black robe stepped from a side door, and the crowd hushed. Accompanied by the ponderous notes of an organ, he passed in front of three enormous bursts of flowers and stopped at the lectern, discreetly touching his forehead with a handkerchief.

From an unseen loft, organ music swelled and then faded as the minister began the service. The thick air blurred his words.

Laura turned when the rear doors opened, and a processional shuffled into the room. The pallbearers sweated beneath a mahogany coffin fitted with gleaming brass. Such tasteful splendor. Rita had done a good job of being a senator's wife, right to the end.

The closeness of the air made Laura's head ache, and her stomach churned at a whiff of body odor eddying sluggishly around the pallbearers. One of them wobbled slightly, or maybe that was an illusion of the heat. No; the man stumbled to one knee. It was the Republican state central-committee chairman, a former legislator well into his seventies. What maniac had allowed him to go through this ceremonial hard labor?

The coffin began to tilt. The entire church sat paralyzed, helplessly watching an old man crumble and a sacred ritual turn cruelly to slapstick.

Greg pushed by Laura into the aisle. She heard his concerned query and the chairman's hoarse reassurance, and then Greg set his shoulder beneath the edge of the casket and straightened.

Onward the procession went, on and on. It must be a momentary dizziness making her imagine she saw a great dome open up overhead. Dimly, she perceived gilded cupids and brown-horned shapes, darkening the vast space with the whirr of wings.

Laura squinted to see the pallbearers through smoky air. Their figures stooped and coarsened as they moved, the tailored suits transforming into the rough woven cloaks of peasants. Wizened figures from another world. Where were they taking the body?

Her hand grasped the railing beside her seat. She must not run after them. This was an illusion. If she focused hard enough, she could break through it.

The procession stopped at the altar and lowered the coffin in front of a black silhouette. The shape of a goat, its arms upraised, reaching out . . .

"Cruise Long was a great man, a towering figure fallen in the midst of life."

It was the minister speaking, his arms raised and his nose shining with sweat. Not a goat, but a stocky, balding man in a black robe.

The pallbearers merged quietly into the side aisles, leaving the magnificent casket set among an honor guard of flowers. Greg slipped back into his seat.

Laura clasped her hands together so he wouldn't notice her trembling. Damn it, why was her mind playing tricks on her? She had always been clearheaded and intensely rational. In journalism school, it had usually been Laura who came up with the most pointed questions, who hit to the heart of any issue. Now, her brain was turning fuzzy on her.

Laura got through the rest of the service by concentrating on the pastor's words, one after another.

Greg stood up as soon as the service ended. "I'm going to have a few words with the vice president, if I can get close enough." He worked his way down their row to the outside aisle, unmindful of the glares of other guests.

As soon as an usher came by, Laura stood up on cramped legs and joined the crowd in the aisle. She felt stretched and dry.

"Miss Bennett?" Bob Fillipone touched her elbow. "This way, please."

He spoke as if she must have been expecting him. She followed him through a private door to a plush dressing room where Rita Long sat drinking a cup of tea.

"I'm sorry," Laura said. "That was so awkward, that man stumbling."

"Your editor came to the rescue." Rita waved her into a chair. "Bob, could you leave us for a minute?" The press aide paused as if to caution her, then nodded and left. "He's very protective," Rita said. "Can we talk off the record?"

"Yes, of course."

"I've received some threats." The widow's forefinger tapped against a pack of cigarettes, but she didn't draw one out. "I can't tell you the exact nature, but the gist is that something terrible will happen to me if I agree to fill my husband's position."

"Has it been offered to you?" Laura asked.

Rita glanced at her sharply. "No. Maybe it won't be. That would simplify things."

It was cooler in here; the air-conditioning must be running again. "Do you have any idea who would threaten you?"

The full lips tightened. "I wish I did. Someone seems to read my thoughts in almost a . . . supernatural way. And—this is strictly confidential, you understand?"

Laura nodded. What she felt was something like elation, and something like dread. Supernatural, Rita had said. Laura wasn't the only one who felt something odd lay beneath the surface of events.

"The first threat arrived before Cruise died." Rita pulled out one of the cigarettes and twisted it. "It wasn't specific, just a . . . kind of warning."

"You think this person who threatened you killed your husband?"

The widow shrugged. "It sounds so bizarre, I'm not sure I *can* believe it. But I don't know what else to think."

"Have you told the police?"

"No one." The cigarette broke open, spilling out squiggles of brown tobacco that Rita brushed off her dress. "I don't even know why I'm telling you. I thought . . . you might hear something. You get around, you can ask questions without anyone getting suspicious. You know, it occurred to me that it might have been Joe Pickard, but I got another threat after he was arrested."

"He could have accomplices," Laura said dubiously. The two women looked at each other. "You don't believe that, either, do you?"

A shake of the head scarcely disturbed the carefully arranged dark hair. "No. It's someone a lot craftier, a lot more . . . wicked. I have this strong sense of evil. I've never been religious. Are you?"

"No." A weight had been shifted, ever so slightly, from Rita onto Laura. "If someone's watching you, he's probably here today. He probably saw me come in here."

Rita took a quick breath. "I didn't mean to put you in danger."

"I might be already. I've been running around interviewing people who might be offered your husband's job." Laura wished, suddenly and intensely, that Lew were here to advise her. Instinct told her not to hold back with Rita, but if she went too far, she might sound crazy.

"Who else have you talked to?" Rita asked.

"Joe Pickard, before he got arrested, and a superior-court judge named Lewis Tarkenton. Do you know him?"

"We've met briefly. At a reception at our house, a year or so ago." Rita pulled out another cigarette, fumbled with a match, and got it lighted. "It's occurred to me I might be wise to turn the job down, but it riles the hell out of me. What am I supposed to do with the rest of my life?"

"You could adopt a charitable cause, I suppose," Laura said. "You don't need money, do you?" She waved her hand. "Forget I said that."

For the first time, Rita smiled. "It's all right. I don't need money. The problem is, I *want* the appointment. Do you understand? I want the power. I think I could handle it. I've got a lot to learn, but I've also got Cruise's staff, and they do most of the work anyway."

Rita might make a surprisingly good senator; she owed no political debts and was tougher than people would expect. "If I find out anything, I'll let you know."

"Here's my private line." Rita wrote the number down for her. "And here's the car phone. If it's urgent."

Laura took out a business card and put her own home number on the back. "Maybe you ought to hire a guard."

"Maybe I ought to, but I won't." Rita tucked the card into her purse, along with the pack of cigarettes. "People would talk. Besides, I have this feeling that whoever it is would get around them."

There was a discreet tap at the door, and Bob Fillipone came in. "The limo's here, Mrs. Long."

"Thanks." Rita shook hands with Laura, her grip firm but brief. "We'll talk again."

Laura went out through the chapel. In spite of the heat, she shivered.

At the newspaper, it was hard to focus on writing up the mundane details of the funeral after Laura's conversation with Rita, but she managed to get through it in a couple of hours.

The Sunday editor came in and turned on the newsroom TV to check the coverage of the summit. Logging off the computer, Laura paused to watch the camera pan over a brownish building with narrow, white-edged windows.

"More than a dozen of the world's leaders, including French president Giroux and Li Song Yen of China, are arriving here in Perth for tomorrow's unprecedented summit," said a British-accented male voice. "It's a stellar lineup such as this quiet city hasn't seen in centuries.

"The 'Fair City,' as it's called, was the capital of Scotland until 1437, when James I was murdered here and his widow moved the court to Edinburgh."

At the mention of murder, something cold touched Laura's spine.

And yet, there couldn't be many cities in Europe that didn't have a bloody past.

"We're looking at Huntingtower Castle near Perth, where James VI of Scotland was kidnapped in 1582 by angry Protestant noblemen," the announcer continued. "The city has a long and colorful history. . . ."

She tucked her notebook into her purse and went out into the late-afternoon heat. Once, Laura had aspired to become a foreign correspondent, to cover the great events of her time. But Long's death and the ugly threats against Rita made her wonder if she had the stomach for it.

It wasn't until she parked in front of her apartment that Laura remembered about the biography of Goya and reached into the backseat for it.

The book was gone.

CHAPTER SIXTEEN

Draper Dagmar was not a happy man that Saturday night as he showed his lawyer out of his sprawling Huntington Harbour home.

"I want my case assigned to another judge," he repeated. "I don't care how you do it, just do it."

The lawyer, Ted Lopez, stood on the front porch, backlighted by a streetlamp. "I told you, I've had no luck. Mr. Dagmar—"

"Then I'll get me another lawyer." Dagmar slammed the door in the man's face. Hell, he was paid to take that kind of abuse.

Draper Dagmar, born Dudley Tubbs in a public hospital in East Los Angeles, stalked through the living room to the den at the back of the house, where he stood glaring through a broad glass wall at the harbor.

Lydia was in Europe, their daughter was in summer camp, and he was in a hell of a mess.

He hadn't thought he would ever get caught. He'd been careful along the way, not like a lot of assholes. He'd greased the right palms. If the governor weren't in so much trouble himself, he might have helped, but as it was . . .

Damn Lewis Tarkenton! Not that the other judges were corrupt, but most of them were . . . influenceable. They had their soft spots; at least, they'd grant continuances automatically, let his lawyers drag things out until Fisher's problems blew over or the D.A. had bigger fish to fry.

Draper stalked to the mirrored bar and poured himself a glass of straight bourbon.

He was only forty-five years old. He couldn't plead ill health or the dangers of prison life like some of those old farts did. And it was only a few years since the money had really started to blossom, not just on the books but in his private bank accounts. He didn't intend to spend the next ten or twenty years behind bars while his wife blew it on clothes.

Draper clenched his hands, feeling the gritty roughness left from years of laboring on construction jobs. Until he'd finally caught on that it wasn't enough to work hard. You also had to work smart.

He'd got his start as a management spy at union meetings and moved up to foreman while earning his contractor's license. Along the way, he'd picked up the things they didn't teach you in class: how to substitute one grade of steel for another, how to tinker with the plans after they'd passed through the vast red tape of California planning agencies. The stuff that made the difference between just scraping by and raking it in.

Draper's real education had begun, though, when he moved into management. When he began making up budgets and learned the art of creative bookkeeping.

If you were wise, you didn't cheat, not so it could be caught in an audit. You simply assigned expenses so projects took years to show a profit, maybe never. Everybody did it: movie producers, hell, even the U.S. government. You paid two thousand dollars for fancy paper clips your own subsidiary manufactured, threw in another thou for coke and hid it under "office supplies."

If you needed a little zone change or a piece of land annexed by the right city, that's when you had to know which government official to take out to lunch, maybe treat to a massage. The kind where the masseuse had big boobs and locked the door. And there was that fat envelope for the guy to carry home afterward, all wrinkled old bills that couldn't be traced.

Of course, sometimes you ran into one of those yapping citizens' watchdog groups you couldn't shut up. Draper hadn't taken it seriously enough, the whining about migratory birds and estuaries. He'd got complacent, hadn't hidden the money carefully. Some damn accountant who hated developers had tracked the paper trail and turned it over to the D.A. Then, suddenly, the grand jury was handing down an indictment.

It was no use trying to buy off the witnesses; those environmentalists were a bunch of shithead zealots. He had to concentrate on the judge. Which was why he'd hired a private detective.

Draper smiled a little as he shoved his empty glass into the metal sink at the bar. He'd enjoyed the photo shot through a window of the judge with that hot little newspaper reporter. Unfortunately, it wasn't really illegal, just embarrassing, and Lewis Tarkenton wasn't likely to fold that easily.

Draper was beginning to sweat. He hadn't thought things would get this far. But the courtroom had been assigned, and the date set. Only six weeks away. Hell, he'd thought it took years to get anything to court. Why hadn't somebody told him that was only for civil cases?

Criminal. The word echoed in his head until his temples throbbed. *Criminal. Criminal.*

He could have sworn someone was whispering that word. It was coming from the harbor, the marina made for rich people. For the beautiful people, not for Dudley Tubbs. He'd shed his name and thirty pounds, had his acne scars planed off and his hair replanted. But he was still Dudley.

Draper slammed out through the French doors onto the deck, down the steps to the pier. It swayed on the water, mocking his footsteps. He stood by the cabin cruiser and listened to the long-ago voices of children. *Nobody loves/Dudley Tubbs/If you touch him/Put on your gloves.*

There was a way, of course. Set fire to the boat. Make sure his wallet was on board, maybe his shoes. Not tonight, of course; on Monday, after he'd had time to visit his safe-deposit box, the only money that couldn't be traced.

Then what? Safely dead, where could he go? Being poor and anonymous would be almost worse than going to jail.

I'd sell my soul for a way out of this mess.

The phone was ringing. Draper turned back toward the house with a snarl. Damn the world full of people interrupting his privacy. But it might be important.

He raced up the steps and into the den. "Yes?"

"Mr. Dagmar?"

"Who wants to know?"

The voice had a muffled sound, as if the man were speaking through a handkerchief. "I'm calling on behalf of Judge Tarkenton."

As surely as he'd always known which officials were crooked and which union leaders could be bought, Draper knew it was the judge himself. He flicked on the answering machine and pressed the "record" button. "This is Dagmar."

"The judge would like to arrange a private meeting with you."

"Yeah?" Was Tarkenton setting him up, trying to lure him into offering another bribe? Draper didn't think judges acted as bait in sting operations, but he'd learned long ago not to trust anyone. "Like when? And what about?"

"Somewhere private. Your home would be fine, if you're alone."

"Tonight?"

"No. You'll need to make a phone call first."

The guy wasn't trying so hard to disguise his voice. Draper had heard him speak once at a Rotary luncheon. It sure as hell sounded like Tarkenton.

"A phone call? Like to my lawyer or what?"

"To Sacramento, Mr. Dagmar. You're a smart man. You figure it out."

Jesus, he couldn't be hearing what he thought he was hearing. "You want Long's seat?" he said. "What if Fisher's already decided on somebody else?"

"Then you change his mind, Mr. Dagmar. You'll be hearing from me." The line went dead.

Draper tossed the phone into its cradle and rewound the tape. He'd missed the first few sentences, but he was almost certain an expert could identify the judge's voice.

Not that Draper didn't intend to make that phone call. It would be a lot easier if he could just keep everybody happy.

But if he couldn't, he had the goods on Tarkenton.

Heading home on the freeway from Los Angeles, Lew changed stations on the radio half a dozen times until he realized he was too irritable to listen. He turned the damn thing off.

Kyle and Terri's foster parents kept the curtains drawn so their house was always dark, and even the accumulated clutter couldn't hide the thinness of the carpet or the marked-up paint on the walls. He always found the place depressing, even though the foster mother herself did seem to care about the children.

But that wasn't what bothered him tonight. It was the children's chatter about Daddy—how he'd taken them to Burger King, and then bought them a big bucket of Legos. How much fun Daddy was. Daddy this and Daddy that.

Maybe he was jealous.

No. He didn't think so, and Lew prided himself on his objectivity. What he hated was that Butch, who had abandoned his kids three years ago and left Sarah to scrape by on her teacher's salary, was trying to buy their love to win custody. He'd joined AA and dried out, but how long would that last?

This whole custody business had come up at a bad time, Lew reflected as he changed lanes to get out of the way of a speeding semi.

When he'd started thinking that someday he might run for governor, it had seemed so far away. Not something to interfere in his relationship with Laura while it was still tentative. And now this Senate business had come up.

What disturbed him most was the uneasy feeling that things were getting out of control. Lew had a keen mind, one capable of sorting through the fine twists of the law with speed that would shame a computer. He saw the logic of things that to other people appeared chaotic.

Only he couldn't find the logic in this.

Item: Courthouse staffers, including his own presiding judge, claimed that Lew himself had declared his ambitions. Which he would never have done.

Item: Laura claimed to have seen him in a parking lot when he hadn't been there. Laura might occasionally rely too heavily on her intuition, but she was a trained observer. A reliable witness, so to speak.

And then there was the matter of the file. And the trip meter.

Lew glanced uneasily at the dashboard. He knew exactly how far it was to the foster home, based on previous visits. He'd set the trip meter at zero before he left, and so far it was right on course.

Wednesday had been one of those weird little flukes that people claimed happened sometimes, where you lost a chunk of time. You were driving along one freeway and—snap!—you found yourself ten miles further along, on a different one. Nothing unusual.

Except that it didn't fit with Lew's knowledge of himself. He didn't lose blocks of time, not even five minutes, let alone . . .

When he'd slid into his car Wednesday afternoon, he'd noticed the file folder lying on the dashboard. He could swear he'd left it on the seat, and he opened it to see if anything had been removed.

Inside, he found the probation report complete, except that the page he'd turned upside down to mark his place had been righted.

Remembering what Laura had said about seeing him at the supermarket lot, Lew had checked the trip meter. He'd bought gas on his way to court that morning and reset it to zero. The gas station wasn't more than half a mile from the courthouse.

The meter read 12. Enough miles to have driven from Santa Ana to San Paradiso and back.

Lew climbed out and examined the car for any sign of forced entry. He kept his Regency immaculate, so it would be easy to spot a greasy fingerprint or a scrape mark.

Nothing. Not on the door or the hood. Besides, Laura hadn't just reported seeing his car; she'd reported seeing *him.*

Now, as he steered off at his freeway exit and headed for home, Lew told himself there had to be an explanation.

At his condo complex, he sat in the dark for a moment, centering himself. Wednesday's events would yield their own rationale, sooner or later.

His nagging sense of disorder abated. He was home.

Still, inside the condominium, Lew checked for any sign of an intruder.

The cream draperies stood half-open, as he had left them. The white carnation in the vase on the table still leaned at the same angle. The air smelled a little musty, but that wasn't surprising. All was as it should be, Lew decided with a twinge of relief that he refused to acknowledge.

He decided to call Laura. It didn't seem right to spend Saturday night without at least talking to her.

When he walked into the bedroom, Lew noticed a slight indentation on the bed, next to the phone.

Not so strange, of course. He'd sat there himself this afternoon when he called to confirm his appointment with his niece and nephew. But he usually straightened the bed when he got up.

Lew reached down to smooth it and stopped in disbelief. Damn, the place felt warm, as if he'd only got up a minute ago.

And someone had doodled on the pad beside the phone.

Such a strange drawing. The pointy face and furred texture made it resemble some mythological man-beast, an effect emphasized by the two small horns. And those eyes. Alert eyes, studying him with calculated cunning.

Lew forced his breathing to slow down. Obviously, the apartment manager must have come in for some reason and had to use the phone while he was here.

The guy certainly possessed artistic talent, Lew decided, glad to have found a reasonable explanation for the drawing.

Still, it might be best not to call Laura tonight. Not while he was so susceptible to these panicky reactions.

When he talked to her, Lew wanted to be fully in control of himself.

CHAPTER SEVENTEEN

Should I have trusted her?

Rita lay in the recliner in the upstairs den, her neck resting against a hot-water bottle that so far had done nothing to soothe the throbbing. She didn't want to take painkillers, not after that hallucination on Friday. She needed a clear head.

On TV, the weatherman blathered on about the record heat wave. Rita's thoughts played back to the dressing room at the church, to her meeting with Laura Bennett. Had she told her too much? Or too little?

Rita felt as if she could trust the reporter, although Cruise had impressed on her even before they were married that never, under any circumstances, was she to say anything in the presence of the press that couldn't be published.

There was a quality about Laura that made Rita think she, too, had secrets. Having grown up as an outsider, Rita could sense the same uncertainties in another human being.

This all means something to her, apart from her job. If I'd been more open, maybe she would have been, too.

They'd have to talk again soon. If nothing else, Rita intended to call if she was offered the appointment. She wanted to get Laura's reaction before making a decision.

The wheeze of bagpipes interrupted her thoughts. Rita rolled her head so she could see the screen, where a clump of men in kilts were puffing into what looked like vacuum cleaners.

"Here at the Perth City Chambers, excitement is high and security is tight as a dozen world leaders gather," the announcer said.

The camera cut to a stained-glass window. "These windows, which date from the last century, depict scenes of Robert the Bruce, who captured Perth in 1311," the voice said. "But for centuries now,

Perth has been a quiet city in the Highlands. Its very remoteness is one of the reasons it was chosen for the supersummit."

Rita was about to flip channels when the scene switched to a line of limousines arriving in front of the city chambers. Out climbed men and women in hand-tailored suits, looking serenely self-important as they shook hands and—judging by the half-smiles on a few faces—exchanged witticisms.

How invulnerable they looked as they marched into the chambers, attended by their aides. Like Cruise. He'd been feeling his way toward a presidential bid, something he'd discussed with only a few supporters, Bob Fillipone, and Rita. She hadn't looked forward to it, to the endless campaigning and the intense scrutiny, but she'd never told him so. She knew he was a politician when she married him.

She'd been afraid for Cruise, afraid of terrorists and crazed loners. How ironic that he had died right there next to her, in their home county, among people they thought were friends.

Instinctively, Rita reached into the pocket of her bathrobe and touched the butt of the pistol. She carried it all the time now. After she told him about the photograph and the threats, Bob had taken her out to a practice range and made sure she knew how to use it.

There was a tap at the door. "Mrs. Long?" Ramona poked her head in. "Barbara Long is on the phone."

The muscles twitched in Rita's neck. "Tell her I'm resting, would you? I'll call her back later." Much later.

"Yes, Mrs. Long." The housekeeper went away.

Rita had to face her stepdaughter sooner or later, but not right now. In her present mood, she might let Barbara browbeat her into giving up all of Cruise's antiques, and heaven knows what else.

The drone of the announcer's voice was wearing her out. Rita let her head sag and her mind clear, and within minutes she fell asleep.

Laura stopped by B. Dalton in South Coast Plaza on Sunday to ask if they had the Time-Life book on Goya. A saleswoman directed her to a section on art books, but she didn't see anything on the Spanish painter.

Wending her way out through the hordes of shoppers and refugees from the heat, Laura passed the Carousel Court and turned toward Brentano's.

There, a young man told her the book had been out of print for years, and that her best bet would be a used-book store. Laura thanked him, glanced through the displays of glossy game sets and gift books, and wandered back into the mall. She doubted she'd find a used-book store open on Sunday.

People bustled around her, pushing baby strollers, chatting with companions, rustling their shiny shopping bags. The air smelled of coffee and cinnamon.

Laura decided to skip lunch and pig out on chocolate instead. Waiting in line at the candy counter, she watched two children press their noses to the glass and argue the merits of truffles versus turtles.

Today, for the first time in weeks, she felt normal. There was nothing old here, nothing that echoed. The lighting was flat, the merchandise new and dustless, the cafés along the mall gleaming with brass and oak. The only pain came from looking at the price tags, but then, that was the only source of humor, too.

Before she'd begun dating Lew, Laura used to come to the mall occasionally on the weekend just to kill time and people-watch. It was like an old-time Main Street, except that she hardly ever saw anyone she knew. She kind of liked it that way.

The saleslady came to take her order, tucking the chocolates into a paper bag and adding a free chunk of fudge. Laura thanked her and strolled out, nibbling thickly.

She'd already read the Sunday paper, and she had no plans for tonight. She wished she needed some clothes or shoes, something to shop for. Something to take up the time, to justify staying here a while longer.

Laura's skin began to prickle. She stopped, surveying the shoppers around her. Nothing strange, nothing out of the ordinary. Only that, just ahead, people were halting in front of a display of television sets inside Sears. A blue-jeaned young man stood with his arms folded; a young woman stared at the screens, oblivious to the kicking toddler in her stroller. Two older women balanced on high heels, one of them twisting distractedly at a scarf.

In ancient agoras, people must have gathered this way around sweating runners who raised their arms for silence. *Our fleet has been scattered. . . . The king of Macedon is at the gates . . .* Laura had seen the crash of the *Challenger* in a discount store in Cincinnati. She had watched in a student union lounge at Northwestern as the bodies of 241 Americans were carried out of the marine headquarters in Beirut.

The crowd was solidifying around the TV sets. She walked over, peering between the onlookers. Across tiers of small screens raced little figures like toy soldiers, dodging through the fairy-tale streets of Perth amid the rattle of automatic gunfire. "What's going on?"

The man next to Laura just shook his head.

The battle scene was replaced by the face of a TV anchorman. "For those of you just joining us, we're getting conflicting reports from Perth, but apparently there's been some kind of armed assault. It isn't clear yet whether any of the world leaders have been harmed, but military helicopters of unknown origin have landed in large numbers at the North Inch Park.

"An estimated two hundred soldiers from the helicopters have attacked guards protecting the summit. The guards, which include both U.S. Marines and British forces, appear to be temporarily overwhelmed, although they're putting up a stiff resistance. The attackers are described as Middle Eastern in appearance but . . . Let's go to Lucy Sager in Washington."

A young woman stood in front of the Capitol Building, microphone in hand, her flyaway hair attesting to the suddenness with which she'd been called into action. "Vice President Whiting has just announced that U.S. forces have been mobilized . . ."

"Excuse me, Lucy, this just in." The anchorman's image replaced hers on the screen. "We are getting confirmation that at least one world leader has been injured, and others were taken prisoner by the attackers, but we have no details."

"My God," said the man next to Laura. No one else spoke.

She felt the chocolates squish inside her paper bag. But she wasn't, after all, just an observer. She was a reporter.

Digging in her purse for notebook and pen, Laura set grimly to work, getting people's reactions. Those who would talk were shocked, angry, fearful. Why-weren't-there-more-guards, I'll-bet-the-Ruskies-are-behind-this, My-daughter-and-her-friend-are-traveling-in-Scotland-my-God-I hope-they're-all-right . . .

Finally, she flipped the notebook shut and headed for the newspaper.

Greg was already there when she arrived, along with a scattering of metro and copy editors. They were getting a head start on tomorrow's paper, putting together a special section.

The editor stopped by Laura's desk. "Thanks for coming in. I'm putting you in charge of the local reaction. Call around, see what you can dig up."

Laura waved her notebook. "I was at South Coast Plaza. I got a start already."

"Good." Greg stared at the bank of TV screens, each monitoring a different newscast. "What a fucking mess." He turned away toward the copy desk. "Mary, let me handle the wire reports."

Mary Trueblood, the copy chief, looked up from her computer. "*The New York Times* says President Giroux of France is dead, and Graves of Canada was seriously injured."

No one, she said, seemed to know about the others, but there were at least twenty-five guards and a dozen terrorists slain, along with four civilians.

Greg began opening files on one of the terminal screens. "Okay. I've got it."

Laura picked up the phone and just held it for a moment, listening to the dial tone. For the first time, she didn't want to report on a situation.

She wanted to grieve with the rest of the world. The hope represented by the summit had been crushed, and with it the sense that responsible leaders could still guide the fate of the world.

Self-discipline and duty finally winning out, Laura began to dial.

Whenever she had a spare moment from calling civic leaders, restaurants, police, and anyone else who might have something colorful to say about how people were reacting, Laura read through the incoming wire stories in the computer. The invading helicopters had taken off; radar was attempting to track them, but they had scattered and were conducting low-altitude evasive maneuvers.

As for President Harkness, Soviet leader Karponov, and the heads of state of Great Britain, Egypt, Israel, India, China, Japan, Jordan, and West Germany, they had vanished.

An emergency meeting of the U.S. Senate was to consider a declaration of war against Arabia if the attack could definitely be linked to Al-Hadassi, while the UN Security Council scrambled into a meeting of its own. In nations around the globe, unfamiliar faces and names cropped up as the temporary new heads of state. Everywhere, Laura knew, in cities like Bangkok and Johannesburg and Sydney, people were huddling inside their homes, staring at their TV sets with stark disbelief.

It was as if the world had suddenly been taken hostage.

CHAPTER EIGHTEEN

"When he did open the sixth seal, I looked and lo, there came a great earthquake, and the sun blackened, the moon swelled red as blood, and the stars fell from the sky to the earth as the fig tree drops its fruit when shaken by the storm; the sky rolled up like a scroll, mountains shifted and islands sheared away. Then kings and commoners, great men and soldiers, the rich and the powerful and everyone, slaves and freemen, hid their faces in the caves and among the rocks. . . ."

Madeleine closed her Bible carefully, her fingers tracing the frayed old binding. She had hoped, in rereading it, to find the confidence she needed. Because something had to be done, and quickly.

It was late now, almost midnight, but in Europe it was morning, and the television continued to whisper its nightmare rumors. The helicopters had landed in Libya, or they had crashed into the ocean, or they had set down in Arabia.

There was talk of an enormous ransom, of a demand for nuclear weapons. There was even a rumor that Ayatollah Al-Hadassi was a CIA operative.

Madeleine believed all of it and none of it. The hollow-eyed newscasters hadn't even come close to the truth yet.

Oh, that cursed painting.

The nightmare was still there, waiting behind Madeleine's eyelids. That night when James thought she was asleep, while Laura lay near death in the hospital. He'd unrolled the painting and tacked it on the wall and stood there staring, and she'd seen the door crack slowly open, heard the snarling grunts, and felt the rumble of the earth's fabric parting.

An unholy scarlet flame had lighted James from within, turning his skin transparent, like a Chinese lantern. Within that roiling evil glow hung bloated cells, distended faces. A swirl of the viscous liquid and she saw that one of the faces was James's, the mouth crying out an indistinct gurgle, the features contorting into one needle-sharp instant of pure agony.

She must have fainted; when she awoke, the air was cool, the painting was gone, and James slept by her side.

The next day he disappeared, and Laura vanished from the hospital. It was weeks before they came back, looking so normal. But she had noted the change in his voice when he talked about the child. An undertone of darkness, of secrecy.

Oh, God, he was lying, wasn't he? He hadn't really taken her to doctors in England.

Another person might have seen no connection between James and his painting and the terrible events racking the world. A conventional person would reject any possibility that the biblical prophecies were coming true. Good and evil, battling it out at the last . . .

But Madeleine knew that there were many rooms in the Father's mansion, and that some of them lay hidden behind curtains. This earth was not as it seemed; James had given her that horrible glimpse into hidden realms.

When he died, she had stifled the impulse to fly to America and seek out the painting, to burn it. She knew the thing must have masked itself somehow. That it would never be found until the right moment, when Laura was grown.

Still, Madeleine had to be sure. Absolutely sure. She had been, when she bought the dagger, when she took it to the Vatican to be blessed, and when she brought it here.

Sure that she knew the name of the demon, and that she could kill it. Now, sometimes, she began to doubt. What if she killed an innocent person?

And worst of all, what if she hung here suspended by her uncertainties and then found out, too late, that she'd been right?

CHAPTER NINETEEN

"They did what?" Daryl Wilkinson shifted the phone against his shoulder, wondering if he'd heard wrong. "What does the judge have, shit for brains?"

"That hotshot defense attorney from L.A. dug up some witnesses," Captain DeWitt shouted above the clatter in the courthouse hallway. "A young couple claim they saw Pickard at Kentucky Fried at five-thirty the evening Marla Rivers was killed. And he can prove he didn't leave city hall until five-fifteen."

"Jeezus." A quarter of a million in bail might be a lot for a common criminal, but Joe Pickard ought to be able to cough it up from somewhere. Maybe he already had.

"They're using the same line he gave you—that somebody was trying to frame him," DeWitt said.

"Yeah? We got the guy's fucking fingerprints, for Christ's sake!"

"He claims somebody planted the purse in his car. Said he didn't even know about the murder until after he'd thrown it away, and then he got scared." There was grudging admiration in the captain's voice. "The guy's smarter than I gave him credit for."

Daryl still couldn't believe it. "We'll put a tail on him the minute he gets out of jail."

"That's why I called. Get on it." DeWitt rang off.

Daryl checked with Orange County Jail and found out Pickard was due to be released in half an hour. He grabbed Norm Hertz off another case and sent him out there with instructions to step on it.

The files were still sitting on his desk. Hell, they hadn't even officially solved the murders of Gina Lopez and Kiki Bellaga. Now, the bastard was out on the street, free to kill another one.

There was something weird going on here. The whole fucking world was turning upside down—maniacs kidnapping the president and all those other heads of state. He'd heard on the radio today that the Russians might be behind it, that they'd pretended to snatch Karponov just to make it look good. And those pantywaists in the Senate were still haggling over whether they wanted to declare war, and if so, on whom. Whiting might be acting president, but he'd never have the guts to take on Russia, and neither would those weak nellies in the Senate.

What this country needed was a real leader, somebody who wasn't afraid of a fight. Only where was he going to come from?

Daryl picked up the phone and dialed Detective Briana Kew. It was her day off, but she'd be needed to spell Norm on the mayor's tail. Maybe he couldn't solve the world's problems, but he could make damn sure Joe Pickard didn't get away with murder again.

The house on Beatrice Lane looked even shabbier than usual as Joe mounted the steps. He'd only been away four days, but already the weeds were wilting and the front porch seemed to be shucking its paint at record speed.

But God, the place looked good. Compared to jail, hell would look good.

Joe unlocked the door, forcing himself not to turn around and stare at the plainclothes cop parked down the block. The guy was just doing his job. Besides, it could work to Joe's advantage, having a witness to his whereabouts.

It was just luck, that Mr. and Mrs. Simms turning up to vouch for him. Nice people, ordinary citizens doing their duty. Why hadn't the police found them? Not trying very hard, maybe. It had all been so neat, a solution those hack TV writers would be proud of. Three murders tied up in time to get on with the commercials.

He swung the door open and braced himself for a blast of hot air, but it wasn't nearly as bad as he expected. Maybe the weather had cooled down this weekend; in jail, he hadn't been concerned about stuff like that.

Joe pulled off his tie and turned on the air conditioner. He'd never been so scared in his life. Closed in, surrounded.

They'd put him alone in a cell. Public officials and sex killers weren't real popular among the prisoners, one of the guards had told him, grinning a little, enjoying the fact that Joe was nearly shitting in his pants. One wrong move and he was a dead duck, the guard said. Good thing, too. Save the county the cost of a trial.

He'd known they were out there. He could smell them, the stink of b.o. and urine through the thin mask of disinfectant. He'd heard their whispers in the night. *We're gonna get you, Mr. Mayor. Gonna cut off your balls first and let you watch the rats eat 'em.*

Joe shuddered again. He'd kept thinking about Kiki, replaying that night, wondering what he could have done differently. Stood guard, or warned her. Something. He should have done something.

In the bedroom, his old hack-around slacks and Angels T-shirt lay across the rumpled bedspread. He didn't remember setting them out. He'd been arrested at his office Friday afternoon. What the fuck?

My head's all screwed up. It's a miracle I can take a pee without hitting the ceiling.

He put on the comfortable clothes, took the pee with reasonable accuracy, and headed for the refrigerator.

Well, that was a nice surprise. Two six-packs of Coors. He seemed to recall being low on beer Thursday night. God, he was really losing it. He must have run out to the 7-Eleven before he went to bed.

Joe leaned against the counter, drinking beer, smoking, and wondering what to do next. He didn't want to go to city hall. For all he knew, the council was planning to replace him at tonight's meeting. He'd be about as welcome as a preacher in a whorehouse.

When he'd emptied the can, he put in a call to Rhondie, who assured him everything was under control at the law office. But she passed on a message to phone the state bar association.

"I'll get back to them," Joe promised. Not until after the trial, though. Not until he'd proved he was no murderer.

On the other hand, there was no point in kidding himself. He'd have to drop by to pay Rhondie for the next few weeks and give her the option of finding another job or taking a long vacation.

Joe played back the messages on his machine. There was only one, from Mel Kawakami at the Governor's Office, and that had come in this morning.

He returned the call.

"Joe." Mel spoke the name abruptly, as if not wanting to let it sit in his mouth too long. "About what we discussed last Monday." He meant having Joe drum up more support for Fisher in that campaign-funds mess. "Under the circumstances, it might be best if we put it on a back burner."

"Yeah, I gotcha." You couldn't blame them, but it hurt. That reporter from the *Herald,* she'd thought he might get tabbed for the U.S. Senate. What a joke.

"We'll be back in touch," the aide said. "Oh, and congratulations on getting out. We know you'll be cleared." He sounded about as sincere as a cat chirping to a pigeon.

"Thanks." Joe hung up and went for another beer.

Yeah, well, fuck them all. And Emma, wherever she might be. At least he had witnesses now. And a few old friends, people who owed him favors. They'd get their bail money back. He wouldn't forget, either, when things got better. If there was one thing Joe believed in, it was loyalty.

He clattered around in the cupboard and pulled out a can of chili for lunch. It occurred to him, as he dug into the beans with a plastic spoon, that in books and movies the falsely accused hero usually went out and solved the crime himself.

Only movie heroes didn't have cops on their tail. Besides which, the last thing Joe wanted was to be anywhere near the real murderer. Or even to lay eyes on another woman, until this thing was settled.

He was going to stay right here, except for a few trips to his office and the grocery store. He might as well use the time to fix things up a little, maybe clean the place. Read the newspaper, pay some bills.

It struck him that he hadn't seen any mail out front. Joe set aside the can of chili and went out to check.

Empty. Well, great. Maybe the cops had been reading his stuff.

He glared down the street at the unmarked car and then went back into the house, into the second bedroom to see if the cops had been considerate enough to leave the stuff on his desk when they were done with it.

Well, whaddaya know, they had. Without even bothering to pretend they hadn't opened it. Some of the advertising circulars had been tossed in the wastebasket, and a couple of bills sat open on the battered surface of the old desk.

Sons of bitches.

They'd better have a search warrant, or the whole case might get thrown out of court. Which wasn't exactly what Joe wanted, to be cleared on a technicality. But why would a judge issue a warrant for them to read his mail? What did they think, he was getting letters of application from potential victims?

Damn stupid, nosy assholes.

As he bent down to make sure nothing valuable had been dropped in the wastebasket, Joe noticed something peculiar.

His checkbook, which he'd left at the office, was sitting on the desk. Not only that, but somebody had started to fill in one of the checks in his handwriting.

He had a distinctive way of slanting his letters that would be tough to copy. Not to mention how hard he bore down on the pen; he used to snap off pencil points all the time in grade school.

It sure as hell looked like his handwriting. But the date on the check was Saturday. And he'd been in jail Saturday.

The clothes on the bed. The Coors in the refrigerator. Joe sat down heavily on the swivel chair.

Somebody had been living in his house. Somebody who used his clothes and drank the same kind of beer and knew how to write like him.

Maybe somebody who was real fond of knives. Jesus. It gave Joe a squirmy, damp feeling, as if he was being watched.

He swung around in the chair, but he couldn't see anything. Just a faint swirl of dust in the light from the window.

CHAPTER TWENTY

The newsroom was subdued on Monday except for the chatter of the TV set and the almost nonstop ringing of phones. People called for updates on the president's kidnapping, or they wanted to check out rumors, from unconfirmed reports of a nuclear explosion to sightings of UFOs. Or just to make sure the newspaper was still there.

Another 5.3 quake struck near Paris, but nobody took much notice. It wasn't as if the world was functioning with anything approaching normality.

Even Steve Orkney sat staring numbly at his keyboard, although, Laura thought, he might merely be pondering the mystery of Joe Pickard's release.

As she sat down at her terminal, an anchorwoman on TV repeated that there had been no definite news of the missing world leaders since the previous day. "It's as if they were swallowed up, as if they had somehow walked off the edge of the earth," she said.

Laura closed her eyes. For some reason, she felt as if the edge of the earth weren't very far away.

"You okay?" Orkney leaned around his screen. "You need a coupla Tylenols?" He rummaged through his desk drawer, coming up with a sticky red roll of Lifesavers instead. "How about a sugar rush?"

Laura's thought vanished so completely she couldn't even remember what it had been, just a vague sense of danger. She waved away the candies. Steve shrugged and ate one himself.

It didn't seem so important anymore, who would replace Cruise Long. Not in view of yesterday's events. But it was Laura's assignment.

She ran through her notes, indifference gradually shifting into perplexity. There was a kind of pattern emerging, now that she'd got a little distance on it.

Rita Long had been threatened even before her husband's death.

Joe Pickard's fingerprints identified him as a killer, but two apparently objective witnesses said he'd been elsewhere.

Someone was gabbing about Lew's ambitions in a way likely to destroy any chance he had of being appointed.

It looked as if all three of them were being knocked out of the running. But it didn't make sense. No one person could have arranged all these bizarre circumstances.

Restlessly, Laura keyed her terminal to page through the computer's California Queue, a compendium of today's state wire-service stories. She wasn't even sure what she was looking for. Another clue, maybe, something that would help shake the puzzle pieces into a different and perhaps recognizable order.

She skimmed a story out of Oceanside about a Christian sect whose long-bearded leader had proclaimed the coming Day of Judgment. Last night, he and twenty-seven of his followers, including five children, had waded out into the ocean to offer themselves as sacrifices for the sins of the world. The leader and twenty members of the sect, including four of the children, had drowned.

On the political side, Governor Fisher had appointed seven panelists to investigate the campaign-funds charges against him. To Laura's surprise, he had selected a bipartisan and apparently unobjectionable group from around the state.

For the first time, the governor had admitted there might have been some irregularities, due to "the overzealousness of some of my aides." Not a particularly noble way to disentangle himself, but a lot slicker than the huffing and bluffing of Fisher's previous remarks. He might even get out of this one with his political reputation intact, Laura realized.

But there was nothing about a senatorial appointee, nothing that could clarify her sense of unease.

She glanced at Greg's office and saw through the window that the publisher was just leaving. Waiting a minute to make sure Greg was alone, she went and knocked on the door.

"Come in." Unlike the rest of the staff, the editor looked almost cheerful, Laura noted as she stepped inside. With experience from Watergate to Vietnam, he must feel in his element when the world was falling apart. "Good story on the funeral," he said.

"Thanks." Laura sat down. Along one office wall, three TV sets had been tuned to different stations, with the sound off. "I'm stuck on something. You have a better instinct for political infighting."

"Shoot."

"It has to do with the Long seat." Laura weighed her words

carefully. "Some strange things have been happening. Almost as if somebody's trying to manipulate the situation."

"Such as?" Greg folded his hands on the desk.

She told him about the threats against Rita, and the conflicting evidence about Joe Pickard. "Am I imagining there's some connection?"

"What about Tarkenton? He sounds like odd man out."

"He's been assigned the Draper Dagmar case," Laura said. "How would it look if he accepted an appointment from the governor?"

"Lousy," he agreed.

"And then . . . well . . . what if it wasn't a heart attack? What if Senator Long was murdered?"

"Whoa," Greg said. "I think you're getting a bit far afield here. But I'm pleased with you, Laura. You're coming along."

"Coming along?"

The editor smiled. "Getting more devious. Becoming paranoid—the mark of a good reporter."

"Thanks, I think," Laura said.

"I may have a chance to sound out one of the governor's aides," Greg said. "If I hear about any other contenders, anyone who might have engineered at least a few of these things, I'll get back to you."

Laura went to her desk. She knew she should hang on to this story like a bulldog, worrying and chewing on it until some brilliant insight came up.

Except that, for the first time in her career, a story was getting too close to home. Too close to whatever truth she'd been running from for almost twenty years and was only now becoming aware of.

She sat at her desk for a long time, staring at the computer screen and feeling like a stranger to herself. Feeling like a fraud, a reporter who probed other people's secrets and hid from her own.

Finally, knowing she was cheating, she began phoning her usual list of contacts and working up a story on routine political fund-raisers.

There was something reassuring about the fact that, even in the face of world cataclysm, people in Orange County went right on worrying about the next election.

Draper clicked off the tape recorder and leaned back in the reclining chair, staring past his desk out the broad window of his office ten stories above Newport Center.

He must have listened to that tape twenty times since Saturday. Listened to a voice that he was almost certain belonged to Judge

Tarkenton, asking for a bribe. A unique and subtle bribe, to be sure, but a bribe.

It was time to make a decision. The judge would be calling back soon, expecting an answer.

His street-fighting instincts told him to nail the guy, play the tape for the district attorney and get Tarkenton thrown off the bench. But Draper didn't just work smart, he fought smart, too. It wasn't hard to figure out that he'd get only a marginal benefit from having his case transferred to another judge. Another guy might go a little easier on him, especially if they asked for a nonjury trial. But then again, there were other tough judges.

This way, he'd have Tarkenton in his hip pocket. The edges of his lips curled in satisfaction at the thought of the D.A. haranguing and pontificating in front of a judge whom Draper already owned.

He dialed the Governor's Office.

Mel Kawakami got on the phone almost immediately. "What can we do for you, Drape?"

"Armand around?"

"The governor's tied up this morning."

Draper could feel the chill in the air. "I, uh, had a little question for him. About who's going to fill out Long's term."

"That isn't public information."

"And I'm not the public, Mel. Cut the crap."

He heard a sharp intake of breath at the other end of the line. "Look, Drape, you've got to know, this indictment thing is exactly what the governor doesn't need. He's got troubles of his own."

Draper had bulldozed Armand Fisher into two minor appointments—payoffs for favors done—over the past few years. But this, he could see, was going to be different.

"I didn't want to suggest anything he wasn't already considering," he said carefully. "But I've been hearing some good things down here about a judge named Lewis Tarkenton."

"We're aware of him." Mel sounded a shade friendlier. "This is strictly between you and me, got it? He's on the list for consideration. But the widow's got an edge. She's a perfect nonpolitical choice. As a matter of fact, I'm having lunch with her tomorrow."

"I see." Draper grunted to himself. Shit, he should have realized this wouldn't be like getting a pal named to some environmental board. What did Tarkenton expect, anyway? "Hey, I'm just trying to help."

"Is Tarkenton hearing your case?" Mel wasn't slow on the uptake.

"Looks that way."

"I see." The aide didn't speak for so long that Draper wondered if they'd been cut off, and then Mel said, "I'll tell the governor what you've said. We really appreciate all the support you've given us down there. We won't forget you."

"Good," Draper said. "Thanks, Mel."

For the rest of the day, in the back of his mind, he kept wondering what he was going to say when Tarkenton called. Hell, maybe the guy would just let it drop. That might be for the best, after all. He'd keep that tape under lock and key, and use it only if he had to.

One thing was for sure. When it was all over, if he was going to jail, he'd make sure Lewis Tarkenton was going with him.

CHAPTER TWENTY-ONE

It was the third time in as many days that Barbara Long had dialed the number that used to be her father's. Sitting on the edge of the bed, her long red fingernails digging half-circles into the hotel's end table, she could feel the anger boil up in her stomach.

"Ramona? It's me." Barbara had sensed the first time she called that she had the housekeeper's sympathy. Some servants, those accustomed to working for important people, took on a certain importance by association. Ramona, Barbara could tell, didn't relish being left as handmaiden to a jumped-up B-movie actress. "Is she ready to talk to me yet?"

"She's not here," Ramona said. "She went out for lunch."

"Where?" Barbara didn't particularly want to make a public scene, but she was tired of waiting around. She had a beautiful home in San Francisco to get back to and a wedding to plan for. And she had no intention of leaving empty-handed.

"She didn't say." There was a pause, and then the housekeeper added, "But I think she'll be a while. She was meeting someone from the Governor's Office."

Barbara couldn't see what the governor would want with Rita, but that wasn't her concern. "When did she leave?"

"A few minutes ago."

It would be going too far to expect Ramona to put her job and her references on the line by letting Barbara in, but then, Barbara didn't need to be let in. She had a key. "You wouldn't happen to be going out yourself, would you?"

"I usually do some grocery shopping on Tuesdays." Ramona sounded as if she were having a brief struggle with her conscience. "I was planning to leave in about fifteen minutes."

Barbara glanced at her watch. It was ten minutes after one. "Well, have a good time."

"It usually takes me an hour."

"Thanks, Ramona. I owe you one."

Barbara went to check herself in the mirror. Her blond hair needed a bit of brushing, and her lipstick had to be touched up, but other than that, she looked just about perfect.

She hadn't changed much since her debutante days. Twenty-seven was still pretty young.

The same age that slut was when Dad married her.

Barbara picked up her white leather purse and stepped out into the heat. She could hear the *thong-thong* of tennis balls and the splash of a diver cutting into the swimming pool, but a profusion of plants and the hotel's terraced setting provided privacy.

It wasn't as if she were going to do anything really wrong, Barbara reminded herself. She was just going to look around, make a list of things that had belonged to her grandmother. Things that Dad obviously would have wanted her to have.

She wished her brother, Beau, had more sense of his position, but he'd flown back to New York immediately after the funeral. Beau seemed to nurse a sneaking sympathy for Rita, which Barbara couldn't understand at all. True, the woman hadn't actually stolen their father, but their marriage had been an insult. A tramp like that, taking Mom's place as Mrs. Cruise Long.

Barbara gave her key to the valet and waited for the rental car to be brought around. Standing there in the hot sun, she felt her temper begin to rise. Who did Rita think she was, anyway, refusing to take Barbara's calls? As if she were really devastated with grief, when everybody knew she'd only married Dad for his money.

And when everybody knew he'd only married her for sex. Too bad that, in today's conservative climate, smart politicians didn't keep mistresses anymore.

It took longer than Barbara had expected to find the house. She'd been there a couple of times and thought she knew the way, but the roads twisted and the signs were hard to read, and it was after one-thirty when she arrived.

Even so, Barbara was careful to walk up and ring the doorbell, in case Ramona hadn't left yet. Or in case Rita had come home unexpectedly.

Who knows? She might even be giving the governor's aide a free tumble. Barbara wouldn't be surprised.

The doorbell echoed through the house. There was no answering tap of footsteps, no sound of voices within.

Barbara glanced back at the street, but nothing stirred. Carefully, she fitted her key into the lock.

"Would you like to go ahead and order?" The waitress stopped by Rita's table, taking in the almost-empty margarita glass. "Maybe your friend got held up."

Rita checked her watch. Mel Kawakami had arranged to meet her here half an hour ago. It hadn't been an unpleasant half hour, watching boats sail by in the harbor, eavesdropping on conversations from behind the safety of her dark glasses, but she was getting edgy. Still, planes could be late. "Perhaps I'll have a shrimp cocktail."

"Right away. Ready for a refill?"

She shook her head. Mel hadn't said what this meeting was about, but she certainly didn't want to be tipsy. "Just more water, please."

"Coming right up."

Rita rested her chin on her palm. She felt steadier than she had two days ago, despite Barbara's annoying refusal to give up and go home. At least she hadn't received any more threats. She was beginning to wonder if they hadn't been merely a crude attempt to extort money, after all.

Three young men in business suits walked by, chuckling at a remark. Nice hard bodies under those suits, and young faces, not more than thirty-five. Men she would have fantasized about taking to bed once upon a time, a week ago.

"Mrs. Long." Startled, she looked up and saw a stocky man of Japanese descent standing beside her table, impeccably dressed in tailored gray silk. "I'm Mel."

"Pleased to meet you." They shook hands.

"Sorry for the delay." Mel slid into the seat opposite her and signaled for the waitress. Rita took off her dark glasses. "The airline overbooked, and I had to fly into LAX and drive down."

"I hope the traffic wasn't too bad." Rita was glad the next few minutes were occupied with ordering. She felt ill at ease, the way she had the first time Cruise took her out on a date.

"Well." The aide handed his menu to the departing waitress. "I suppose you're wondering what this is all about."

"I am sort of curious," Rita said. *He's going to tell me they're establishing a memorial for Cruise. Or that the governor wants me to campaign for him. Something innocuous like that.*

"I won't keep you in suspense." Mel smiled, and she could see that he enjoyed the power he held by proxy. "The governor asked me to find out if you would consider accepting an appointment to fill the next two years of your husband's term."

Rita turned her head, and the sun glinted off the calm water of the harbor directly into her eyes, so that the world turned white. She wanted to say yes. Hell, she wanted to jump up and down and shout like a kid. Instead, she sat there with all the dignity she could muster, blinked her eyes to clear away the dazzle, and said, "Tell me more about it."

The house felt cool to Barbara after the heat of the August day. She stood in the marble-floored entrance, letting the cold-stone smoothness close in around her.

From somewhere upstairs came the tick of a clock. The clock her grandfather had made with his own hands. She plucked a small spiral notebook from her purse and put the clock on the top of her list.

Two doors led off the foyer. The smaller one, she knew, would take her to the dining room and the kitchen. Mom had kept most of the valuable china and silver serving dishes after the divorce, so there wasn't much point in looking there.

Instead, Barbara turned left and walked through the double doorway into the living room.

It was obvious Rita hadn't had much to do with decorating it. Barbara noted with approval the blue-and-white color scheme, although she wasn't impressed by that Expressionist painting Dad had picked up at Sotheby's.

Moving quickly through the room, Barbara made note of the twin oversize Chinese vases that flanked the fireplace. They hadn't actually belonged to her grandmother—Dad had bought them during his second marriage—but Rita probably wouldn't know that.

Barbara also jotted down, *oak sideboard.* And, for good measure, *silver candelabrum,* although she really wasn't that crazy about it. But then, she didn't expect Rita to give her everything on the list, either.

She paused to follow the mutter of a car as it came up the street, then swished on by. Barbara was surprised to find her heart thudding noticeably. What was she afraid of, anyway? If Rita came home and discovered her, she could brazen it out. After all, she *was* in the right.

Her father had assured her once that she was always welcome to stay here, that they'd love to have her come visit, but of course she hadn't. That would be treason to Mom, who had never taken down Dad's portrait from over her mantel, who still signed her name *Mrs. Cruise Long,* who refused to let her children speak a word against him. Those other two women had been concubines, not wives.

Barbara wanted to go through every room, pry into every corner of the downstairs den, the breakfast nook, the laundry room, to make notes of everything she could possibly lay claim to. But time was short. She wanted to get on to the jewelry upstairs.

The steps creaked as Barbara mounted slowly. The air seemed to thin out as she climbed, as if she were ascending a great distance. It took more and more effort to suck air into her lungs. It was just nerves. Nerves and distaste at being in a house where Rita lived.

At the top, Barbara looked around. She'd never much liked the old-fashioned layout of the long upstairs hallway off which half a dozen rooms opened. Somebody ought to burn this place down. She might even consider it, except that the oak sideboard and all that other stuff would go up in smoke. Besides, she suspected it was harder to set a fire than it looked in the movies, and easier to get caught.

Barbara walked into the bedroom, drawing the door half-shut behind her. It would give her extra time to hide, if she had to.

The room had been decorated in gold and brown. Ramona's work was obvious in the carefully made bed, the tidied dressing table, the smell of lemon cleanser from the bathroom.

But it was still a whore's room.

Barbara strode over to the closet. Here were her father's clothes, meticulously lined up along one side. And there, on the other, were the seductive silk nighties, the flirty off-the-shoulder gowns and the satiny high heels Rita had used to ensnare him. A spice-and-musk fragrance wafted up from them, a scent so strong it had survived dry cleaners and washing machines.

Her father had always been a handsome man; Barbara remembered her high school classmates sighing over Dad as if he were some kind of movie star. She didn't like to think of him rutting with Rita on that bed, and yet it fit somehow. Mom was too pure, too good. Rita had the ripe flesh for satisfying a man's needs. But why did he have to go and marry her?

A creak from the hallway made Barbara whirl, her hands clenching. She waited, but there was nothing more, and gradually she let the tension out of her muscles.

She'd better get this over with.

A jewelry box stood on Rita's dressing table, a gaudy oversize thing with etched-glass doors and velvet lining, but there wouldn't be anything much in that. Just a few trinkets and baubles for everyday.

Barbara knew her father well enough to guess that the Picasso print on the wall near the bathroom wasn't there merely for decoration. She lifted it down to reveal the shiny surface of a wall safe. The kind with a combination, thank goodness.

Her parents had lost the combination to their safe once, and it had taken a locksmith several hours to break into it. Dad had vowed that next time he'd use numbers he couldn't forget.

Barbara whirled the knobs through variations of her father's birthdate, but that didn't work. Then she tried Beau's, and then her own. It seemed like a good omen when it clicked open.

The board in the hallway creaked again.

She froze. If Rita or Ramona had returned, surely they would have made some noise coming up the stairs. Barbara could hear only the rush of her own pulse.

Damn nerves again. She'd never been a nervous person. But she'd never broken into a house before, either.

She lifted a cedar box out of the safe and opened it carefully. It occurred to her that she should have worn gloves, but it was too late now. Her prints would be all over the painting and the wall. Besides, she wasn't actually going to take anything.

The cedar smell of the box reminded her of pet hamsters she'd owned as a kid. In fact, this whole escapade was like one time she and Beau had sneaked into their parents' bedroom and had a grand time playing dress-up until the nanny caught them and gave them what-for. It had been worth it.

Smiling, Barbara opened the box. Ignoring the rubber-banded papers and securities, she began unrolling black velvet lengths and opening the small jewelers' boxes.

God, he'd spent a lot of money on that bitch. Look at the necklace, diamonds edged with pearls, and the big emerald-and-diamond earrings. Now that antique gold necklace had been Granny's. And come to think of it, the diamonds in the earrings might have been recut from her grandmother's rings. Barbara recognized one of the bracelets, too, although it wasn't terribly valuable, jade and amber. Still, she put it on the list.

Rita had no right to any of this stuff. Dad couldn't possibly have meant for her to keep it. On the other hand, Barbara wasn't sure she wanted to go so far as to steal it.

She didn't even intend to tell Rita she'd been here. She would say she'd had a few days with nothing to do but tap her memory and draw up a list. Rita would probably believe it.

The slow groan of the door edging open sent her heart slamming into her throat. Oh, Jesus!

Barbara spun around, dropping one of the rings onto the floor. "Rita?"

Her father stood in the doorway.

"Dad?" Barbara closed her eyes and then opened them again. He was still there. "What's going on, Dad? They told me you were dead."

"I'm afraid we had to do that." Cruise smiled, that old, confident smile, only it didn't look quite the same. As if he were an actor playing the part of himself. "There was a plot to kill me, a plot by some very powerful people. We decided it was better if I laid low for a while."

"Does Rita know?" Barbara asked.

He shook his head. "Not even Rita."

That was good. He knew better than to trust his life to that woman. Maybe she was even part of the conspiracy. Barbara wanted to ask him a lot of things, but she remembered that Rita and Ramona were likely to come home soon. "I was just making a list . . ."

"I know what you were doing." Her father nodded indulgently. "And you're right. I *did* mean for you to have your grandmother's things. Go ahead and take them."

"Just . . . take them?"

"That's what I said."

Dubiously, Barbara put the necklace and the bracelet in her purse, but hesitated over the earrings. "Were these . . . ?"

"Your grandmother's diamonds. Go ahead."

There was something strange about this. Dad should have been angry at her for sneaking into his house. On the other hand, if Rita was conspiring against him . . . "Did I overlook anything?" Barbara asked.

He gestured toward the dressing table. "The silver mirror and brush. We had new glass and bristles put in, but they should go to you."

"Okay." There wasn't room in her purse, so Barbara clutched the pieces in one hand. "I'd better go, Dad. I won't tell anybody."

"I know," he said.

"Thanks." She didn't know what else to say. But then, she'd never known how to talk to her father.

"The others will be back soon," he said.

"'Bye." Barbara stood on tiptoe and kissed his cheek. He didn't smell of after-shave lotion and toothpaste, the way he usually did. In a funny way, he smelled of dust. "God, I'm glad you're okay."

"I'll walk you down." Her father held the door open, and Barbara headed toward the staircase. Her purse felt heavy, and the mirror and brush were awkward to carry. She didn't really want them, not after

Rita had used them, but it wouldn't do to hurt Dad's feelings. Besides, they were probably worth a lot.

Her mouth was dry, and the air felt thin again, as if something funny had happened to the atmosphere. The staircase looked so long, more than one story; it seemed to descend as far as she could see, down down into distant fire. Barbara's chest squeezed tight and she started to turn. "Dad, I'm scared. . . ."

"Good-bye, Barbara." The force of his shove caught her with one foot in the air. She didn't have time to scream, couldn't even break her fall because her hands were gripping the purse and the silver brush. The mirror shattered; shards of cruel light shot around her, the earth was spinning away, the back of her head slammed into a riser, her skirt hiked up around her thighs, she was all bent and twisted, hurtling into darkness and then softly enveloped by silence.

"Ramona? Is someone here?" Rita opened the kitchen door hesitantly. She didn't recognize the Cadillac in the driveway, and she hadn't seen Ramona's car in the garage. Maybe it was thieves; but thieves didn't usually drive Cadillacs, even in Newport Beach.

She ought to go for the police. Or wait until Ramona got back. But it might be Bob Fillipone; she seemed to remember Cruise giving him a key to the house, a long time ago. He usually drove a Porsche, but it could be a loaner.

"Bob?" She wanted to talk to him, to tell him about the appointment. Of course, she hadn't accepted right away. She'd said she needed time to think about it. So she wouldn't look too eager. Besides, it would be a good idea to confer with her staff first, to make sure they were willing to stick with her. Not that there was much doubt of that.

No one had answered.

Rita drew the gun out of her purse and took the safety off, then thought the better of it. If there *were* thieves here, she didn't want to go shooting them. How would it look, a senatorial appointee gunning down someone in her own house, maybe a teenager? Cruise had always said you wanted to avoid any sort of scandal, any hint of wrongdoing. There were always people waiting to seize on it.

Rita put away the gun and stepped outside. A car was coming up the street, slowing down, turning into the driveway. A battered old station wagon. Ramona's car.

"Ramona! Thank goodness." Rita started toward her. "I think there's someone in the house."

"Oh?" Ramona took a long look at the Cadillac as she got out, almost an angry look. "Well, now, I wonder who that could be?"

"I thought it might be Bob, but—" Rita shook her head ruefully. "Why didn't I think of that? Barbara. Of course."

"I'll bet it is." Ramona's usually unexpressive face tightened. Why would she be angry with Barbara? But then, Ramona took pride in the house. She probably resented the intrusion almost as much as Rita did.

"We'd better go in together." Ignoring the housekeeper's protest, Rita helped her collect the bags of groceries. They walked into the kitchen amid the rustle of paper sacks.

Rita set her load on the table and went into the dining room. "Barbara? There's no point in hiding. We know you're in here." Her words echoed oddly, as if the walls had gone hollow.

"Maybe I'd better go in first." Ramona stepped past Rita. "If you're the one who finds her, well, she could be unbalanced. Maybe do something foolish."

It hadn't occurred to Rita that her stepdaughter might have come here armed, might claim that she'd been startled and mistaken Rita for a burglar.

"Thanks." She thought about taking out her gun again, but didn't want to overreact. Ramona was just being cautious.

She waited while the housekeeper went into the hall. The footsteps stopped abruptly, and then Rita heard a low, gurgling noise rise slowly into a scream. "Ramona?" She forced herself forward.

"Oh, sweet Lord! Barbara!" The housekeeper knelt by a crumpled figure at the foot of the steps. "My God, look at her! She must have fallen the whole way down!"

The evidence spoke for itself. Barbara's purse had broken open, spilling out a necklace and bracelet that had been heirlooms. Rita's silver mirror lay shattered, glass everywhere, and the brush had skittered down the hall.

The damn fool must have panicked when she heard Rita drive up and tried to run down the stairs. "Is she breathing?" Rita crouched beside the housekeeper, who shook her head. "I'll call the paramedics."

She wondered, briefly, as she gave the dispatcher her address, how this would look in the newspapers and whether it would make Governor Fisher reconsider his offer. But why should it? She wouldn't tell anyone about the dispute over the heirlooms. It was a simple accident. Made careless by grief, Cruise's daughter had lost her footing while alone in the house and fallen to her death. That was all.

How did she get into the safe? Why would she take the dresser set Cruise bought me on our honeymoon?

Ramona was sobbing in the hallway, still crouched next to Barbara. "It's my fault. It's all my fault."

"What do you mean?" Rita hoped the woman wasn't going to be hysterical.

"She called—I mentioned you were out, that I was going to the grocery—I—I should have known she might try something. I should have stopped her. It's dangerous, this house. I hear things, ever since I started working here."

The heat-racked kitchen, the voices. "There's no such thing as a haunted house, Ramona. Besides which, nothing bad ever happened in this house before, as far as I know."

The housekeeper swallowed her sobs. "I'm sorry. I'm not superstitious, Mrs. Long. And I like working for you. But there's something wrong with this house."

"Well, it's too big for me anyway. I'll probably sell it and buy a condo." Sirens wailed toward them. "Thank goodness."

"I'll let them in." Ramona hurried to the front.

Left alone with the body, Rita stared down with horrified fascination. Barbara's blond curls looked like a skewed wig against the doll-like head and twisted neck. Her eyes were still open, her mouth twisted as if in a scream. She smelled foul, as if she'd been touched by something evil.

She didn't just fall.

What if Barbara had been pushed? She had died while the governor's aide was offering Rita the appointment. It seemed too much of a coincidence.

The paramedics burst into the hall, equipment beeping, two-way radios blaring. Just like the day Cruise died. Just as efficient, just as useless. Too late again.

It could have been me.

In a flash, Rita knew she was being warned for the last time.

CHAPTER TWENTY-TWO

"I did *what?*" Joe stared at his secretary in disbelief, "Wait a minute. You'd better start over."

"Well, I wasn't there." Rhondie passed one long polished fingernail through her tight red curls. She was an efficient woman in her early forties, not given to idle gossip. "You know Chipper Doyle?"

"Slightly." Chipper was the wife of Manny Doyle, mayor pro tem of San Paradiso and the man Joe had expected to be named mayor last night.

"She called this morning to congratulate you on that speech you made to the council. Something about proving your innocence and knowing they'd stand behind you. She said you rose above yourself and everyone was impressed." Rhondie shifted from one foot to the other, as if unsure whether to sit down or remain standing.

It was the first time Joe had left his house since noon yesterday, when he got out of jail. He didn't like hearing that he'd been at last night's council meeting, even if he had impressed everybody.

"I wasn't there," he said. "Rhondie, someone's posing as me."

She looked at him dubiously. "But all those people know you. Joe, are you feeling okay?"

"I'm fine." Damn it, who did she think she was, his mother?" I'm not crazy, Rhondie. I swear I'm not. I was home all night. I watched that movie on TV, what's it called? *Dead Heat.* Want me to describe it?"

She shook her head. But then, of course, he could have seen the movie some other time. Or taped it and watched it later.

"I'll tell you what." Joe folded his arms. "There's a cop tailing me. It was a woman last night. She could testify that I didn't leave my house."

"A cop?" Rhondie began to look convinced. "Really? Gosh, I wish I'd been there. Next council meeting, I'll go. I could tell the difference, even if you had an identical twin you didn't know about."

"I'll call you if I hear of anything coming up that the mayor might attend." Joe was relieved. Rhondie would be able to describe exactly what this imposter looked like, how he acted. "But be careful. He's a killer, Rhondie."

"Oh." Her pale eyes widened. "I forgot about that. Maybe we ought to tell the police about this guy posing as you."

"I already tried," Joe said. "They didn't believe me. You can reach me at home if you need anything. Forget what I said about taking unpaid vacation. I can pay your salary for another month. Maybe they'll catch the bastard by then."

"I sure hope so." Rhondie followed him to the door.

"Lock it after me," Joe said. "We need some kind of signal in the future, so you'll know it's me. On the phone, too." He thought for a minute. "I'll say, 'It's just good old Joe.' Okay?"

"Okay." Rhondie nodded for emphasis. "'Good old Joe.' Now you take care."

He repressed the sudden urge to give her a hug. He had damn few friends in this world. It was good to know at least one person still believed in him.

"Be careful," he said. "Don't forget to lock the door." He waited outside until he heard the bolt click into place.

Joe sat in his car for a while in the parking lot, playing the radio and watching to make sure no one who looked like him was sneaking back there. He wished to God he'd done the same thing for Kiki.

The cop—a man this time—was parked on the street, pretending to read the newspaper. His presence was reassuring. If they needed help, it would be close at hand.

With one ear, he listened to the newscast. "Vice President Whiting today offered himself as a hostage in exchange for President Harkness. There was no immediate response from the kidnappers. . . ."

Bunch of shithead bravado. Who'd trade in a president for a veep?

"In France, meanwhile, a curious choice has emerged as the likely successor to slain President Giroux in the upcoming elections. Public sentiment seems to be uniting behind rock star René Dubois, head of the new Strong France party. He's an outspoken critic of how the French government has handled the earthquake crisis, but his views on most issues are unknown.

"We'll take a look at the weather in just a minute. . . ."

Joe flipped channels and started the car. No point in sitting here all day. But he'd call Rhondie when he got home, just to make sure she was okay.

"I can't believe you let him get away from you. Somebody might have been killed." Lieutenant Grover, his face deeply lined and his eyes haggard from another night at his wife's bedside, glared over his desk at Detective Briana Kew.

Daryl had already made that point himself, after he learned this morning about Joe Pickard's surprise visit to the city council while Briana was still at her post in front of his house.

She told Grover the same thing she'd told Daryl. "I could swear it wasn't Pickard. It's not that big a house, and there's not much cover. I could see someone moving around inside, behind the shade. And his car was there."

"Maybe he's got an accomplice." Grover looked as if all his red corpuscles had gone on vacation.

"An accomplice for what?" Kew was a dependable cop, and not bad-looking, either. She'd been a little shaken when she heard the news this morning, but she was sticking to her story. "He didn't commit any crimes last night. Why sneak away from us to make a public appearance? He ought to know we'll just watch him harder."

"None of this makes a hell of a lot of sense," the lieutenant had to admit. "But damn it, you were supposed to stay on him."

"I don't want to beat a dead horse," Daryl said from where he leaned in the doorway, "but do you suppose it's possible there really is someone else who looks like him running around? Some kind of twin? Maybe the guy was adopted or something and never knew about it."

"Check it out," Grover said. "Anything's possible, I suppose."

"Yes, sir." Daryl held the door for Briana and followed her out.

Shit, why did that judge have to go and let Joe Pickard out of jail anyway? This past weekend was the first one in a long time that Daryl hadn't had to work overtime. He'd picked up a doll named Nina on the beach, a student from Sweden, and they'd had a hot time at her apartment. Had another date tonight, and he didn't intend to miss it. He still had a lot of lost time to make up.

He went through Pickard's file, found out where he'd been born, and began making some routine checks. Only you were talking about fifty years ago, which made it hard to track things down. By midafternoon, he'd turned up a birth certificate and no record of adoption. Finding out if the guy might have a brother or cousin who looked like him would be damn near impossible. If there was an obvious candidate, surely the mayor himself would have hit on it.

Daryl carried on a long struggle between his conscience and his sex drive, and the conscience came in first. But not by much.

Tonight, he'd help out by watching the back of Pickard's house. They'd make damn sure the guy was where he was supposed to be.

He tried Nina's number, but there was no answer. Probably out on the beach again. Those Swedish girls loved to get the darkest tans they could. He just hoped he could reach her before he had to go out in the field.

Draper liked working out at his club. He liked the masculine smell of sweat, the echoing thud of weights and equipment, the sharp *whang-whang* of the racquetball caroming off the walls. He liked to watch the girls, the way the sweaty T-shirts clung to their breasts, the way they sucked the air in and out and their nostrils flared. A couple of times he'd picked one up. They melted like butter, already hot; they'd hardly been able to wait till they were alone in the hotel room before they started stripping off their clothes.

It wasn't like cheating, not really. Just another kind of exercise, something a man needed once in a while. And a woman, too. Not his wife, of course. But then, she cared more about clothes than sex.

He was coming out of the sauna, a towel wrapped around his waist, when he heard his name over the loudspeaker. "Telephone call for Mr. Draper Dagmar."

Who would call him here? His lawyer, Ted Lopez, maybe. His secretary wouldn't have told anyone else where he was.

"Yeah? Dagmar," he growled when the attendant brought him the portable phone.

"You know who this is." That smooth voice again.

"How'd you know I was here?"

"Does it matter?" The guy sounded as if Draper had said something stupid. It irritated him, but he tried not to show it.

"I guess not." No sense in calling the judge by name; portable phones could be listened in on. "I made that call. You don't want me to tell you about it now, do you?"

"Tomorrow night," Tarkenton said. "Your house." The phone clicked off. Damn arrogant son of a bitch. He didn't even say what time.

Draper fumed silently as he showered and dressed. He was tempted to turn the guy in just for the sheer pleasure of it. But that *would* be stupid.

How would Tarkenton react when he learned he wasn't a shoo-in for the job? He couldn't expect to back out now. Draper had done his part. And he had the evidence.

It would be a relief, anyway, to meet the guy face-to-face, without that intimidating courtroom and that black robe getting in the way. To see Lewis Tarkenton shrunk down to ordinary man-size.

Draper could handle him. The guy might be a judge, but he had a lot to learn about how the big boys operated.

Who could tell? Tarkenton might turn out to be a useful contact. Even if he didn't get the appointment, there might be favors Draper could trade.

Maybe in the long run he'd pay off even better than Fisher.

CHAPTER TWENTY-THREE

The pressure must be getting to Steve Orkney, Laura reflected Wednesday morning. His desk was always a mess, but today the amount of junk food had elevated it to health-hazard proportions. There were not one, not two, but three cups of machine coffee perched atop the pile of papers, along with a scattering of half-eaten Twinkies, an open bag of cheese-and-jalapeño tortilla chips, and three untouched double packs of Reese's peanut-butter cups.

"You look lousy," she said, which was true. Dark circles shadowed his eyes, and his skin had a sallow cast. "You're killing yourself, Steve. Dammit. How many friends have I got?"

"I couldn't sleep last night." He leaned on the pile of papers, nearly dislodging one of the coffee cups. "I couldn't turn the TV off. The prime minister of Canada died—did you know that?"

Laura shook her head. "When?"

"Died of injuries about ten P.M. our time." Steve was a news junkie; Laura had visited his apartment once and found it sparsely furnished except for three TV sets, side by side in the living room, each tuned to a different channel. "And then there's Barbara Long's death."

"There wasn't anything strange about it, was there? She just fell, I thought."

"Just fell. Only what was she doing there alone?" Steve said. "She and Rita hated each other."

Laura just watched him.

"What?" he said.

"It's getting to you," she said. "I never thought I'd see the day."

"Well, you're seeing it."

The phone rang, and she picked it up.

"It's Rita." The usually controlled voice shook nervously. "Can we talk?"

"Sure." Laura opened a file in the computer. At the next desk, Steve went back to his work. "On or off the record?"

"On. At least for starters." There was a deep intake of breath at the other end of the phone. "I have the governor's permission to tell you that he offered to appoint me to fill out my husband's term. I appreciate the generosity and sensitivity of his offer"—she sounded as if she were reading from a statement —"but I have decided to decline."

"Why?"

There was a brief pause. "I have no experience in office, and this is a very important position to the people of California. I think it should go to someone with more expertise, someone who will make sure Cruise's agenda is carried out as he would have wished."

"What are you going to do?"

Laura heard rustling, as if Rita were setting down a piece of paper. "I—I like that idea of yours, Laura. I'm going to devote myself to a cause that's—that's concerned me for a long time. You can print this. I'm on the board of an organization called Love and Cherish Kids —LACK, for short. We're trying to help neglected kids, who often get overlooked with all the publicity about abused children. But sometimes the neglected ones suffer just as deeply."

"I didn't know you were involved with that." Laura could type almost as fast as Rita was talking, but it still took her a minute to catch up.

"I'm on the board of several charities, you know, a figurehead kind of thing. But I'm going to take a more active role in LACK from now on."

Laura reread her notes quickly. "Excuse me if I'm being insensitive, but does this decision have anything to do with your stepdaughter's death?"

She heard the click of a cigarette lighter. "This is off the record."

"Okay." Laura stopped typing.

"I don't believe it was an accident." Rita paused to blow out a puff of smoke. "If I accepted this offer, I'm pretty sure I'd be next."

"Jesus." Laura swallowed thickly. "Do you have any idea who it is? Even a wild guess?"

"Not even. But I'm not entirely giving up. If I can, I'll make sure my husband's job goes to somebody who really cares about it, somebody Cruise would approve of."

"The governor didn't indicate who he might tab?"

"I didn't ask. I don't suppose they would have told me if I had." Laura heard the housekeeper's voice in the background, and then Rita said, "There's someone downstairs to see me. I have to go."

"Good luck," was all Laura could say.

"Who was that?" Steve didn't miss much.

"Rita Long. She's turning down the appointment." Who had killed Barbara? The same person who murdered those other women? "Steve, she—off the record, she doesn't think Barbara's death was an accident. But she doesn't have any proof."

"Did she tell the cops?"

"No."

"I don't blame her. That would make a big stink." Steve tapped his fingers on a Twinkie, seemingly unaware he was mashing a hole in it. "I'll nose around."

About to start on the story about Rita, Laura remembered she ought to call the Coroner's Office. After she spent several minutes on hold, the spokesman came on the line.

"I have a statement to read." Laura waited, fingers poised over the keyboard. "Toxicological tests indicate the death of Senator Cruise Long resulted from a lethal dose of an analogue of heroin."

"An analogue of heroin?" She was so startled she almost forgot to type.

"It's chemically similar, but man-made. Alphamethylfentanyl is its scientific name." The spokesman seemed to enjoy displaying his knowledge. "It's an isomer—a variation—of fentanyl, which is widely used in hospitals as a painkiller—has few aftereffects, and it's fifty to one hundred times as potent as morphine."

"Could it have been administered at the hospital?" She answered her own question: "No, it's not exactly the same drug, right? How big a dose did he take?"

"At least a milligram. That would cause death in about half an hour."

Half an hour. That meant he could have taken it—or been given it—before his speech. "Was there any evidence he was an abuser? Or could somebody have slipped it in his drink? Does it have to be injected?"

"It can be administered orally or by injection," the deputy coroner said. "There've been more than a hundred such deaths recorded in California. Only two out of state, and both of them had visited Orange County. Frankly, if he'd died in another state, it might have gone undetected. Death looks natural at autopsy. You have to test specifically for the drug."

"Where does this thing come from?" Peripherally, Laura saw Steve Orkney walk around and begin to read the notes on her computer screen.

"A mobile lab. First we got a cluster of deaths in Stanton, then San Diego, then Monterey. God knows where it's coming from now."

Laura could still see Cruise staring at her, pleading for help, or maybe warning her. Like her father.

Dad. He'd died in 1974. It didn't seem possible there was any connection with the drug, but her reporter's instincts made her ask anyway. "How long has alpha-whatever-it-is been around?"

"Since the early seventies," the spokesman said. "Excuse me, I've got another call."

"Thanks for your help." Laura hit the "save" button, and the computer whirred.

"Shit." Steve shook his head and waved to the metro editor. "Bill, you'd better look at this."

A couple of other reporters and editors drifted by, and soon a small, silent knot surrounded Laura. They parted as Greg came through. He stood behind Laura's shoulder, reading her notes.

"I'll call the governor," Greg said. "He'll appreciate getting the news, and he might say something interesting."

"I'll phone Rita back," Laura volunteered. "See what she has to say about the coroner's report. And, oh, Greg, she turned down the appointment."

"Okay. Get on it. Looks like we're going to have a Long family front page today."

Rita's housekeeper answered on the second ring, and Laura identified herself.

"Just a minute, Miz Bennett."

It wasn't Rita who picked up the phone a minute later but Bob Fillipone. "The coroner called me this morning, and I came over to break the news," he said.

"Can I speak to Rita?"

"I'm sorry, but she's in seclusion."

Damn and double damn. "Do you have a statement?"

"Nothing yet. I'll call you when we do." He took down her number. "But I doubt if she'll want to comment. Let me just say for print that it's a terrible shock. Okay?"

"Thanks." Laura made a face and hung up.

A message from Greg popped up on her screen. *This from Fisher: "I extend my deepest sympathies to Mrs. Long on this terrible disclosure about her husband's death, and I want to say how sorry I am that she has decided not to accept the appointment to the U.S. Senate. The death of Senator Long's daughter is yet another great tragedy. I can only hope that, if there was any wrongdoing involved in either of the deaths, the perpetrator is quickly brought to justice."*

Laura messaged back an acknowledgment. It was kind of odd, though. Fisher sounded as if somebody had helped him prepare a statement, but that wasn't possible unless he'd already known about the coroner's report.

Well, if they'd notified Bob Fillipone, maybe they'd notified the Governor's Office, too.

The next two hours passed in a mental tunnel. Laura led with the autopsy report, and sidebarred the appointment. At the next desk, Steve punched furiously at the keys, burying Barbara. He was the fastest hunt-and-peck typist Laura had ever seen.

By the time she forwarded the second story to Bill White, Laura felt tired and hungry. She reached back to rub her neck muscles, then stood up slowly. Her head ached, as if she were coming down with something.

Laura paused by the filing cabinets, looking out the newsroom window. Sunlight bleached the parking lot to a shimmering gray-white. California sunshine. August.

Behind her, the clicking of computer keys from the newsroom stopped suddenly. The chatter of reporters, the scuffling of footsteps, everything fell silent. Except the TV set.

Laura turned, thinking at first the bulletin was about Cruise Long's cause of death. But that wasn't big enough news to break into a network in the middle of the day. Not when the president had been kidnapped.

The anchorman looked stunned. "We've just been handed this bulletin from the Associated Press. A videotape delivered today to a Paris television station appears to show the execution of Soviet leader Aleksei Karponov."

Someone let out a low, grim whistle. Somebody else said, "Shit."

"The tape showing the firing-squad execution of the Soviet leader is believed to have been delivered by followers of Ayatollah Al-Hadassi, but there was no indication why Karponov was killed or what has happened to President Harkness and the other missing leaders." The anchorman seemed to be having some trouble getting the words out. "Another report from Arabian radio indicates the CIA may have had something to do with Sunday's debacle. However, U.S. sources are denying these reports. In Washington today, First Lady Dorothy Harkness appealed to the kidnappers. . . ."

. . . *there was no indication why Karponov was killed* . . .

Because he was in the way, Laura thought. They were all in the way—Dad, Senator Long—but whose way? For what?

The newsroom faded, and she became sharply aware of the framed photographs lining the walls. Brightly clothed children tossing a beach ball; a bum sleeping in a doorway; lightning jagging through the sky above the ocean. The world as Laura knew it.

A world with, somewhere, an unsuspected door in it. A door to the unthinkable.

Over at the copy desk, Greg was remaking the front page. The copy editors poked at their keys with grim concentration, shoehorning in Karponov's death and the stories about the Long family. They looked normal and familiar.

These were real events, real tragedies that needed no supernatural explanation.

Jerkily, Laura reached the door and went outside. She had to calm down, have lunch, pursue a follow-up story on Senator Long's cause of death. There was plenty to keep her busy.

Halfway to her car, she realized what she was doing. Running away from her own buried memory. The one that wouldn't stay dead, the one that could explain these strange shifts of consciousness.

The one she'd been fleeing all her life.

She was being forced to confront it. Fitting the key into her car, Laura's hand began to tremble.

Today, after work, she would find another copy of the Goya book.

CHAPTER TWENTY-FOUR

Rhondie Harper examined the two bottles of nail polish carefully. Red and white. She was getting tired of painting her nails the same old colors. What if she alternated them? Would people think she was some kind of aging hippie, or would it look sharp?

She'd always wanted to have a sense of style. You'd think, reading all those magazines month after month, that you'd get a clear idea of what it took. But just as soon as she thought she knew—it had to do with colors, or fabrics, or accessories—some designer would start a new trend and throw the whole thing out of whack.

Might as well try it and see how it looked. It wasn't as if she had anything else to do.

Rhondie wiped off her old polish and was angling her cuticle scissors into position when a soft knock at the door startled her. Her hand jerked, and the tip of the scissors ploughed across her thumb, leaving a welt and a prick of blood.

Damn, who could that be? Annoyed, she lifted her injured thumb to her mouth and sucked it. Well, at least he'd come before she painted her nails, so she didn't have to worry about smudging them on the knob.

Rhondie heaved herself up, cuticle scissors in hand. The window air conditioner wasn't making much inroad into the sullen air. "Who is it?" she called near the door.

"It's me," said a man's voice. "Just good old Joe."

Maybe it was all those warnings he'd given her, but something made her hesitate. That was the code, all right . . . but it didn't sound quite like Joe's voice. It had a tinny ring, like something synthesized by a computer.

"Joe?" Rhondie called.

"That's what I just said." He didn't bother to hide his impatience. "It's hot out here. Open the damn door."

She turned the lock and cracked the door open to peer out. Yes, that sure looked like Joe. "Listen—"

He wasn't looking at her. He was staring at her thumb, at the little pill of blood welling up.

"Joe?"

His nostrils flared like an animal scenting something. Blood. Dear Lord, he wanted her blood.

"Get out!" Rhondie's voice rose to a shriek as she shoved at the door. It was the killer! Exactly like Joe except not really him. Not really human. "Go—"

He lunged forward, slamming the door into her hip. Rhondie cried out, and the creature nodded as if pleased.

"Who are you?" she gasped. "*What* are you?"

The Joe-thing smiled and pushed harder against the door. God, it was strong. Inhumanly strong.

Rhondie tried to scream again, but her voice caught. Surely someone would notice the struggle, somebody from one of the half-dozen other businesses in the strip. If she could only manage to scream.

The killer leaned away for a split second. Before she could react, he kicked the door so hard it split down the middle.

Rhondie staggered back into the room and felt her ankle twist under her. She grabbed desperately, but found nothing to break her fall. Dear God, the thing was on top of her. . . .

Nobody had been in a good mood all day at the PD.

Ever since the news about Karponov's murder came on the radio, a weird kind of depression had fallen over the whole detective bureau. Even Daryl couldn't quite figure out how to blame this one on the communists. The way things were going, there was going to be a war. He hadn't thought that would happen again, not in his lifetime.

Lieutenant Grover dozed over his third cup of coffee, worn out from another death vigil at the hospital. He ought to take some leave, Daryl thought, but the timing was bad. The other detective sergeant, Mike Guinness, had gone sailing up the coast to Oregon on vacation before the first murder broke, leaving them short-handed.

And the chief had called Captain DeWitt into some kind of emergency meeting ten minutes ago. That couldn't mean anything good, either.

Daryl stared blearily down at the reports stacked in front of him, wondering what Nina had thought when he failed to show up last night. He'd called twice, once from a pay phone and once after he got home. She hadn't answered.

That could mean she'd given up and gone out. Or that she was home with somebody else and didn't feel like taking phone calls.

Nina wasn't exactly movie-star material. Her nose had a little bump on it, and her cheekbones were kind of broad, and one of her front teeth leaned slightly to starboard. But oh that body. It just didn't quit.

Joe Pickard hadn't stirred from inside his house all night. Which meant Daryl's sacrifice had gone for nothing.

He heard his name, and turned to see Captain DeWitt gesturing him and Lieutenant Grover into his office.

Sure enough, it was more bad news. Senator Long hadn't died of natural causes after all. Unless the guy was some kind of drug abuser, which didn't seem likely, he'd been murdered.

"We'll be getting some help on this from the FBI," DeWitt said. "But we're going to do everything in our power to solve it ourselves. This is a homicide in our jurisdiction, and I don't want the feds to come in here and make us look like wimps."

"Any chance Joe Pickard was involved?" Daryl asked, half-humorously, until it struck him that the mayor probably *had* been at the luncheon.

DeWitt grunted. "He'll have to be questioned. Along with a bunch of newspaper editors, and you know what that'll be like. They've all got lawyers on retainer."

"And the widow," Grover said.

"What's the motive?" Daryl could see he wasn't going to get anywhere near Nina or her pants for a while, even if she was still speaking to him. "Who'd have anything to gain? You suppose it was a grudge?"

"He was being talked about as a presidential candidate." The captain paused to let the significance sink in. "Let's do the legwork first. If it's intramural greed, that would really simplify things."

"What about his daughter's death?" Grover said. "It's Newport's case, but they could be linked."

They looked at each other. "I'll see what I can dig up on Mrs. Long," Daryl said.

He'd scarcely got back to his desk when the phone rang. It was Steve Orkney, letting him know, after swearing him to secrecy, that Mrs. Long didn't think her stepdaughter's death was an accident.

Well, great. That made their prime suspect suddenly not so

prime. If she'd staged the thing to look accidental, she'd hardly go tipping her hand to reporters, would she?

There was one good thing about all this, anyway. He didn't see how the day could get much worse.

That was before the phone rang again.

It was the desk sergeant. "I just took a call from a woman named Rhondie Harper who says she's Joe Pickard's secretary. Apparently, she was attacked a few minutes ago by a guy she said could be Joe's double."

"How does she know it wasn't Joe?"

"She couldn't really say. She was kind of hysterical. I figured it might be related to these murders."

Daryl took down the woman's phone number and address, which turned out to be Pickard's office. "I'll get right on it."

He checked in with the lieutenant and then headed out.

"I had this scissors in my hand—if it hadn't been for that—I kept stabbing him. And then somebody pulled into the parking lot—just turning around, I guess, but it scared him off. Oh, God. I thought I was dead."

Rhondie Harper was a pale woman with fading red curls. Right now, she hovered on the brink of hysteria, gulping down coffee and twisting hair around her finger. She'd come damn close to being victim number four.

"How can you be sure it wasn't Joe?" Daryl wished the damn chair weren't so hard. What kind of office was this, anyway, for the mayor of San Paradiso? Bare and shabby-looking, although at least it was neater than the guy's house. "Other than his voice sounding a little tinny?"

"Well, when I looked out the window, I saw him running off, and Joe's car wasn't there. And neither was that policeman, the one who's been following him."

So much for secrecy. "But his car could have been parked nearby," Daryl pointed out.

"Yes, only . . ." Mrs. Harper clutched her hands together in her lap. "I went right to the phone and called Joe first thing. And he was home. He couldn't have gotten back that fast. It's over a mile. He wasn't even out of breath."

Norm Hertz was tailing Joe again today. Was it possible old Pickard had sneaked out twice, on two different detectives, without being spotted? "It couldn't have been some kind of taped message, could it?" Daryl knew he was grasping at straws.

"I don't see how. I mean, we had this conversation. He was really worried. Sergeant, that *wasn't* Joe who attacked me. It didn't—it didn't smell like him. I mean, it doesn't sound nice, but Joe sweats. It's real hot out there today, and he must have walked a ways from his car. I don't know who it was, and if I'd seen him across a room, I couldn't have told the difference, but it wasn't Joe."

She stared down at the cuticle scissors on the desk. "And that's another funny thing. There's no blood. I mean, there *was* blood when I was stabbing him, but there isn't a sign of it anywhere."

"Probably all on his clothes." Daryl closed his notebook. "Mrs. Harper, if there's someone who looks exactly like your boss running around, I think you should find a nice safe place to hide out for a while. Maybe with some relatives? Just be sure you let me know where you'll be."

"Thank you, Sergeant." She locked up the office, and he walked her to her car.

Jesus, this was crazy.

Daryl radioed in and got patched through to Norm, who'd already been apprised of the attack. Norm confirmed that Joe had never left the house.

DeWitt and Grover didn't look too happy when Daryl told them there really was a man going around pretending to be Joe Pickard. Of course, it didn't prove anything one way or another about the murders. Joe's fingerprints had been on that purse, and you couldn't fake fingerprints.

They put out an APB for anyone resembling Joe Pickard, and notified area hospitals in case Mrs. Harper's nail scissors had done any real damage. Grover went out to Pickard's house, but he didn't learn much. The guy had his lawyer present, and all he would say was that he'd been home all day and that, to his knowledge, he didn't have a brother or a cousin who looked like him.

Daryl spent the rest of the afternoon digging up a list of people who'd been at last Tuesday's luncheon, especially those who'd sat at the head table. Which led him right back to Joe Pickard and, maybe, Mrs. Long.

It was almost five o'clock when he tried Nina's number again.

"Hallo?" She sounded cheerful, which he took as a good sign.

"Hi, it's Daryl. About last night . . ."

"I've been thinking about it all day," she practically purred into the phone. "You were wonderful. When can we do it again? Tonight?"

"I was *what?*" Daryl frowned.

"You men." She laughed. "You always want to be flattered. Can you come over tonight?"

It hit him suddenly how tired he was. Which might have something to do with only sleeping about two hours last night. His mind must be going fuzzy. Had he really dropped over sometime yesterday? Or had she got the days confused, or what? "Not tonight. I'm wiped out. How about Friday? Seven o'clock?"

"Okay." She sounded disappointed, then brightened again. "I'll get some more oils, the ones you like."

Oils? She must have him mixed up with somebody else. Maybe she knew two guys named Daryl. On the other hand, he still might get some action Friday night, which was better than nothing. "Sounds great."

"See you then."

After she hung up, he stared at the receiver for a minute before replacing it in the cradle.

Now that was strange. But on the other hand, it was a bit of luck he hadn't counted on.

Maybe today hadn't been a total loss, after all.

CHAPTER TWENTY-FIVE

On TV, the shock waves from Karponov's assassination reverberated all afternoon. Fingers pointed, mostly at Arabia, but countries whose heads of state remained in jeopardy grew vocal in their criticism of the United States. There were references to bungled CIA operations over the years and to the fact that Al-Hadassi had changed his methods so abruptly a few years ago, without apparent cause.

The State Department didn't trust the National Security Council, and nobody trusted the CIA. Secret operations, arms deals, a semiautonomous band of superpatriots gone haywire—accusations flew. The NSC scheduled an emergency meeting, and Whiting wasn't available for comment.

In West Germany, a bomb went off near a U.S. air base, killing two soldiers and five civilians. In Jordan, the eldest son of the missing king publicly declared that he blamed the United States for Karponov's murder. The Egyptian ambassador to Washington was called home for "consultations." In the United Nations, China urged a special session to be held, not in New York but in Geneva.

After work, Laura steered north toward Fullerton, to a used-book store Steve had told her about in a once-deteriorating open-air mall now dominated by discount stores. She parked in front of a bargain boutique and walked along a concrete path to the Book Cellar. The glass windows displayed rare volumes, and inside she found a huge room packed floor-to-ceiling with books. The air smelled of dust and old leather.

Laura stopped by the desk. A sad-eyed man with a beard looked up from his computer. "Can I help you?"

She gave him the name of the book, and he typed it in. "Yes, we have it. Just a minute."

The World of Goya was an oversize volume, with $21.95 handwritten lightly inside the cover. "That's as much as it must have cost new," Laura said.

"You can't find it new," the man pointed out. "It's been out of print for twenty years."

Laura fished the money out of her purse, took the book to her car, and drove home with the doors locked.

At the fourplex, it didn't surprise her that Madeleine emerged from her apartment as Laura reached the foot of the staircase. She knew the Frenchwoman must be watching.

"Hello." Laura paused on the second step, glad for the slight advantage of height.

"Be careful," the red-haired woman said in a monotone, like a small child just learning to speak. Her eyes were opaque in the late-afternoon light. Oddly, Laura had the impression that it wasn't really Madeleine.

"Of what?"

"Why, of me." She seemed to expect Laura to understand some subtext.

"You're warning me about yourself?"

"You should always be careful with strangers, especially strangers you think you know," the Frenchwoman said. "You must get ready."

She moved away down the sidewalk, a mesh plastic shopping bag dangling from one arm. Laura flashed back to that strange episode with Lew in the parking lot. Or with a man who looked like Lew. But there couldn't be someone who looked just like Madeleine, too.

All the same, she locked the door behind her before opening the Goya book.

She recognized some of the pictures at once. A horrible titan figure looming in the sky; an old woman leering from within a hooded robe; the sensuous Maja, reclining on a couch. She had seen them before, not in a book but as another layer of reality. Something projected from within herself.

Laura dropped the book onto her lap. Carefully, she surveyed the room around her. The aging shag carpet looked exactly the same shade of brownish-green as always. Tan sofa, cheap rented table, and lamps with pleated shades. Late-afternoon light slanted in, dancing with dust motes. Was it possible to be insane and still perceive everything so normally?

She glanced down at the book. It had opened to a foldout painting sprawled across three pages. "The Witches' Sabbath."

She knew it already. There was the goat-devil, silhouetted before the dark, haunted faces of its listeners. Above its head, Laura could make out some kind of squiggle, a blur of paint. No, not a blur; those were lines.

The painting was rearranging itself before her eyes. It *was* a door, slightly ajar, letting out a sliver of red, flickering light.

Laura knew she was only visualizing the door in this reproduction. Remembering it. Remembering—what?—on the other side. An impression, a childish nightmare of scarlet monsters she had seen once, in what seemed like another lifetime.

Only . . . she remembered Daddy carrying her out, clutching her tightly in spite of the revulsion written on his face. And she remembered turning to look back as the door shrank behind them, a door in a smoky void that imploded as she watched.

But she didn't remember going in. Only coming out. As if she, or some part of her, had been born in there.

Tension radiated across Laura's throat and neck, up, up, into the base of the brain. Her skin felt as if it were being sucked into a vacuum cleaner, as if the cells were turning inside out.

The light shifted into a red zone, blurry like film shot through some heat-sensing camera at night. Some alien consciousness was looking out through Laura's eyes.

She shuffled onto the balcony and gazed down at a world that boiled and shimmered. Below, a thin figure scrabbled up the walk. A pinkish old thing, not much blood left in it. Frail bones that would crunch in her jaws. Barely a morsel, but she longed for that unique taste. Red blood, red pain. The delicious, ephemeral heat of human life. Oh, God, the overwhelming hunger—new, and yet familiar. She needed to feed, to fill herself and transform herself until the metamorphosis became irreversible. . . .

No! Within this haze, it was hard to find a landmark to the world she knew, but Laura fought for one. Lew. His face came strong and real into her mind. If she could only grasp that image . . . the way his mouth curled when he looked at her, the sharp emotional definition of him. Something to hold on to, something to guide her home.

Her eyes burned and whirled. Her skin crackled as if an electric current had run through it, and Laura sagged against the railing until the vertigo passed.

When she looked down again, she glimpsed Madeleine's face turning up, its black-rimmed eyes narrow with suspicion. Human eyes, ordinary flesh, an old woman for whom she felt a certain compassion. Not prey. Not a hideous temptation to whatever lay within herself.

Laura retreated into the apartment. It terrified her, not knowing what had happened when they entered that hell. Something so terrible it had blocked out her memory. Something that was still happening.

Why had Daddy taken her into the painting?

In one of his last letters, he'd written something peculiar about fearing a war. Reading it the first time, Laura had concluded unhappily that her father had indeed suffered a breakdown.

Now, she crossed to her desk and sorted through the faded letters until she found it.

The letter was dated October 10, 1973.

> *Dear Ellen,*
>
> *Do you feel sometimes as if we're living in an age of chaos? I've been reading about Agnew's resignation, thinking about the past half-dozen years, Robert Kennedy and Martin Luther King, Nixon, Vietnam. So many deaths, such abuse of power, America on the verge of becoming a police state. Nothing makes sense. The systems that have guided us for centuries are breaking down. . . .*

"This is crazy," Kate said, setting her spoon down next to the empty shell of her soft-boiled egg.

She was looking at him that strange way, the way she'd regarded him frequently since his second trip to Madrid.

"Think about it." James tried to keep his voice even. It *did* sound insane, a doctoral student in art history declaring over the breakfast table that he had a mission to prevent a world war. But he felt such urgency, he could barely restrain his impatience. "I know you're not much for reading the Bible—"

"And you are?" Kate's mouth set in a thin line.

"I have been recently." He did his best to ignore the sarcasm. "Matthew twenty-four. It talks of 'wars and rumors of wars,' famines and earthquakes, false prophets and darkness."

"And from this you conclude that the millennium is at hand?" Kate glanced toward the bedroom where Laura slept. "James—have you been using drugs? Please. I'd rather you told me the truth."

"You have to have faith in me! You, of all people." He jumped up and paced across their small sitting room. "I've been having dreams, Kate. About—about Napoleon."

"Napoleon?" Her voice cracked. "Oh, James."

"Please, please hear me out." He needed her. He wasn't strong enough to handle this by himself. "Goya—he lived in an age like ours. Old values being tossed aside, democracy struggling with tyranny."

"Honestly, James, that's the way life's always been."

"But I keep having these dreams." He ached to make her see how real they were. "Only they're not really dreams. It has to do with the painting and with something the painting pulled out of me. It needs me. Needs me to open the door."

His wife's eyes glistened.

"I'm not crazy." James heard the pleading in his words. "Kate, this door in the painting—is it something evil that's going to come through, or is it our salvation? I have to find out. I don't know why I've been chosen; I'm no hero. I need you to help me."

Kate just sat there.

"Think!" he said desperately. "What if I'm right? What if we're all going to die because I didn't—"

"Mommy?" A small figure padded into the doorway, brown hair tumbling sleepily around her face. "Is something wrong?"

"Oh, honey." Kate shot James a reproving look.

"Nothing for you to worry about." James picked up his little girl and swung her high into the air. "How about a drive?"

"I want to see Princess Grace," she said.

Even Kate smiled at that.

"We could drive to Monaco." James set Laura back on her feet. "I can't promise the princess will put in an appearance, but they have a wonderful marine museum. What do you say?" He looked at Kate.

She nodded slowly. "I suppose . . . yes."

I had to write you before I lose my nerve. Ellen, I need for you to understand, too. You remember how mother was. I'm not like that. *You can tell the difference, can't you?*

Kate and Laura and I are going to Monaco today, as soon as they get dressed. We can all use a break. Please believe in me.

Love,
James

That was the night Mommy had died. The one person who might, somehow, have stopped him from opening the door.

The letter slipped out of Laura's hand and floated onto the desk.

Less than a year later, he'd died, too. In Washington, where he'd gone . . . to do what?

Grimly, she dialed her aunt's number. When Ellen answered, she said, "Could you tell me everything you remember about Dad's death?"

"You're dwelling on those letters again, aren't you?" The clatter of a game show faded in the background as her aunt turned down the volume. "I don't know much. We got a call from the hotel where he was staying, in Washington. The Madison, I think it was. The housemaid found him slumped on the carpet."

"What was he doing in Washington?"

"I never really knew. Laura, this is all water under the bridge."

"They're sure it was a heart attack?"

"Of course it was." Ellen sounded shocked. "Why should you think otherwise?"

"He must have gone there to see someone," Laura said. "That idea he had, that a war was imminent and that someone might come through the painting to start or stop it. Maybe he went to warn somebody."

"He didn't say." Her aunt clucked into the phone. "Honey, it was so long ago. Obviously, we didn't have a war, did we?"

"He didn't have any visitors?" Laura asked. "At the hotel, before he died?"

"Not that I know of," her aunt said. "Besides, what difference would it make?"

"None, I guess," Laura said. "Oh, Ellen. Dad didn't—he didn't ever mention the name Cruise Long, did he?"

"That senator who died? No. Why?"

"He would have been a congressman back then," Laura said, more to herself than to her aunt. "Never mind. There's probably no connection."

After they hung up, she studied the newspaper she'd brought home from work. The front-page stories were Karponov's assassination, Cruise Long's cause of death, Barbara Long's fatal fall, and Rita's turning down the senatorial nomination.

All linked in a way she couldn't piece together. A puzzle whose crucial missing piece might lie somewhere in Laura's memory.

Lew, she thought. In 1973, he'd been in college, a war protester. Marching on Washington. He'd remember who the political players were. Maybe he could help her pry loose the right name. Some antiwar leader, maybe, to whom James might have gone for help.

She dialed and found his line busy. Well, at least he was home.

Resolutely, Laura walked out of the apartment, leaving the Goya book on the floor.

CHAPTER TWENTY-SIX

All day, Draper Dagmar had an uneasy sense of being out of control. That damn judge sure knew how to keep the upper hand, not even specifying a time. Which meant Draper had to be home all evening; he picked up a steak dinner at the Sizzler and ate it in his own dining room, which meant he couldn't make repeat trips to the salad bar.

Fuck Lew Tarkenton, anyway.

It might have been a good idea to have Ted Lopez hiding in a closet and eavesdropping. On the other hand, there were things Draper wasn't sure he wanted even his lawyer to know. It all depended on how the meeting went.

To own a U.S. senator. That sure would be nice. Maybe Draper's suggestion to the governor would carry more weight than Mel Kawakami had let on. Especially now that, according to the paper, Rita Long had turned down the job.

He checked his watch. It was getting on seven o'clock.

Restlessly, Draper wandered into the second den and began racking the billiard balls. Might as well get in a little practice while he waited.

Crack! His first shot went wild. Damn, but he was edgy. He wanted this whole business over with.

Something about it smelled fishy. Like the guy was setting him up and some cop would come in his place. Or maybe Lew Tarkenton was the kind of jerk who got his jollies throwing his weight around, making other people dance to his tune. Maybe this was the creep's way of whacking off.

He probably wouldn't show.

After three wasted shots, Draper gave up on billiards. He went to the bar and poured himself a bourbon.

The electronic scream of the doorbell startled him so the liquor slopped onto his wrist.

Shit. Draper mopped it up with a paper towel and tossed it in the sink. "Yeah, be right there," he shouted, but took his time walking to the front door. It went against the grain to let this bastard see how uptight he was.

Laura parked in one of the guest slots near Lew's condominium and strode along the walkway toward his unit.

There was a light on in Lew's living room. She paused to listen for voices, in case he had guests, but heard only the soft strains of Vivaldi.

Tightening her grip on her purse, Laura pressed the buzzer.

Draper felt a sudden surge of reassurance as he opened the door. The man standing there in the porch light was unquestionably Lew Tarkenton.

The uneven lighting made his eyes look flat and gave his skin an unhealthy pallor. But hell yes, Draper would have recognized the son of a bitch anywhere.

"Come in." He gestured his visitor toward the back den, with its view of the harbor. "Like a drink?"

"No, thanks." Draper was reaching to switch on the light when he heard the judge say, "Leave it off."

He's afraid of being spotted. The evidence of Tarkenton's anxiety gave Draper's confidence another boost.

"Sure, whatever you say." He could afford to be genial now. "Mind if I have one?"

"If you like."

Draper went around the bar and clattered the glasses to cover the soft sound of the tape recorder being switched on, then poured himself another bourbon. "I guess you'd like to know what the governor's aide said."

"He said I'm on the list, but Mrs. Long came first." There was a note of contempt in the smooth voice. Okay, so it wasn't hard to figure out what Kawakami must have said, but did the guy have to be so arrogant about it? "Well, she's out of the running. Now, I want you to make another call."

Draper bit back the urge to tell the guy off. Tarkenton was still a judge, and he was still hearing Draper's case. "Yeah, okay."

"Tell them if I don't get the appointment, I'll nail you to the wall and the governor with you."

"Now wait just a goddamn—"

"You'd be surprised how much information I have access to." The guy sure was full of himself. Didn't he know that Draper could nail *him* to the wall?

A funny look crossed the judge's face, and he raised his hand to stop Draper's reply, as if he'd heard something suspicious. Surely, he couldn't have picked up the ultrasoft burr of the recorder.

"Just a minute," Tarkenton said, and half ran out of the room.

Laura pressed the buzzer again. It occurred to her how awkward it would be if Lew had brought a woman home, like a scene out of a bad soap opera. But he wouldn't do that.

Finally, she heard footsteps on the carpet. There was a pause as he observed her through the peephole, and then the door swung open.

"Laura?" Lew wore the gray velour robe she'd given him for his birthday. He stepped back to let her inside.

"I tried to call, but your phone was busy." She led the way into the living room, where a briefcase rested against the side of the couch and papers lay scattered across the coffee table.

"That must have been when I was sending out for pizza. It should be here any minute." Lew hesitated, as if there was something he couldn't bring himself to tell her.

That wasn't like him. "So?" Laura said. "Listen, if I'm interrupting anything—"

"No." He went into the kitchen and, watching her across the breakfast counter, poured two beers. "It's not that." Abruptly, he added, "Tell me why you're here."

"I need to pick your brain," she said. "About who my father might have gone to see in Washington before he died."

"Beg pardon?"

"I've been reading these letters," she began.

Draper stood there feeling like an idiot, holding a glass of untouched bourbon and waiting for Tarkenton to come back.

He didn't hear the front door open or close, so he knew the guy hadn't left. Maybe he was taking a leak.

"Hey!" Draper's voice rang back to him as if from a great distance. "Hey, Yer Honor!"

No one answered.

Damn. Draper put down the glass and went to investigate. He paced through the house slowly, which took a while, because it was over five thousand square feet with four johns. But there was no sign of Judge Lewis Tarkenton.

Disgusted, Draper checked out front. No car.

He wasn't sure how the asshole had managed to leave without making any noise. And he still didn't know why. There was no one else around, not in front and not out on the harbor. Nothing to spook the guy.

It had to be some kind of double cross.

Angrily, Draper went back to the den and turned off the recorder, then dialed Ted Lopez's home number.

"Hello?" Two children were shouting at each other in the background.

"It's Draper. I want you over here, now."

"It might take a while." Lopez sounded harassed. "My wife's out of town, and I was about to put the kids to bed. I'll have to call around to find a sitter."

"Oh, hell." That could take hours. "Where do you live?" Lopez gave him the address in Newport Beach. "All right. Put the kids down, and I'll be right over. This is urgent."

"What's up?"

"I'll tell you when I get there." Fuck Lew Tarkenton and his sources of information. Draper hung up and played back the recorder, just to make sure it had picked up the conversation with Hizzoner.

Clear as a bell.

"Gotcha," Draper said, and headed for his car.

"So you think your father went to Washington to warn someone about this painting . . . which was going to—what did you say it was going to do?" Lew's mind buzzed as if he'd read too many pages of a law brief late at night. System overload.

"If I'm interpreting it right," Laura said, "and if he saw what I think I remember seeing, he believed it was the gateway to hell. And that the—the creatures on the other side wanted to come through and start a war."

"Which would lead to Judgment Day?" Lew finished.

She nodded mutely.

He stared down at the one remaining slice of pizza on the table. "Laura, do you know how this sounds?"

"It sounds like I'm crazy," she said. "But tell me this: Why would anyone poison Cruise Long? It wasn't the act of some typical fanatic. And the way Rita and Joe Pickard are being set up, it's as if someone were trying to rig the senatorial appointment."

"Cruise Long was important, but not *that* important," Lew said. "Even if he planned to run for president, whoever replaces him will be a newcomer."

Laura sipped thoughtfully on her beer. It had always amused him, that she preferred beer rather than white wine with dinner. He supposed it came with being a reporter.

"Okay, suppose it works this way," she said. "Harkness gets killed. Whiting has to pick a vice president, so he picks the junior senator from California—and then Whiting dies. Look at Gerald Ford. He was appointed vice president, and he ended up in the White House."

Ridiculous, the whole conjecture. But this was Laura speaking, and he respected her. "Whiting isn't going to pick some newly appointed senator as vice president. It doesn't work that way, Laura."

"Not if things were proceeding logically and normally," she said, and then stopped as if she'd had a shock.

"What?" He leaned over and touched her hand.

"Lew," she said. "Think about it. All over the world, all those leaders. The ones who die, they'll have to be replaced. What if the new ones, the new leaders, aren't . . . human?"

Lew pushed the pizza carton away from him. "Dammit, Laura, that's enough of this nonsense."

"Don't patronize me!"

About to argue, he hesitated. During those final, wrenching fights as his marriage to Sharon disintegrated, she'd accused him of a lot of things that weren't true, like selling out, and a few things that were, like arrogance. He wasn't about to repeat that mistake now. "All right." He took a deep breath. "You want to know who your father might have gone to see in Washington."

"Right," Laura said.

"I suppose you've already thought of Cruise Long."

"Or someone connected with him?"

"Hell, it could be anybody," Lew said. "Some fire-and-brimstone reactionary, maybe. No, they didn't have much political clout until the Reagan era."

Laura was no longer listening. She stared out the window as if gazing into a crystal ball. "Lew, if the governor offers you the job, would you take it?"

"I'd be a damn fool not to," he said.

Draper had never liked driving at night. The glare of headlights had an odd, diffusing effect on his vision. He especially didn't like the stretch of Coast Highway that ran between his house and Newport Beach. It was high-speed and spottily illuminated. Beachgoers seemed to appear from nowhere, and oncoming cars had a way of swerving into his lane.

Damn that Lopez. Draper would never have allowed his wife to go out of town when their daughter was young. Taking care of the kid was her job.

He gripped the steering wheel of the Porsche and stared straight ahead as he drove. The moon and stars were bright tonight, leering in over the ocean.

Now, he was really getting spooked. Jeez, he didn't like this business with Tarkenton. Something about the whole thing didn't sit right. Why would the judge think Draper had that much influence? Didn't the judge have other contacts, legitimate ones, who could speak up for him with the governor? And why the disappearing act?

Come to think of it, Draper couldn't recall seeing a car out front when the judge arrived. But then, he hadn't looked.

Maybe the guy'd come in a cab. Maybe he was walking around Huntington Harbour right now, looking for a phone. But why?

None of it made sense. It was almost as if the guy wanted to piss Draper off. He must be assuming Draper wouldn't have the nerve to turn him in, or that nobody'd believe him. You'd think a guy bright enough to be a judge might figure he was being taped.

Holy shit! Draper jerked the steering wheel to the left. Where had that girl come from, anyway?

In the moment that he realized he'd missed her, he couldn't help noticing what a looker she was. A real tidy little brunette with huge bazooms hanging out of her bikini top. He'd sure like to get his hands into that.

Now that the danger was past and the girl shrinking in his sideview mirror, he felt steadier. And, would you believe it, horny?

Maybe after the tapes were turned over to Lopez, he'd find himself some action for the night. A guy had to be careful these days, but Draper had plenty of condoms.

He might come back and see if that brunette was hanging around one of the fast-food joints. Ask if she needed a ride somewhere. Yeah, he could use a little release. Work off his frustrations.

"You make it sound like becoming a senator would be setting myself up as a target," Lew said. "Laura, that's preposterous."

"You think I'm crazy, don't you?" She crammed paper napkins and cups into the pizza box and carried it across the kitchen, where she stuffed it angrily into the trash. "Like my father. And my grandmother."

"I would if I didn't know you," he said.

"In other words, don't go shooting my mouth off to anyone else, is that it?" she snapped. "Lew, I need someone to back me up, in case I ever do have to go public with this. Someone responsible that people will trust, even if they don't trust me."

"Go public?" He couldn't believe she meant it.

If he stood before the press and said he believed the Day of Judgment was at hand and demons were about to pour into the earth through a window in a painting—a painting nobody could find, by the way—it would mean the end of his political career. Maybe the end of his judicial career as well.

"You have to understand." Laura stood by the garbage can, balancing on one foot like a little girl. "I can't back away from this, Lew. I don't have a choice. It's all . . . revolving around me. It might even be because of me that these things are happening in San Paradiso. If I'd moved somewhere else, Barbara Long and that librarian and that waitress might still be alive."

There was a technical term for what she was experiencing, he thought. *Megalomania.* The sense of being omnipotent. Except that this was Laura, one of the sanest people he knew.

Lew kept flashing back to Sharon. They'd split up when he decided to attend law school rather than join a commune with her. She'd accused him, shrilly and repeatedly, of selling out.

She'd refused to believe he wanted to work within the system, that he still intended to fight for peace and justice and all the other ideals of the sixties. What had finally cut the deepest and made him realize he couldn't live with Sharon anymore was her complete lack of trust in his integrity.

He couldn't do the same thing to Laura. And he couldn't keep denying the evidence of his own eyes, either. Just as someone appeared to be setting up Rita Long and Joe Pickard, someone had been monkeying around with Lew's reputation. And God only knew what else—borrowing his car, using his telephone.

Maybe she was right about the appointment, after all. Maybe he'd be a damn fool to take it.

"Some strange things have happened to me, too," Lew said.

After checking around for cops, Draper let the car pick up speed. He wanted to get to Newport and take care of business so he could move on to the fun. Just thinking about that beach bunny made his pants feel tight.

Then something caught his eye, a dark, buxom figure standing on the right edge of the highway. Damn if she wasn't built just like that brunette back there.

He slowed down to get a closer look. Hell, she could be that chick's twin. Big dark eyes and even bigger tits. He thought he could see the nipples poking out through the wet bikini top. Getting him hard.

Only . . . something weird was happening to her face. It sagged, wrinkled, folded in on itself. God, what was wrong with her? She wasn't a girl at all but a pathetic old hag, her skin drooping obscenely out of the narrow folds of cloth. She walked toward the car, crooking her finger as if to signal him over.

Jesus, he must have drunk one bourbon too many. Draper stepped on the gas and swerved away from the approaching figure.

The pavement was slicker than he'd figured, and the sudden acceleration sent the car into a skid, fishtailing around so it smacked right into the old crone. She splatted onto the windshield as if she were nothing but a bag of blood. Holy shit, the windshield hadn't busted, but there was blood all over him, hot and sticky and pungent. He couldn't see, and the car was still spinning, and as if from far off he heard the wail of a truck horn, screaming to a sudden explosion that shattered the world into a thousand pieces.

CHAPTER TWENTY-SEVEN

A kind of numbed normality descended on the newsroom by Thursday morning. It seemed almost natural now for Laura to sit calmly at her terminal writing up the latest nonleads into Cruise Long's death while on TV the world unraveled.

"In Moscow, Kremlin watchers were surprised by the choice of a previously little-known party functionary, Ivan Ivanov, to replace slain leader Aleksei Karponov," the newscaster said.

"One of Ivanov's first priorities is expected to be sifting through the conflicting stories regarding his predecessor's death," the narrator went on. "Ivanov is believed to take a hard-line stance regarding the United States."

Laura turned her attention to her story. "Police today questioned editors and others who had contact with the senator during the hour before his death," she wrote.

"Meanwhile, on Wednesday afternoon, the body of Long's daughter, Barbara, was flown to San Francisco for burial. Newport Beach police said there is no evidence to indicate her fall was anything other than accidental."

She pressed "save," to make sure the computer didn't eat her story, and waited for the file to close.

A previously little-known party functionary. Who was Ivan Ivanov, really? Or René Dubois of France?

And if Cruise and Barbara's murderer became president of the United States . . . Was that really possible?

At least Lew believed in her. He was even willing to suspend his natural disbelief, to admit the possibility that there wasn't a rational explanation for the strange things that had happened to him.

Except . . .

There was one thing she hadn't discussed with him, because it frightened her so much. The fact that she couldn't remember entering the door in the painting, only coming back out. And that during the final year of his life, her father had drawn away from her, had barely touched her, as if afraid.

He must have seen the same alien spirit that had gazed out through Laura's eyes last night and turned the world red. Whatever it looked like. Whatever it was . . .

The painting had released it once, then left it to fester within her all these years. What would happen if she entered the door again?

Finally, after finishing the article about the Longs, Laura returned to the matter of who was going to replace Cruise Long. Not a story anymore, but an obsession.

After only a moment's hesitation, she dialed Rita's number.

The housekeeper put the call through. Rita sounded sleepy when she picked up the phone.

"I'm sorry to disturb you," Laura said. "My short list of who the governor might appoint has dwindled to zilch. I thought maybe you'd heard something."

"You don't give up easily." There was a rustle, as if Rita were sitting up in bed. "Actually, I did make a recommendation to the governor, but I'm not at liberty to disclose who. Someone close to Cruise, who's familiar with his agenda. Someone I trust to do a good job. But that doesn't mean he'll get it."

No, it didn't. Fisher would try to get any advantage he could out of the appointment, whether it was paying off an old debt or trying to sidetrack some potential rival. Which probably left Rita's choice out in the cold. "Thanks. Are you doing okay?"

"My doctor gave me a tranquilizer last night," Rita admitted. "This is off the record, of course. I was upset because some police sergeant came by to talk to me about Cruise, whether he ever used drugs, which of course he didn't, and whether I might have seen anything suspicious. I kept feeling as if he suspected *me.*"

Laura felt a surge of protectiveness. "For what motive?"

"Well, money, I suppose," Rita said. "But there weren't any problems between Cruise and me. I guess detectives have to suspect everyone."

"You still have my home number, right?" Laura waited while Rita searched in a drawer and confirmed it. "If you need any help or if—if anything strange happens, let me know."

Rita would understand what she was talking about. Those threats she'd received hadn't been ordinary threats. "Yes, I will, Laura."

Yes, I will, Laura. After she hung up, Rita wondered again whether she should tell the reporter about the photograph and that bizarre episode when she might have been drugged. But why bring it up now? No one was threatening her anymore.

They got what they wanted. Damn them.

What she wanted most was to burrow back under the covers, but Rita had spent enough time hiding out. She needed to get on with whatever was left of her life.

She couldn't face going down to the health club. She didn't want to talk to anyone, and she hated the thought of those pseudo-cheery instructors urging her to bounce a little higher and pump a little harder.

Before his heart attack, she and Cruise used to run together. With luck, it wasn't too hot yet this morning.

Rita pulled on a designer jogging suit and tied back her hair. On her way out, she saw Ramona's nod of approval. Since Barbara's death, the housekeeper had seemed friendlier, for some reason.

Outside, the heat shimmered off the roadway, but there was still a hint of a breeze. Besides, Rita didn't plan to run very fast.

She started off down the sidewalk at a fast trot. The sprinkler in the next yard swished over her as it made its rounds; the momentary coolness filled her with exhilaration.

She was glad to be alive. Even without Cruise.

At the bottom of the hill, Rita was just rounding the corner when a car, about to turn toward her house from the opposite direction, instead pulled to the curb alongside her.

It wasn't the kind of car you saw around this neighborhood much—an old, beat-up Volkswagen convertible. Inside it sat three young men.

When she recognized them, Rita stumbled. She reached out for some kind of support, but there wasn't any.

The UCI students. The ones from the photograph.

"Hey, hey, Rita!" The Hispanic youth in the front passenger seat leaned out with a broad grin. "Whatcha doing out here?"

"Jogging." Why wasn't there anyone around when she needed someone? Why had she ever been stupid enough to go running by herself?

"Well, get in." The blond man in the backseat flung open the door.

"I—I'm afraid I can't." What were they doing here? She didn't want to make them angry, not three against one. Especially not when they obviously expected something.

The driver, dark-skinned, Middle Eastern perhaps, took off his sunglasses. "Then why did you call us?"

"Why did I *what?*"

The three men looked at her and then at each other. "Is this a game?" said the Hispanic.

"No—I—" Rita took a deep breath. "I'm sorry. What are your names?"

"I'm Rick." The front passenger gestured to the driver. "That's Gaddi. And Rafe's in the back. Are you getting in, or what?"

"I didn't call you," Rita said, "but I'm sure someone did."

Gaddi tapped his sunglasses against the steering wheel. "You got us all ready for more of same, Rita, babe."

From the back, Rafe slid out the door and sauntered toward her. Rita stiffened, but there was nowhere to run. "Now, come on, honey." He took her arm. "Let's go have some more fun, okay? Like, we've been whacking off over those photos you gave us. Let's take some more, okay?"

Rita pulled her arm away, trying not to show her repugnance. "I know this sounds crazy but"—hadn't it been a hallucination after all, that twin in the kitchen?— "someone's trying to blackmail me. I think there must be another woman who looks like me. I got one of those photographs in the mail. But believe me, I wasn't—I wouldn't—I mean, I didn't do those things with you."

Rafe glanced over at Gaddi and Rick. "Are you bullshitting us?"

"We're not your goddamn little toys." Gaddi's face had gone hard.

"You must think I'm schizophrenic or something." A sudden prickling behind her eyes warned of tears, but Rita fought them back. "My husband just died—do you think I'd . . . for Christ's sake." A hot stream ran down her cheek. She brushed at it angrily.

The boys exchanged glances. She could read their thoughts: The woman's bonkers.

Rafe backed away.

"Wait," Rita said. "Please. This person who's trying to blackmail me. He's, or she's, very, very dangerous. Maybe a murderer. Please . . . where were the pictures taken? Who took them?"

"Forget it." Gaddi put the car in gear.

"Hold on." Rick leaned out. "You sure as hell look like the same girl, but you don't act like her. Anyway, we took the pictures at that house up the street—that's yours, isn't it?"

Rita nodded dully.

"In the basement," Rick said. "Kind of musty. Down one hell of a long staircase. She sneaked us in from the back."

"We don't have a basement." Rita could hear the quaver in her voice.

"We took the pictures on your camera," Rick went on as Rafe slammed himself into the backseat. "You asked us to."

Gaddi took the brake off. "Listen, babe. Do us a favor. You get horny again, don't call."

"If you see her, that woman, could you try to get a license plate or something?" Rita said. "It's very important."

"A murderer, right?" Rafe plopped his feet up over the back of the seat. "I'll tell you what. We'll tattoo her ass for you."

"Give me a break." Gaddi hit the gas with a squeal of tires. "The rich bitch is fucking us over."

Rita barely made it up the hill again, and when she got to her room, she snatched off the jogging suit and hurried into the shower. She spent a long time scrubbing herself all over, and shampooed her hair twice.

"So what's going on with the oil fields?" Jane Lomax, the courts reporter, plopped a pile of transcripts on the desk beyond Steve's.

"The oil fields?" Steve said. "Nothing as far as I know."

"Well, I just drove up Beach Boulevard, and there's this funny black cloud hanging over it," Jane said. "And over Paradise Park, and kind of shifting in this direction."

"Hey, Bill," Steve called. "There's some kind of black cloud over the oil fields. Want me to call the oil company?"

"Damn right," the metro editor said. "Laura, you up? Try the Air Quality Management District. And maybe the U.S. Geological Survey. Send your notes to Steve."

The two of them got on the phone. San Paradiso, like much of southern California, covered rich pools of oil. From Beach Boulevard, motorists could watch the pumps churning constantly up and down. But there'd never been a serious problem with fumes in Laura's experience.

From time to time, in between her own inquiries, she called up Steve's file to check on his progress. They were both finding out the same thing.

A fissure had cracked open in the fields an hour ago, releasing an undetermined amount of an unknown gas. It was rapidly dissipating in an ocean breeze, and wasn't expected to pose any serious health hazard.

As suddenly as it had appeared, the fissure had closed.

"Good riddance," Steve said as he sent his story to the copy desk. "Let's just hope this isn't some new earthquake indicator they don't know about yet."

He was getting edgy, but not any edgier than Laura. She didn't want to sit here and worry about unexplained geological phenomena in San Paradiso. Besides, she was starving. "How about lunch?"

"You think I'm going out there and get poisoned?"

Laura pointed to the window. "Looks clear."

"It's probably silent and deadly, like farts," Steve said. "Oh, hell, why not? A person's gotta eat."

The minute she stepped outside, Laura knew the gas hadn't gone.

She couldn't exactly smell it, but she could feel it. A kind of density to the air, like something packed tight, ready to burst.

"Burger King or McDonald's?" Steve said. "Or how about pizza?"

"You pick," Laura managed to say.

As they drove to the restaurant, she couldn't shake the feeling that something was building inside the earth. Something was going to happen.

She wished she could believe it wasn't going to happen to her.

CHAPTER TWENTY-EIGHT

Joe sat in front of the TV drinking his second beer of the day, or maybe it was his third. He couldn't concentrate on the soap opera, so he didn't mind when it was interrupted by yet another news bulletin.

"This just in," the anchorman said. "A television station in Rome has received a videotape appearing to show the execution of British prime minister Lucinda Basker by a firing squad. There was no indication where the murder took place. Vice President Whiting immediately extended condolences to her family.

"In London, Colin Edwards, the deputy head of the Labor party, assumes the post of prime minister. Edwards is a little-known quantity, having risen quickly through the ranks of the party."

The world was going to hell in a handbasket. It almost made what was happening to Joe seem not so bad after all.

He got up to make himself a salami sandwich. He was running low on mayonnaise, but he didn't want to go out, not even with his police escort. Not until they caught that bastard who attacked Rhondie.

This waiting game was wearing him out. He just had to hang on, survive the boredom, and get through the next few days. Somewhere, somehow, the killer would tip his hand and get caught. And then Joe would be free.

He ate standing up in the kitchen, looking out the window. The yard sure looked like a wreck. As long as he was stuck here, he could at least get some gardening done. It was hot as Hades out there, but the flowerbed along the side of the house lay mostly in the shade. He'd heard something on the radio earlier about a gas leak, but apparently it hadn't amounted to anything, not enough to keep people indoors.

Joe changed into a pair of stained overalls and went out. The air was intensely dry; he could feel it sucking at him. The ground looked too hard to dig, with cracks radiating around the brittle bodies of dead azalea plants, so Joe turned on the hose to give it a good soaking. Emma always said it ought to be wet right down six feet deep, so you could dig a grave if you wanted to. That was her idea of a joke.

He went back to the shed to get some seeds. He hadn't planted anything for a few years, but he remembered stashing away some packets of marigolds. They might still be good; marigolds were tough.

The potting shed had been Emma's idea, during her brief gardening jag. Long and narrow, it was lined with mostly empty shelves, the storage room in back filled with spiderwebbed clay pots and rusting tools. A half-light filtered through the dusty sloping glass over the shelves.

Probably mice lived in here, maybe even a possum, one he'd seen around the neighborhood from time to time. Joe stopped in the glassed-in section and listened. Yeah, there *was* something back there, something that kind of snuffled. Like a mangy old dog. Or like somebody laughing, and trying to stifle it.

Dense with dust and heat, the air closed in around him like a net. He had to get out. But it might be dangerous to turn his back on whatever was hiding in there.

The thing in the storage room grunted softly. Joe didn't know whether possums made a noise like that.

Maybe he ought to go out and get the cop. Oh, yeah. That would give them a good yuck down at the station. Hizzoner the mayor, spooked by a . . . what?

The dust motes down by the storage room spiraled upward. No, that couldn't be right. Dirt didn't fall up. Joe reached out, and his hand closed over a spade. He felt as if someone were setting him up.

Not this time, you bastard.

He knew who was in the storage room now. The imposter. The guy must have moved out quick when Joe came home from jail, into the shed where he could keep an eye on things. The son of a bitch who'd turned his life into hell. The motherfucker who'd butchered Kiki.

He looked around for another weapon and found a length of rusty wire. Not much, but you could strangle a man with it. It might make more sense to go yell for the cop, but the creep could get away. Besides, they had that woman watching him today, and everybody knew broads were no good in a pinch. He was going to take this one out himself.

The swirls of dust were getting thicker, spinning around in the weak sunlight, forming a kind of column. Funny thing, it was the size of a man. A large man, about Joe's build.

Now wait a minute.

He wished he hadn't had so many beers this morning. Or that he'd had his eyes checked. Or that he'd stayed in jail.

He was watching himself take shape out of particles of dirt.

You could see the general outline first, the thick stomach and broad face. The middle seemed to solidify, leaving the top and bottom vague.

It was as if somebody were sketching him out of charcoal, roughing in the head and legs and then going back to fill in details. The cuffs of the overalls, the way his socks collapsed over the rim of the loafers. Then up to the sloppy jawline, the blank eyes.

Those weren't his eyes. They didn't belong to anything human. Light didn't glint off them.

"Hi, Joe." The flat voice didn't echo. Otherwise, the tone sounded a lot like his.

"Who . . . ?" Joe's throat constricted.

"Sorry about all the trouble I've caused." The jowly face softened into a semblance of a smile. "You know, I haven't meant any harm." So smooth, so hypnotic. You felt sleepy, unresisting.

"Get the hell out . . ." Again, the words stuck.

"I've come to arrange a little transfer." The dust-thing nodded toward the spade and wire in Joe's hands. "Now, those aren't going to do any good, you know."

But he remembered that Rhondie had chased the guy away with a scissors. When it was solid, it was vulnerable. At least, he hoped so. Only it didn't make sense to lunge at the thing. That would give it the advantage, and put Joe off-balance. He waited.

"You just want to cooperate with me," the thing went on in its monotone. "This won't hurt much."

"Fuck off." The sound of his own defiance heartened him. Joe gripped the spade tighter.

"That's the trouble with you." The thing that looked like him still wore that easy smile. "You're too crude, Joe. You don't know how to take advantage of things. Mayor of the city, a lawyer, why, the opportunities are limitless. Do you know what I could do in your place?"

"Murder a few more girls?"

"We could work this out together." The thing edged toward him slyly, like a cat. "Make a kind of team. We're going right to the top, Joe. It may be too late for that Senate seat, at least for you and me, but there'll be other chances. I'm not going back where I came from. I like it here."

A hand shot out, heel first, catching Joe under the ribs. Air gasped out of him, but the layer of fat softened the blow. He lashed around with the wire, and the thing snatched back its arm with a red welt running up it.

"Tough guy, aren't we?" it snarled. Now that he was getting used to it, Joe could see how the dust-thing looked a lot like his brother. His big brother, Sam, who used to push him around and tell him he had the smallest weenie in the West. Only it couldn't be Sam, because Sam had died in Korea.

"Get out." Before he lost his nerve, Joe swung the spade as hard as he could toward the thing's neck. It dodged back into the semidarkness of the storage area.

"Coming?" it asked.

Joe's shirt was soaked with sweat. All those fantasies he'd had about attacking people, he hadn't realized how hard it would be in real life.

"If I kill you," he asked, "will you stay dead?"

The thing laughed, a hollow rattling sound. "But I'm not alive, Joe. You see how useless it is? You must be tired. You want to lie down and close your eyes. I'll help you, Joe."

The thing went on murmuring to him. *Kiki. Think about Kiki. Think about this slime-bucket chopping up her sweet, pouty face, slamming her around the apartment and slashing the lifeblood out of her. Oh, sweet Jesus.*

The imposter was still whispering when he shoved the spade into the roll of fat around its belly. With a grunt, the thing doubled over, and then suddenly, with a snaky movement of the neck that would have crippled any real person, sank its fangs into his shoulder. Joe brought up his hand, trying to twist the wire around its neck, until the creature grabbed his balls full force.

Joe's shriek choked off as teeth closed over his throat. Shit, men didn't fight like this. He could feel skin and muscle ripping away, and he couldn't breathe. Air. God, he wanted air more than he'd ever wanted anything in his life. He hadn't known there was so much pain in the world, worse than pain. Had to get free, had to get away. Into the dark, yes, the silence, the stillness. That was the only way left out of the pain.

And, mercifully, he found it.

Briana radioed in at two o'clock. With that double running around, the captain wanted an hourly update on Joe's whereabouts, and she didn't need any more trouble.

"Subject disappeared into the potting shed for a while and I was starting to worry, but he came out a few minutes ago," she said.

"What's he doing now?"

"Digging in the flowerbed," she said. "Making a trench is what it looks like. Must be planning on putting in some bushes."

"You can see him right now?"

"Yes, sir. Clear as a bell. Any sign of that other guy?"

"Not yet."

After she signed off, Briana went back to working her crossword puzzle and wishing they had a john in the car so she dared have another cup of coffee.

From time to time, she looked over to make sure Joe hadn't left. It was kind of amazing in this heat, especially with how heavy he was, that he could make the dirt fly like that. It didn't seem worth all that effort.

But hey, the yard could sure use the improvement.

CHAPTER TWENTY-NINE

Someone was looking at her.

Madeleine came awake suddenly, then couldn't be sure she was really awake at all. The room flickered with strange shadows cast by a streetlight outside the apartment.

The clock showed just after 3:00 A.M. She sat up, drawing on her thin robe and reaching instinctively for the dagger beneath her pillow. The only sounds in the apartment were her own breathing, the faint tick of the clock, and a muted mechanical whirr from the refrigerator in the kitchen.

In the early morning half-reality, her seventy years felt like an eon during which she had evolved from a fierce, hot mammal into a small, frail bird. The rattle of her breath resembled the flutter of feathers, the panic of a sparrow that has caught wind of a cat.

Gradually, Madeleine became aware of other noises in the night, from across the street, down the block. Someone shouting; a door slamming; a phone ringing.

What had happened?

She swung her thin legs over the side of the bed and slipped on her tufted slippers. Carrying the dagger, Madeleine went into the living room.

The noises outside thickened as if morning had arrived, but it was still dark. A car started. A TV set blared. A man yelled at everybody to shut up.

A woman shouted back, "They've killed the president!"

Madeleine turned on the TV. It was tuned to an independent channel, showing an old movie. She rotated the dial to one of the networks.

"A statement from Ayatollah Al-Hadassi, received two hours after the videotape, claims that the assassination of President Harkness was not the work of his followers." The newscaster was someone she had never seen before, probably the first person NBC had been able to roust out of bed. "Al-Hadassi blamed the president's murder on a KGB operation. Kremlin officials have denied the charge.

"For those of you just joining us, a videotape delivered to a Tel Aviv TV station today shows what appears to be a gunman shooting down President Harkness as the president was led through a hallway by robed guards."

Madeleine turned off the set.

She had been expecting this. For her personally, the worst blow had been the death of President Giroux, but it was the murders of the two superpower leaders that would have the harshest consequences for the world. Someone else knew it, too. Someone who wanted a war.

Madeleine went back and sat on the edge of her bed, knowing that she no longer wanted to do what must be done. But it might already be too late. She must not allow herself to delay beyond another twenty-four hours.

She got back into bed, leaving the lights on. She listened for noises from upstairs, but heard none.

Madeleine fell asleep gripping the dagger.

Daryl heard about the president's death on his way to work. He was still digesting the news when the announcer said, "Vice President Whiting was sworn in as president at six o'clock this morning. And now this from Toyota of Orange."

Daryl pressed "scan," hoping to get more information, but during drive-time the L.A. airwaves were full of commercials. Wouldn't you know it?

When he got to his desk, he found the one next to it occupied by the ramrod-stiff figure of Sergeant Will Machado from Traffic, who used to be in Detectives. The guy always reminded Daryl of his drill sergeant in the marines.

"They asked me to fill in until Guinness gets back on Monday," he said. Daryl noticed that a stack of folders from his desk had found their way onto Machado's. He chose to assume that Lieutenant Grover had put them there.

The briefing was short this morning. Mostly, everyone seemed to be in shock. They were told to watch out for bizarre reactions; already, two people had been arrested for trying to kill their spouses, and reports abounded of guns being fired into the air.

After they got back to their desks, Machado began plowing through the backup of cases, mostly robberies that Daryl hadn't had time to get around to. It should have been a relief, but Machado kept looking up and asking questions about the Cruise Long investigation and the Joe Pickard case. As if he didn't believe Daryl was bright enough to think of all the angles.

The way Daryl kept his temper was by looking forward to tonight, all the things he and Nina were going to do. Oils. He could get into that kinky stuff.

It was the middle of the afternoon when Rhondie Harper called and asked for Sergeant Wilkinson.

"I thought I told you to hide out," he said.

"I am." She sounded nervous. "I mean, I'm at my sister's in Westminster. I didn't think Joe knew her name or address, but he came over here a little while ago. He just left."

Daryl straightened up. "How did he act, Mrs. Harper?"

"Well, that's the funny thing." She had a tentative little voice with a trace of a whine. "It's not as if he did anything wrong. In fact, he was real . . . jovial, I guess you'd say. He seemed to think it would be all right to go back to the office; he wants to get cracking on some briefs. He said he's going to install a new alarm system, so I'd be safe."

"I don't think that's such a good idea." Why would Pickard set his secretary up where she might get killed? "Are you sure it was Joe?"

"That's why I'm calling," the woman said. "I mean, that policewoman's car was outside, so I knew it had to be him. And he wasn't threatening or anything. But—Sergeant, I tried to get a look at his hands, where I stabbed him with the scissors, and the funny thing is, he was wearing gloves. Isn't that weird? I mean, nobody wears gloves. I wondered if—if it was possible the double managed to sneak into Joe's house and kill him or something, and then take his place."

Hell, maybe they ought to go out there and fingerprint the guy, just for good measure. Of course, his lawyer would insist on being there. Besides, what had the guy done? He'd probably claim harassment and try to get his case dismissed on a technicality, the way things were going these days. "I'll look into it, Mrs. Harper," Daryl said. "In the meantime, why don't you find somewhere else to hide? Just be sure to let me know."

"Thank you, Sergeant."

As soon as he hung up, Machado came over to find out what was going on. Daryl told him.

"Sounds like a nut case to me," he said. "Have you done any background on her?"

Daryl had to admit he hadn't. He made a note to get on it, which seemed to satisfy Machado.

But he didn't really think Rhondie Harper was crazy. In fact, he was wondering if he shouldn't get a search warrant and go over to Joe's house.

Only that meant he'd have to cancel out on Nina tonight. Besides, he wasn't sure he could convince a judge to issue the warrant. It was just this funny feeling Rhondie Harper had, and Daryl had, too.

He already planned to work most of the weekend on Long's death. And after all, the Pickard case was up to the D.A. now, really. As long as nobody else got attacked.

Daryl decided it could wait until Monday.

CHAPTER THIRTY

Laura could hardly get any work done on Friday.

The announcer on the TV prattled on about how the speaker of the House was the most likely nominee for vice president, but political analysts believed Whiting feared being overshadowed come the next election. She wanted to climb up there and grab Whiting's lapels when he pontificated on the need for someone with no vested political agenda, someone who could bring a fresh outlook to Washington.

Didn't he know he was being set up to get murdered?

At Bill White's suggestion, she phoned local civic leaders for their reactions to Harkness's death and their recommendations as to how Whiting should proceed. It would make an interesting story, Laura supposed. But the only way she could keep her concentration was by probing each person she interviewed, searching for a clue to who might be the next senator from California.

No one had any idea.

From time to time, the TV news continued to intrude on her awareness. There were shots of wild revelry in Rio de Janeiro, Hong Kong, and Copenhagen, as people reacted to the sudden breakdown of world leadership. In other places, in Moscow and New Delhi and Canberra and Washington, masses of people gathered outside the seats of power, simply standing and waiting as if for a revelation.

At some level, they must sense what Laura had already concluded: that the assassinations were as much a natural cataclysm as the earthquakes in France and the famines in China.

And that there would be worse to come.

The pope called for a worldwide prayer vigil tonight. Around the globe, Christians of various denominations, as well as Moslems, Jews, Hindus, and Buddhists, planned to take part. According to one commentator, calls by extremists for a last-ditch holy war to convert the infidels to Islam before the final judgment were rejected by most

Moslem leaders, who were no more eager than anyone else to see the world come to an end.

At the *Paradise Herald*, the usual clicking of keys punctuated the overhead broadcast. Laura could hear snatches of monologue from other reporters on the phone. Jane was tying up the remnants of a court case, Steve pushing to find some new angle on the murders.

A message popped up on Laura's screen. *Come see me. Greg.*

She gathered her notes and went into his office.

For once, even the editor was staring at his TV in dismay. "I didn't believe they'd really do it," he said. "They took the president prisoner and shot him down like a dog."

"Who's behind this?" she asked. "Your best guess?"

He stared blankly through the window into the newsroom. "Somebody who wants us to blame the Russians and vice versa." The pencil in Greg's hand snapped, and then he shrugged. "Well, that wasn't what I called you in to discuss. We've still got a paper to put out, and we've got local news to cover. Anything on Cruise Long's replacement?"

They discussed the strongest possibilities—a Republican assemblyman who was a former aide to Senator Long, and a congressman from Newport Beach who had sponsored a couple of Long's Senate bills in the House.

"And there's Long's aide, what's his name?" Greg said. "Bob Fillipino?"

"Fillipone."

"Right. Dig up his background; what he's done, who he knows."

Somewhere a siren went off, not the usual shrill police warning but a deep-throated boom like a foghorn. "What's that?"

"Civil emergency." Greg pushed past her into the newsroom. "Bill?"

The metro editor said something into his phone and swiveled around. "That fissure in the oil fields just ripped open and spewed out a whole ton more gas. They still don't know what it is or whether it's toxic, but they're asking everyone to stay indoors."

Greg strode across and sat on the edge of Bill's desk. With a few quick orders, he pulled the reporters off their stories and set them on this one. Call the Air Quality Management District, the state emergency services agency, the police and fire departments. Check hospital emergency rooms to see if their admissions are up, call Caltech in case there's any unusual seismic activity, find out what the weather bureau says.

Through the newsroom window, Laura could see a dark haze rolling in, turning the sunny Friday afternoon into premature night.

"What the hell is that stuff?" Steve Orkney muttered.

The air of another world. She didn't know where the thought had come from, or why she felt so certain, but she didn't doubt it. Inside her, something churned as if gathering strength.

Greg jumped to his feet. "I'm going out to see what it smells like. Be right back." Laura waited with hands clenched, reminding herself that this was the man who had survived five years' covering Vietnam. He came back a minute later, looking none the worse for wear. "It feels hot and wet, and it smells like old socks."

"Did it sting when you breathed it?" Bill asked.

"No. Although I've probably just upped my chances of getting lung cancer by ten thousand percent."

"Whatever it is, it's hotter than Hades," Bill said. "Or else the damn air-conditioning's broke again."

Heat. Laura could almost see droplets of it bleeding through the thick walls. Not the dry California heat they'd baked under all these weeks, but something moist that made her clothes stick to her skin. Across the room, women tugged at their panty hose, and men loosened their ties.

Laura had to struggle to inhale, as if phlegm blocked her nasal passages.

The news reports weren't encouraging. Similar rifts had opened up across the globe, in Denmark and Australia, Swaziland and Japan. Danish and Australian authorities had ordered evacuations, but officials in southern California, accustomed to bad air, took a more cautious approach.

On a Los Angeles broadcast, the anchorwoman said, "The AQMD has just announced that there doesn't appear to be any immediate danger from the San Paradiso gas cloud. They're suggesting that companies send employees home a few at a time, to avoid traffic jams."

Only Steve, who was putting the story together, still typed feverishly. Greg looked up from where he and Bill huddled with the copy deskers. "Most of you live close by. Steve will stay on the story. The rest of you, go home."

A few scattered cheers, as well as some grumbling, greeted the announcement. What good was a long weekend if you couldn't go to the beach?

Laura put through a call to Lew's chambers. The bailiff who answered recognized her voice.

"They adjourned early," he said. "The judge just left for the day. Things are . . . kind of hairy around here. One of the marshals freaked out and attacked a defendant, yelling about evil incarnate—that's not for publication, you understand."

"Of course. Thanks." Laura hung up and called Lew's condo, where she told the answering machine she was going home for the day.

Then she forced herself to go out into a world as shadowy and distorted as Goya's darkest painting.

It was the second time in Madeleine's life that the future, that imaginary path that stretches ahead like the Yellow Brick Road, had ended suddenly in a blank wall.

Then, too, the night the Nazis rolled into Paris, there had been those who responded with frenetic debauchery, abandoning all moral restraint. At the apartments across from Madeleine's in Montmartre, drunken shrieks and laughter had pierced the air, disturbing her sleep. In the morning, a girl was found lying broken on the street; it was never discovered whether she had fallen or been thrown.

Now, in this unnatural dark afternoon, she caught glimpses from time to time through her window of figures cavorting, creating a garish travesty of a carnival with their painted faces and wild hair. Stereos fought for dominance, while in a convertible across the street a man and woman copulated, oblivious to onlookers.

It was so hot, one had to leave the window open, even though the air stank of sulfur. Madeleine finished her second shower of the day and knelt, still nude, to wash out the tub.

She had not yet brought herself to the mental state she needed. Today, she had gone to mass and to confession, had prepared her soul for its final journey. It was not death she feared, but that moment when she must kill.

Pieces crumbled off the sponge as she labored over the yellowing old tub. Madeleine paused in her scrubbing.

Outside, one of the competing stereos stopped abruptly. There came the sound of glass breaking, shouts, and then the cacophony resumed.

In the brief lull, Madeleine heard something stir behind her.

She straightened painfully and turned, holding the sponge in front of her as if it were a weapon. A column of dust was rising in the doorway, whirling slowly toward her, solidifying, taking on her face and her sagging shape. An old woman, her bare body bruised by time. It was painful to Madeleine, to see this aging creature unveiled in three dimensions, and to know it must be her twin.

How stupid. The blessed dagger, which she always kept within reach, lay beside the tub on the floor. She tried to crouch, but her knees were stiff, and the monster could walk faster than Madeleine could bend.

"It's all right," the thing said. "I won't hurt you." Madeleine crossed herself.

The devil-woman smiled and kicked the dagger away, toward the counter. In the same moment, Madeleine snatched up her bottle of cleanser and squirted it into the thing's eyes.

It swung for her blindly, the clawlike fingers raking across her shoulder. Madeleine twisted its arm with all her strength, and the thing fell to its knees. She wished she had the strength and agility to kick it, but she could barely step free of the tub before the beast leaped on her again.

They grappled in silence before the tarnished mirror and the cracked fake-marble counter. The thing was fiercely strong, but limited by its human form. Madeleine caught her hairbrush and shoved it into the devil's mouth. She, too, had unsuspected strength; she hoped it meant that God was with her.

But the beast began doing something with its toes, using them like a talon, bringing up the dagger. There was only one moment of weakness, when the thing bent to transfer the knife from foot to hand, and in that instant Madeleine shoved it toward the wall.

Off-balance, the monster thrust out. The knife slashed Madeleine's hand, but she had the creature's wrist now. Tightly, inch by agonizing inch, she pressed the dagger back. The eyes went red; she had a glimpse, barely a glimpse, of yellow fangs crunching for her throat, and then the knife cut through old flesh and scales, bone and sinew, and with a great gasp the beast dropped onto the floor, jerking and snapping and splitting open to spill its guts across the peeling linoleum, and then the thing was gone, just gone.

Madeleine leaned against the counter and choked in the air. Her knees weakened, and she sat down heavily, still hugging the dagger.

There might be others, but before they came, she would have acted.

As if on cue, from outside she heard the tap of footsteps going up to the apartment above hers.

Laura was home.

CHAPTER THIRTY-ONE

The howls of revelers pierced the yellow-cast gloom on Laura's drive home. Here and there she caught weird flickers of light, candles and leftover Fourth of July sparklers and red signal flares.

The phone was ringing with a shrill edge as she hurried into her apartment. Laura slammed the door, slid the bolt, and grabbed the phone on the fourth ring.

It was Rita. "I'm sorry to disturb you, but I'm scared."

"Where are you?" Laura's heart thudded from running up the stairs.

"At home. My housekeeper has Friday nights off, and I keep thinking I hear noises. In case anything happens to me, there are things I want you to know."

The urge to reassure Rita died in Laura's throat. "What things?"

"The threats. I was sent a photograph of a woman who looks exactly like me, doing . . . lewd things. If I accepted the appointment, it would have been released to the press." A long intake of breath told her Rita was smoking again.

"Exactly like you?" That man in the parking lot had looked exactly like Lew. And Joe Pickard's lawyer claimed he had a double . . .

"Down to a tattoo I never reveal in public." Her breathing came raggedly, a painful mix of harsh smoke and tension. "And one night I had this strange experience, as if I'd been drugged. When I woke up, there was another threat, a piece of paper stabbed into the kitchen table with a knife."

"You think this had something to do with Barbara?"

"I thought she might be behind it." Rita sounded a little less shaky now. "The day she died, she'd sneaked in here to steal some things; she resented my inheriting so much of Cruise's estate. I think someone pushed her down the stairs. I think it was the final threat."

"Why wouldn't they just push you down the stairs?" Laura asked. "Was there something else they wanted from you?"

"Not that I can think of. That's part of what scares me." Ice clinked in a glass, and it was a moment before Rita spoke again. "You believe me, then?"

"Of course."

Distant chimes. "Someone's at the door." Rita's words issued in a croak. "Hold on, will you, Laura? If I'm not right back, call the police."

Long moments ticked by and then Rita came on the line, much calmer. "It's Bob Fillipone. My mother hen. I'll be all right now."

"Call me anytime," Laura said.

After hanging up, she wandered over to the refrigerator. She felt she ought to fix something in case Lew came by, but she'd forgotten to go grocery shopping this week and found only half a loaf of bread, some olives, and an old bottle of pickles, along with an assortment of canned drinks.

Downstairs, the door opened, and the *tap-tap* of Madeleine's heels emerged. Then familiar masculine footsteps thumped up the steps and, below, the door closed again as Madeleine retreated.

Not quite Laura today, are we? The old woman knew about whatever had lain hidden inside Laura all these years. That must be why she'd come here and why she circled so cautiously, probing at Laura whenever they met.

She'd come here to do something about it. But what?

As Lew's footsteps reached the landing, Laura unbolted the door and pulled it open. Before she could say more than "Hi," he enfolded her, his cheek evening-rough against hers, his lips finding her mouth.

"It's good to see you." He stepped into the apartment. "Damn good."

It felt like eons since she'd seen him, although it had only been two nights. Could he have changed, in that time? His kiss hadn't quite felt like . . .

His mouth came down on hers again, and his hands grasped Laura's shoulders roughly. He'd never touched her this way before, like a wild animal seizing its prey. It excited her.

"The bedroom—"

He pulled her blouse open, yanking so hard the buttons flew off.

"Lew, somebody might see—"

"Fuck them." They fell across the couch, draped half on and half off. He pushed his way under her skirt, his pants halfway down his hips. Thrusting, hard. Laura gasped, clutching his muscular forearms.

His breathing came harshly, and she felt the potency of his coiled rage, his fierce, primal need to mate. They rolled off the couch, and the glass coffee table cracked beneath them. Fire seemed to blaze around and inside her, scarlet shapes hissing as they writhed and pumped, flaming into long, snaky extrusions and then simmering into a carmine glow.

For a while, Laura lay on the carpet with her eyes closed. When she did, Lew lay next to her, half-asleep.

Slowly, she began to hear the world again, laughter and shrieks in the street, music blaring, wheels screeching around corners. It occurred to her that this was the first time she and Lew hadn't used contraception. He was usually so careful.

She breathed uneasily. "Lew . . ."

"There's something I'd like you to see," he said. "I'm afraid we'll have to go out in that stuff, but it isn't far."

She wasn't sure she wanted to go with him, and yet she didn't want to be left alone, either. Laura sat up, then realized he'd torn her blouse. "I'll have to change."

"No problem," he said.

On her way to the bedroom, she saw the red light blinking on her answering machine. Someone must have called while they were making love.

Laura played back the message.

"It's Lew," said the voice she knew so well. "Listen, I'm sorry, I can't make it. It's Terri—she fell off a swing at the foster home, suffered a mild concussion. Her bastard of a father showed up at the hospital drunk, took a poke at the foster mother, and got arrested. Terri's hysterical, and she needs me. I've got to go, honey. I'm really sorry. Listen, I'll call you as soon as I know more. Stay inside. I don't want anything to happen to you."

Laura stood motionless through the whirr and click of rewinding.

Finally, she turned around.

"What's wrong?" The eyes regarding her were Lew's. Almost. Except that they didn't reflect the light.

"What are you?" Laura glanced around for some kind of weapon, any kind. She grabbed a metal letter opener.

"We are gathering. We need you."

"No!"

"Need you, Laura." He smiled, giving the words double meaning.

She lunged at him with the letter opener, sickened by the thing, by what she had let it do to her.

As he backed away, his features pinched into a viperish flatness.

A narrow, forked tongue licked out with a hiss of frustration, and then he bounded out onto the balcony and over the rail.

Dashing forward, she saw the hard, metallic glitter of dust in the smoky air, spiraling away into the night. The creature, whoever or whatever he might be, had gone.

She staggered back into the apartment, locking the balcony doors. The room contracted into a huddled, frightened thing.

She had mated with that imposter. Dear God, what had he left inside her?

Nina rolled over on the bed, soft blond hair fanning out as she smiled up at Daryl. "Wow," she said. "Again."

He'd never known sex could feel this demanding. They'd made it three times already. Who did she think he was, Superman?

"I had a long day." Daryl collapsed against the pillows, carefully peeling off the condom and ditching it in a plastic wastebasket. Jeez, he didn't think he'd ever get it up again.

Not that things hadn't been terrific. Nina had met him at the door stark naked except for a thin gold chain around one ankle. It drove him crazy. He'd ploughed right into her, scarcely pausing to shrug off his jacket. They'd done it on the carpet, where the beach sand ground into his knees, and then in the kitchen, and then here in bed, smeared with oil. The bedspread would never be the same.

He'd thought maybe he'd died and gone to heaven, only she didn't want to quit. Even now, her hand was sliding up his thigh.

"Whoa," Daryl said. "Let a guy catch his breath."

She laughed, a deep, throaty sound. "Hey, last Tuesday you couldn't get enough. We must have done it ten times."

Who had that guy been, anyway? She really thought it was Daryl. He couldn't have driven over here in some kind of daze and forgotten about it, could he?

Not bloody likely.

Maybe he was coming down with Alzheimer's or something. More likely, just distracted. No wonder, the way Will Machado had been riding him all day. Asking a lot of questions, poking around in the files. As though he thought Daryl was missing something about the murders.

Was he missing something?

"Hey." Nina pouted. "Don't ignore me."

Daryl sat up, trying not to notice the way his muscles stiffened. "I was going to take you out to dinner, but everybody's acting pretty strange out there."

"Not strange," Nina said. "People get like that when the nights are long."

He resisted the urge to point out that the nights didn't get long in southern California. Especially in August. "Wanna brave the smog and merrymakers for a steak?"

"I suppose." Nina pulled on her clothes without even showering. She'd told Daryl she was twenty-five, but he guessed nineteen was more like it. Maybe she'd get smarter when she got older, or at least a little more concerned about hygiene.

On the other hand, maybe that was the way they did things in Sweden.

The air was sweltering when they went out, and it smelled musty. Daryl's eyes stung a little as he drove along Balboa Boulevard. From the beach a block away came drunken singing interspersed with shrieks. He was glad he didn't work for the Newport PD. Things always got wilder on the beach than anywhere else.

Finally, he stopped at a seafood restaurant near Lido Isle. "I don't want to go too far," he said.

"This is okay." Nina got out and strode ahead of him into the restaurant. Long, muscular legs, nice straight back, floating hair. Everything he liked. Too bad she was such an airhead.

I'm getting old, Daryl told himself. Shit.

By the time they finished eating, they'd exhausted what few topics of conversation they had, mostly the threat of global war, which didn't seem to interest Nina, and the latest rock bands, which did. Daryl couldn't face going back to that cramped, sandy apartment and humping her again.

"Look," he said, "I've got some things I have to check out. On a murder case."

"Oh, poo." Nina curled her legs up on the seat of the booth.

"Yeah, I know." The words came easier now. "Life's a bitch. How about tomorrow night?"

Nina shrugged. "I'm going to Mexico with my girlfriend. We'll be back Monday."

"I'll call you," Daryl said.

After he left Nina at home, he drove off feeling like an idiot. What was wrong with him? He'd been fantasizing about her all week.

He was just preoccupied with work, that was all. It would sure be a pisser if Machado came up with something Daryl had overlooked. He had a feeling that even after Guinness got back, Will was going to keep poking into things. He was that kind of guy.

Besides, Daryl couldn't stop thinking about what Rhondie Harper had said today. What if somebody had killed Joe and taken his place? Was that possible?

A check with the dispatcher turned up the information that Joe Pickard was at this very moment helping lead the prayer vigil at city hall. No way to get a search warrant at this hour, not without any new evidence, but the coast was clear.

Daryl drove by the mayor's house. The porch light had been left on, but everything else was dark. Some parties echoed from the next block, but nothing stirred here.

He parked a few houses away and walked back. A dog yapped briefly in somebody's yard.

It was really dark tonight, darker than he could remember. Clouds, or maybe that gassy stuff, had blacked out the stars and the moon. Daryl's throat felt raspy from inhaling that gunk, and his thigh muscles twinged from thrusting away at Nina. He needed to soak in a hot tub.

As he came alongside Pickard's house, he could smell freshly turned dirt. Using his flashlight, Daryl saw that an azalea bush and one of the burgeoning camelias had been trimmed. It looked like old Joe had finally begun fixing up the place.

He took the walkway along the side of the house. Dirt crunched under his shoes. Jeez, you'd think the guy would sweep up after he finished gardening. Once a slob, always a slob.

Nothing moved in the backyard except for a cobweb hanging under the eaves of the potting shed, twitching a little in the muggy air. Damp circles formed under Daryl's arms.

He walked up to the back windows and peered inside the house. Couldn't see much. What had he expected, anyway?

Still, it didn't feel right. Machado, now, if he were here, he'd think of some damn fool thing to ask. Like, what was an accused murderer doing leading a prayer vigil? And why had Hizzoner the mayor suddenly started doing yard work in the middle of a heat wave?

Daryl walked back around to the side of the house and played his flashlight over the dirt. The guy hadn't even got around to planting anything yet.

Something glittered down in the soil. Daryl started to turn away, sure it was nothing but a shard of glass. The thought of Will Machado changed his mind.

He knelt to check it out. Couldn't see much even with the flashlight, so he reached out and brushed at the dirt. There it was again, glistening. Scrape, scrape. Now, he could see a small, round object made of glass. Like a marble. No, it was flat and it blinked.

Damn if it wasn't the face of a digital watch. Joe must have lost it while he was digging.

Daryl reached into the dirt to pick the thing up. Disbelief shuddered through him as he felt something limp and heavy come up with the watch. A wrist. A hand. An arm that led down into the earth.

This wasn't any flowerbed, it was a grave.

God, he'd better call in before he messed up the crime scene. Get the lab boys out here.

Daryl was straightening up when something hard crashed into the back of his head. The last thing he noticed was the dirt coming up to meet him, filling his nostrils, choking off his breath.

CHAPTER THIRTY-TWO

"She shouldn't have left you here alone." Bob Fillipone sat back on the couch, legs crossed at the knee, swirling scotch and water in his glass. "Night off or no night off."

"Ramona left before we learned about the gas, or whatever it is," said Rita, curled up in an oversize chair. For the first time all day, she felt relaxed.

Four years ago, after her marriage, Cruise's staff had treated her with barely polite indifference. No doubt they'd considered her some floozy who would be discarded as quickly as his second wife.

Only Bob had taken the time to advise Rita where to shop in Washington, what to serve at dinner parties, who the players were at embassy functions. Mostly he'd just been doing his job, but at least he'd given her the benefit of the doubt.

Now, since Cruise's death, he'd provided the support she could get nowhere else. With him, she felt protected and safe. Yet he'd never so much as looked at her flirtatiously. Maybe Bob was gay; she'd wondered, once or twice, since he'd reached the age of forty without marrying. Whatever his sidelines, if he had any, he was relentlessly discreet about them.

Which would be a good thing, if he got the Senate nomination. She wasn't sure her recommendation would carry much weight, but Fisher seemed to be looking for an apolitical choice. And Bob certainly had the experience.

"I hope you don't mind my dropping by like this," he said. "I worry about you."

He seemed to be waiting, giving her an opening to confide in him. And suddenly Rita wanted to. "Bob, something happened yesterday."

He leaned forward. "More threats?"

"Not exactly." Rita fumbled for a cigarette, then decided against it. "I saw the young men from the photograph, down the street; they said I, or someone, had called them. Apparently, this woman not only looked like me, she—she brought them here, to this house, to a basement. I looked last night, but I can't find any door that might lead to it."

Bob shook his head. "There's no basement that I know of. Damn, you mean there really is a woman who looks like you? I figured it was a paste-up job."

"I asked them to watch for her, try to get her license number," Rita said. "They seemed to think I was playing games."

"As long as they stay the hell away from here." Bob grimaced. "Right now, my main concern is your health. Didn't Ramona leave something for you to eat?"

"She mentioned pork chops, but I'm not hungry."

He uncrossed his legs. "We'll see about that. I'll put them in the broiler and toss up a salad to go with it. You've been losing weight, and it's not good for you."

The room's shadows came back as soon as he left. Rita considered going after him, but it might be awkward, the two of them alone in the kitchen, puttering around each other. She didn't want to risk having anything change between them.

She closed her eyes. God, she was tired. Suppose there was a war coming? The past two weeks of her life had wiped out her interest in the summit conference and even the kidnappings, but the president's death, that was something else. She'd met him twice, once just after her marriage. He'd been so kind. . . .

"Rita!" There was a twist of alarm in Bob's shout. "Rita, you'd better—" And then silence.

She stood up, fingers twitching. The gun lay lumpily in her skirt pocket, where she'd thrust it when she went to answer the door. As Bob had instructed.

She couldn't let anything happen to him. Not to Bob, of all people.

In the hall, Rita coughed in the harsh air. Smoke billowed toward her from the kitchen. Fire! Real fire, or another hallucination?

"Bob?" A quavering, thin plea, to which there was no response.

How could she go through this again, the throbbing hallway, the scorching dining room? Everything brilliant with red, echoing with whispers. *Rita, Rita come to us. We know what to do with you.*

"Leave me alone!" she screamed. "Haven't I done everything you wanted?"

The voices stopped. Somehow, in spite of the heat, in spite of the watery fear in her knees, she staggered into the kitchen, breathing in shallow gasps to keep from burning her lungs. Smoke fumed from the broiler. Grabbing a pot holder, Rita turned it off.

She couldn't see Bob anywhere in the smoke.

She called his name again, tentatively. There was a pause, and then his voice came clearly from the depths of the pantry. "Rita, you'd better come see this."

Without pausing to think, she swung the pantry door open.

Inside, a wall of shelves had rotated to reveal a hidden staircase. Rita stood gaping down at it. She felt like a child in some bizarre fairy tale. Houses didn't really have secret stairs, secret rooms. The air coming up from it felt hot and moist.

But Bob was down there. The thought gave her confidence.

There seemed to be dozens of steps, as if she were descending not one story but two or three. At the bottom, she found herself in a room she had seen once before, in a photograph.

Rumpled bed, cheap bureau, floor-to-ceiling blackout curtains. Covering up the fact that this was a basement, that it was in her house.

How could that woman have found it? Did Cruise know about this place? The room couldn't really exist, and yet those boys had come here, and they were real.

She wanted to run.

"Hello, Rita." Bob's voice issued from an alcove to her left. She pivoted, anxious for reassurance.

The woman was with him, the woman who looked like Rita. She wore a lacy see-through sheath, and nothing under it.

"What . . . ?" Disbelief clogged her throat. "Bob?"

She'd never seen that expression on his face before, an evil half-smile.

"Rita, Rita," he said. "You've done everything we asked. We're stronger now, and we don't need you anymore."

She saw everything clearly in that moment. Bob, in this room where the photograph had been taken, with the woman who had posed for it. Bob, at Cruise's side before the luncheon. Bob, whom she'd recommended for the Senate seat.

"No." Rita hated the childlike quaver in her voice. "Bob, please, no."

The woman beside him sauntered forward. "You have so many pretty things, Rita. I'm going to enjoy them."

Her hands, her long red fingernails, reached out for Rita's throat.

• • •

"We beseech you, O Lord, to guide us in these perilous times. . . ."

On TV, sweat beaded the forehead of the archbishop of Canterbury. A short while ago, on his satellite link from Rome, the pope had been perspiring. Heat everywhere, all over the world.

Laura popped the top on another can of soda. She was afraid to open the window, afraid the thing that looked like Lew might come back. The apartment sweltered.

In the street, people clanged pots, and a man mocked the prayer vigil in slurred tones over a battery-operated megaphone.

"We ask You to hold the hands of our new leaders, and to spare the lives, if it is Your divine will, of those still imprisoned," said the archbishop on TV.

Fuzzily, over the megaphone from the street, came words out of the Bible, turned into drunken parody. "And you will hear of wars and rumors of war, you sons of bitches. Nation will fight against nation, which is what the damn commies have been asking for, and you will see famines and earthquakes, and they'll all apply to the good old U.S. of A. for a free handout."

She was getting a headache. Laura switched off the television, but she could still hear the echoes from a dozen turned-up sets around the neighborhood.

Faintly: "You are the light of our hope, the rock of our salvation."

Loudly, from the street, as if in chorus: "The sun will darken and the moon will lose its light, and let's have some fucking fireworks around here!"

"Shut up!" Yelling made Laura feel better, even if it didn't accomplish anything.

The sun will darken, and the moon will lose its light. That had come true today, at least in San Paradiso. All the biblical warnings, the old prophecies . . .

If only it weren't so hot in here. She couldn't think straight. She could hardly breathe.

Laura tried to open the glass doors, but they wouldn't budge. She pulled harder, frantically, but the metal frames stuck as if they'd been painted shut. Air, had to get air.

She turned and stumbled across the room, jerked the door open, and inhaled the damp, sulfur-tainted air from outside.

The minute she did, Laura knew it was a mistake. Something writhed inside her, like a snake that was feeding on this unholy gas.

Inch by inch, she felt herself slipping away. Yielding to—to *what?*

"Help," she whispered. "Somebody help me."

"*Oui.* I will help you." Madeleine spoke from close by, her voice startlingly real.

Laura stared across the threshold into a wrinkled face and knowing eyes. And a knife, a huge, ornate dagger that might have come from an adventure movie.

"What are—what are you doing?" she stammered.

"What I have to do," the old woman said. "What I came here to do. To kill the demon."

CHAPTER THIRTY-THREE

"Well, shit." Briana had only left the council chambers for a minute, to radio in. She hadn't expected Joe Pickard to disappear from the podium.

A rabbi stood at the microphone now, leading yet another prayer. Briana stared around, then asked a man in the back where the mayor had gone.

He pointed to an exit from the platform. "They've got their own private rest room, I guess."

Briana hurried around through the corridor to a room marked PRIVATE—CITY COUNCIL ONLY. She pushed her way inside and checked the head. Empty.

Outside, his car was gone. She called dispatch, told them to alert the captain and put out an all-points. This wasn't going to look good, losing the bastard again.

She cruised through the parking lot. No one stirred, not there or across the street at the police department, as far as she could peer through the fog. Paradise Avenue was nearly empty, too, but as she turned down Avenida Dante, Briana saw misty figures moving back and forth, as if dancing. They didn't seem to care that the air might be dangerous.

There were young women out, some of them alone. Maybe one fewer than there had been a few minutes ago. She started to sweat.

Joe only lived a few blocks down Avenida Dante, but she had to inch along for fear of hitting someone. As she pulled up, Briana was relieved to see his aging Cadillac in front.

Something moved at the far side of the house. A fat, rumpled shape she'd recognize anywhere. It looked as if he was digging again, but in the hazy air she couldn't see clearly.

He gave no sign of noticing her car. After radioing in, Briana unholstered her service revolver and moved quietly toward him.

When she spotted the body on the ground, she shivered. Joe Pickard had found another victim, and it was her fault for letting him out of her sight.

She advanced into easy range. "Hold it! Police!" Briana crouched, combat-style. "Hands up, real slow."

The fat man swung around to face her. In the dark, she couldn't read his expression, but she could see his eyes. They glowed like a cat's. A thin edge of red flame flickered around his thick figure.

He looked like nothing Briana had ever seen before. Like nothing human.

In a minute, this hallucination, too, would go away, Laura told herself as she retreated from Madeleine. But everything felt, sounded, so real. From outside came the blare of a megaphone, the clang of pots and pans, the buzz of TV sets. Laura could feel the carpet cushioning her bare feet as she moved backward.

"I'm sorry." Madeleine stalked her step for step. "Sometimes you seem so human. You've been pretending to be Laura for such a long time, you almost believe it."

"You can't—" Her heel touched the wall. "My father—"

"He wasn't really your father." Madeleine raised the knife slowly. "He brought you back, through that door he opened. After Laura died."

The dagger came at her, glittering with purpose. Laura grabbed for the bony wrist. Lord, Madeleine was strong. All Laura's might was barely enough to turn the knife a little, so it nicked her arm as it came down, drawing blood.

Madeleine began chanting in French. A curse, an invocation. Laura's arm burned. As she tried to edge toward the bedroom, the old woman lifted the knife with both hands. Plunging. Down. Nowhere to go but to lunge forward, block her with Laura's whole body, thud onto the floor, hold on, hold on.

Power surged through Laura, a great, unknown force burning away her fear. So easy, to grasp the old woman like a limp doll, to snatch the knife from her bird-boned hand and smell her horror. Such pleasure, to hear her shriek. The whole world full of agony, concentrated in this one puny form. Savor the heat of her blood just beneath the throat . . .

Laura lifted her head and saw herself reflected in the glass doors, a dark reptilian form writhing inside a molten column. As she gaped, the reptile shape crumbled into a vortex of distended cells with eyes and mouths, one swelling until it filled the shimmering tube. Her own face, eyes blank with terror, mouth open in an endless, unheard scream.

Oh, God. That couldn't be her. Couldn't—

James—the door—a creature disguised as his daughter. Raised as a little girl, imbued with Laura-consciousness until this moment . . .

No.

It couldn't be true, and yet she knew already that it must be. That something else had lived inside her for a long time.

Soon it would obliterate the last trace of Laura, the last longing for Lew's gentle strength, the last sharp leap of intellect as she pieced together her journalistic jigsaws.

While she still thought and felt as Laura, maybe she could stop it. But she would have to move quickly to destroy this body that served them both.

With fumbling, thick hands, Laura raised the dagger. Where was the heart in this maelstrom?

"*Arrêtez-vous!*" Stop! Please!" Purple-veined hands cupped around her monstrous ones. No, around Laura's small hands, and the haft of the knife.

She looked up at the glass doors, and her own face stared back. The dagger slipped to the floor.

Madeleine coughed as she retrieved the weapon and slipped it into her skirt pocket. "James, I saw him. Like you. A torn thing, between two worlds. Not like that demon I killed. But . . . what are you, then?"

Laura curled on the floor, hugging her knees. *Please, God, let me wake up now.* "I don't understand."

"Your arm is bleeding." With a fluttery cough, Madeleine went into the bathroom and came out with antiseptic and Band-Aids. "Sit up."

Stiffly, Laura obeyed. Her head felt too heavy for her neck. Vaguely, she noticed that Madeleine had a bandage on her arm, too.

"You went into a coma, after the accident." Madeleine dabbed away the blood with a damp washcloth. "James had some delusion that the only hope to cure you lay through a door in that painting. And if you couldn't be saved, he told me, he had dreamed you had a twin who lived there, in another dimension, who would come back with him."

Laura closed her eyes to keep from looking into the glass doors.

"One morning, you disappeared from the hospital. James was gone, too," Madeleine said. "For weeks, I heard nothing. Then, suddenly one evening, he was at my door with Laura, all healed. A Laura who stared at me strangely and didn't remember things."

"But I've begun remembering," Laura said. "The accident. I remembered that. Could it be that I'm part demon, like my father? That the two parts of me split when he took me through the door?"

Bony fingers spread antiseptic gel along her arm. She thought it ought to sting, but it didn't. Outside, the drunk was singing "Rock of Ages" through his megaphone while people yelled at him to shut up.

"The next day," Madeleine said, "he told me he'd discovered that the painting was evil. He said he'd taken you to a hospital in England instead. But he kept looking at you strangely, as if he were afraid."

"He *was* afraid," Laura said softly. "He must have seen the—the other me."

The day her father left her with Aunt Ellen in Cincinnati, she'd stood in the doorway crying. He hadn't been able to look her in the eye. He must have been remembering that moment in the doorway to hell, when he witnessed the beast inside Laura.

"I saw him change just as you did, by the painting." Madeleine stretched a Band-Aid along Laura's arm. "But he never saw himself reflected. He must not have realized that whatever you were, he was, too."

"Why didn't he destroy the damn thing?" Laura asked.

"He said he would need it as evidence, to show to someone who could warn the world. But he never said who." Pulling the paper carefully off the ends of the Band-Aid, Madeleine described James's last week in France, before he took Laura home. He had drunk heavily, she said, trying to steel his nerve to go to Washington and risk being locked up as a madman.

As Laura listened, her father shrank from a paternal giant to a timid, bewildered man. A mild academic who found to his horror that he had cracked open the door to hell and only been able to shut it partway before he collapsed.

He had come to believe, Madeleine said, that it was only half-breeds who could bridge the gap between the worlds. He felt Goya might also have been such a gate-keeper, and that the painting had become a focus, a conduit. And a lure.

He was convinced, Madeleine said, that somewhere in the world someone must exist who could close the door, or who might, if he was weak, open it wide. A time would come when the world was ripe, when enough demons had slipped through the door and made their evil preparations, and then they would seek him out, this crossbreed, to unloose the deluge.

"Me," Laura said. "He didn't know it was me?"

"You were only a child," the Frenchwoman said. "If he suspected, it must have frightened him even more. Who knows?"

"I don't want this thing to win," Laura said. "This—this part of me."

Outside, the slurred singing had stopped. The low prayers humming from TV sets formed a faint chant in Latin, Chinese, Arabic, Spanish. Everywhere, people prayed.

While the demons readied their final assault, and waited for Laura.

"I think I know who my father went to see in Washington," she said. "The one who killed him and took the painting. It's an aide to Senator Long, named Bob Fillipone. He's been in the right place, every time."

"Whatever you do, Laura, you mustn't fall into this creature's hands," Madeleine said.

She shook her head. "I have to close the door. I have to confront him. Madeleine, when they take human form, these demons must be vulnerable, or they would have triumphed long ago."

The old woman grimaced. "It's true. I killed one. But they are strong, terribly strong."

"Give me the dagger," Laura said.

Madeleine held it out. The cold metal touched Laura's skin with a faint buzz.

The phone rang.

When she answered it, the phone line crackled, making Rita sound tinny. "Laura? I'm sorry to call you at this hour, but I need you right away. Something awful has happened. You're the only one who can help."

"What is it?"

"I can't—Laura, he's here! Please!"

"I'll be right there." She hung up. "He's waiting for me at the senator's house."

The Frenchwoman touched her shoulder lightly. "God be with you."

"Let's hope so." Laura shoved the knife into her purse. If she weakened, she would have to use it on herself.

Outside her apartment, fog rolled in, or maybe the gas had intensified. Barely able to see a few feet ahead, Laura slogged down the steps as if through mire.

The whole world had turned into one of her visions.

CHAPTER THIRTY-FOUR

Madeleine moved slowly through Laura's apartment, not sure what she sought.

Some little clue to reassure her that this had been James's daughter after all, that she hadn't given her blessed weapon to a devil? No, of course the girl was really Laura; Madeleine had seen the torment as clearly in her as in James, at that moment when the inner demon fought for possession of the soul. Yet she wanted to know more, to understand how such a creature could live for so many years and not realize she wasn't fully human.

Laura inhabited an ordinary place, except for the broken coffee table. Madeleine didn't remember smashing it in their struggle, but she might well not have noticed.

Such normal-looking magazines, *Editor & Publisher, Insight, TV Guide.* Books cramming a shelf, Jane Austen, Orson Scott Card, A. E. Maxwell. A curious mix of classics, science fiction, and mysteries. Mostly home-taped videos, a few Disney cartoons, an exercise tape. And, atop the bookcase, a half-dozen well-worn stuffed animals. If this was a monster, it certainly believed it was Laura.

The phone rang. She picked it up.

"Laura?" Ah, that would be the judge, the man who had so little idea what it was he loved.

"This is Madeleine, from downstairs," she said. "Laura's gone."

A quick intake of breath. "Where?"

"How do I know that you are who you say you are?" she asked.

"What?" His voice took on an impatient edge. "What's going on here?"

It occurred to Madeleine that a demon wouldn't need help finding Laura. "She went to the senator's house. That widow asked for her."

"I—damn it. Why now, in this fog?" Those deep, rich tones must be impressive on the bench.

"If she ever needed anyone, she needs you now," Madeleine said. "There is terrible danger for her in that house. She isn't imagining it."

"How can you be sure?"

"Someone tried to kill me an hour ago," Madeleine said. "A woman who looked exactly like me. My double, you might say. There are creatures on the move tonight who have no business being on this earth, and they are looking for Laura. I think they're waiting for her at the senator's house."

"I'm not sure I can believe this."

"If you love her, you'll think with your heart and not with your mind, this once," Madeleine said, although she wasn't sure what anyone human could do to help.

"I trust Laura. More than I trust my own sanity, right now." His voice faded and then came back. "My niece is asleep, and her foster mother's with her. I'd better get over there."

"You know where it is?"

"Yes. If she calls, tell her I'm on my way."

Slowly, feeling seventy years of accumulated gravity weighting her bones, Madeleine went to lean on the balcony railing and peer into the thickening darkness, standing vigil, as it were, for Laura.

The pillared house in Newport Beach loomed over Laura as she got out of her car. Night and haze furred the white walls with mosslike patches.

The front door stood ajar. Her hand tapped her unzipped purse where the dagger lay. "Rita?"

"In here."

Cautiously, Laura went through the hall and into the living room. All the lights had been turned on, as if for a party. A bottle of champagne stood uncorked on the coffee table.

Rita sat next to Bob on one of the couches. They were smiling, both of them.

"I'm afraid Rita got a bit carried away when she called you," Bob said. "Some kind of prowler. You know how it is out there tonight, everybody going crazy."

"I wasn't thinking straight." Rita held out a champagne glass. "As long as you're here, join us for a drink." She wore an indecently transparent dress, her breasts spilling out.

The hairs stood up along Laura's arm. What had they done with the real Rita?

The house quivered around her like a living thing. Boards creaked in the hall. A faint mustiness wafted into the room, as if dust had been disturbed.

"We're celebrating," the Rita-thing said. "You do understand?"

"Where is she?" Laura asked. She wanted to save Rita, if she could, before she confronted the painting.

The others exchanged glances. "Not persuaded yet?" Bob reached for Laura's arm. "Come with me."

She pulled back. "You lead. Both of you."

Rita shrugged. "You're only making it harder."

"Not really," Bob said. "More fun." He caught Rita's hand, and they walked together out of the room.

The other way, through the open front door, lay a wide, dark world full of hiding places. But not for Laura. Not tonight.

She followed the demons into the kitchen.

The large pantry stood open, shelves tidily arranged with cans of peas and boxes of rice, jars of coffee, plastic-wrapped spaghetti. In the back, a wall rotated to reveal a hidden staircase that couldn't possibly be there.

"This way," Bob called over his shoulder.

He and the woman walked down. At the top of the steps, Laura felt hot, wet air waft up from somewhere not on earth. The basement floor looked solid, but she felt as if it were a quagmire deceptively surfaced, like the La Brea Tar Pits. Ready to trap her and pull her under.

From below came a soft sob, like a wounded animal. Rita. Rita was down there.

Forcing herself to descend, Laura stepped into a disheveled room. A dark-haired figure lay huddled on the bed, wrists lashed together, sides moving faintly. Still breathing.

"We knew you'd enjoy this," Bob said. "Watch." With an expert pull, he loosed Rita's wrists. She stirred and sat up slowly, hair falling over her face. The eyes that stared at Laura had a dull, glazed surface. There were red lines on her throat and a purple bruise on one cheek.

The proud, dignified wife of a senator had vanished. What remained was something out of a B-movie, Rita the Bimbo, skirt hiked up on her thigh, breasts peeping through a torn blouse. A disposable victim, waiting to be violated.

Bob produced a cheap plastic cigarette lighter from his pocket. Flicking it open, he pushed the flame toward Rita.

She scrabbled backward on the bed. "Stop—stop it. Why are you doing this?"

"Laura knows," Bob said.

Too late, she saw the trap they'd set. The bait for a demon. Turn. Run. But oh, the smell of hot blood oozing from the scrapes on Rita's neck. The flame swelling until the room shifted into red. Fire, burning away the surface; blood, pulling, sucking a great scaly thing from Laura's innards.

Standing over Rita, Bob's human shape became a transparent form with a reptile coiled inside, circling flame toward the prey's black hair. Layers of crimson air whorled around them, blurring their edges. Beside him, the demon-Rita watched hungrily.

Laura felt the tight constraint of skin begin to peel away. She was sinking, being pulled inside herself, losing ground. God, she couldn't let the thing win. She couldn't let the monster within devour human flesh.

The victim on the bed gaped at her in disbelief. "Oh, Jesus, what are you?" A gush of noise, nothing more. "You're not really Laura. You can't be." The movement sent blood trickling from a gash in her neck.

The overwhelming silver scent of it slammed through Laura. Ready. Yes, she was ready to feed.

"Laura? Are you down there?" Lew's disbelieving voice came from the top of the stairs. "Jesus Christ, what *is* that thing?"

She was drowning. Trapped in here, little Laura, her mind spinning around and around. No one could hear, no one could rescue her. But this was her body. Take it back, fight, feel the thing thrash and snarl.

The beast contracted in a twist of pain, lashing at her guts as it shrank. Battling cell by cell, draining her strength, wrenching her to the ground. Laura focused with all her spirit. Her temples throbbed; her blood churned and counterflowed, until finally, finally, the thing dropped into some dark pit where she couldn't reach it.

The Bob-thing was pacing toward her.

Where was the knife? In her purse, dropped somewhere. Laura's hands scrabbled across the floor, searching feebly.

The Bob-thing grasped her ankles. The room, the world, flamed around her, while Rita lay motionless on the bed. Bob jerked backward, and Laura's head thudded against the floor as he hauled her—where?—surely to wherever the painting lay hidden.

Not now, please, when she had no energy to fight. She needed Lew, but he must have fled to safety, away from this monstrous woman he had once loved. Away from the unimaginable, which could have no place in his orderly heart.

As Laura tried to catch hold of something, anything, her fingers closed over a smooth leather length; her purse strap. Her hand scrabbled inside and curled around the cool shaft of the dagger, but the Bob-thing only laughed as she stabbed blindly at him. Thud, thud; he hauled her up the steps, her head jolting painfully against each riser.

Halt. Her legs flopped loose, and Laura had to brace herself to keep from falling. Above, someone was struggling with the demon.

Twisting around on the stairs, Laura tried to aim the dagger. The figures above her moved too quickly, kicking and grappling. Cursing, they slipped, fell over her, and landed in a heap on the burning floor. Wavering red light cast them both as silhouettes. Which one was Lew? Which one was Bob?

"Lew!" Laura screamed. A turn of the head. She had to trust that it was him, to drive the blade into the other male body, deep deep. *God, let me have chosen right.*

She heard something like a firecracker and felt a shudder deep within the earth. Air, blessed sharp air, rushed into her chest.

A scaly thing shriveled on the floor. Lew stood by the wall, gasping.

Rita—where was she? There, leaning against the bed, holding a gun over another fallen devil, a black shape flailing and then disintegrating into dust.

"We've got to get out of here." Lew's voice came out in a rasp. "The whole house is going up."

"I don't think I can. . . ." Rita took a step and collapsed. Lew caught her.

"Go on, Laura," he ordered roughly. "Get out. I'll bring her."

Unearthly fire slithered along the concrete floor, circling toward the steps. In the flames, blues and violets danced. If you looked hard enough, you could see great shadowed depths, hollows with eyes. James's eyes.

This time, Laura knew she was hallucinating. Her head pounded.

"Out!" Lew said.

She slogged upward in a daze, hearing his heavy footsteps behind. Flames howled and sucked at their heels until he thrust the pantry wall into place with his shoulder. Tendrils of hellfire crept through the cracks.

He pushed Laura ahead as they half crawled through the smoke. The exit from the kitchen was locked, and the knob burned Laura's hand as she fumbled with it.

There were voices on the other side; neighbors, it must be neighbors, yelling at her to stand back. Amid a staccato of hammering, the door fell open. Laura staggered out to the sweet softness of night air and the nearing shrill of sirens.

Briana stood gaping for several seconds after the red-eyed Joe Pickard lumbered off into the night. Then, reflexively, she fired, but heard only the whine of a bullet gone wild.

The darkness was heavy with the scent of freshly turned earth. For a moment, she considered running after him. But others would be along soon to search, and his victim might still live.

Briana knelt and heard a stifled groan. Playing her flashlight on the huddled body, she saw that it was a man. Then he rolled over.

"Jesus Christ!" She reached down to feel the sergeant's pulse. Strong, thank goodness. "What the hell happened?"

"Somebody hit me." The words came out slurred. Daryl reached back gingerly and touched the crown of his head. "Goddamn."

A patrol car screamed up the street toward them. "It was Joe Pickard," Briana said. "I'm sorry. I lost him."

"There's someone in there." He pointed to the dirt.

"Oh, shit," Briana said. "Wait. Don't move. You might have a concussion."

"When they get Pickard, I'll kill the son of a bitch," Daryl muttered.

"I'll help you," she said, and caught him as he passed out.

CHAPTER THIRTY-FIVE

It surprised Laura how bright the sunshine looked outside the hospital window. In only a few hours, the dark fumes and the night had blown away together.

Trying to ignore the painful stiffness in her muscles and the stinging behind her eyes, she went into the bathroom and sponged off. The other bed in the double was empty, and she had already dressed by the time the nurse came in with breakfast.

"Doctor hasn't been in yet, has he?" the woman said.

"I'm fine." Laura tried to look pleasant. "How do I check out of here?"

The nurse clucked. Laura fought down an irrational surge of anger. She didn't want to sit around waiting for the doctor, or for the police to question her, either, not until she had a chance to talk to Rita and decide what version of the truth to tell them. There was no urgency, anyway. As far as anybody else knew, last night's fire was just an accident.

"Well," the nurse said, "I think the doctor's on the floor. I'll go see if I can find him."

Somehow, by the time Laura finished nibbling at her rubbery pancakes and overcooked eggs, the doctor had been browbeaten into releasing her, and Lew had managed to work some kind of wizardry with the hospital paperwork.

The only hang-up was that Rita was too sedated to talk. Reluctantly, Laura left her in the care of her housekeeper.

"We'll check back later," Lew promised as she climbed into the car he'd brought around.

They headed northwest from Newport Beach toward San Paradiso. On the radio, in a low hum, the announcer was talking about the international sense of hope spreading after last night's worldwide prayer meeting. Laura didn't feel very hopeful, riding next to Lew. Between them lay a silence that had never been there before.

"Laura," he said finally, "what the hell *was* that last night?"

"Me," she said.

"Bullshit."

She let the miles slip by. Maybe it was too much to ask him to accept.

She could still feel that alien presence inside her, like an echo in a cave. "It's not over," Laura said. "I still have to close that door. Rita might know where Bob lived. Maybe he kept the painting there."

Lew stared ahead. "Laura, things like I saw last night don't exist outside science-fiction movies."

"So what do *you* think it was?" she said.

The announcer's excited voice broke in before Lew could answer. "Here's an Associated Press bulletin. In a gesture of reconciliation, a spokesman for Ayatollah Al-Hadassi says the release of the remaining world leaders has been arranged. There's no word as to who is actually holding them, or when they may be—wait, wait! Look at this!"

It took a few seconds for him to calm down enough to go on. "Officials in Athens, Greece, say seven people came ashore from a yacht this morning in Piraeus. They have been identified as the survivors of last week's kidnapping, the heads of state of Egypt, Israel, India, China, Japan, and West Germany, and the king of Jordan. A spokesman said they appear to be suffering from exhaustion but are otherwise unharmed."

Was it possible the worst had passed?

Lew stopped in front of her apartment and killed the engine. He studied his hands on the steering wheel. "Was this because of you? Because of what happened at Rita's last night?"

"I think so," Laura said. "I hope so." She opened the door. "Are you coming in?"

He shook his head. "I need to be alone for a while."

She wanted to insist on his staying, but she couldn't force him. "Will you go and see Rita later? Find out where Bob lived?"

After a long moment, he said, "All right. I'll see this thing through, at least. You go get some sleep. You look like hell."

Laura didn't doubt it for a minute.

The jangle of the phone woke her. In the dim room, Laura fumbled for the receiver and squinted at the clock. Almost noon.

Greg's voice was disgustingly cheery. "Hi, sorry to call you on a Saturday, but we've got a little emergency here."

Laura struggled to sit up. "Greg, I had a rough night."

"I know. Steve's down in Newport covering the fire investigation," the editor said. "He'll want to talk to you later. But right now, they've turned up Joe Pickard's body. I can't reach Steve, and, anyway, you're only a few blocks from the PD."

Laura's mind stretched blearily. "What happened to Joe?"

"Good question," Greg said. "Apparently, he's been dead for a couple of days. Somebody's been running around impersonating him. Which gives an interesting slant to those murders."

Only an editor would think of such a bizarre circumstance as an interesting slant, Laura reflected as she heard herself agreeing to go.

She knew what Lew would say about her heading back to work with her head still throbbing. "Damn reporters."

After she hung up, Laura said it to herself.

Driving to the paper after the press conference, Laura realized that she knew too much. The detective side of reporting, the challenge she had loved for so long, seemed superficial now.

The camera crews jockeying for position, the radio personalities asking questions more for show than for information, the reporters picking over the wording of the captain's statement, they'd reminded her of vultures fighting over a carcass.

None of them had a clue to the truth about Joe Pickard or his double. Neither, for that matter, did the police.

It was a story Laura would never be able to write. As she turned right on Firenze Street, she realized she was losing interest in newspaper journalism.

She wasn't sure what she wanted to do after this, but it would have to be something less confining. Which ought to make Lew happy, if he still intended to be part of her life. If she still had a life.

Surely, Rita would be able to talk by this evening. The painting must be at Bob's home. If it had been hidden in the Long household, they would have confronted her with it last night.

Tonight. She'd have to be strong enough to face it by then.

When she pulled in, there was only one other car in the *Herald* lot. Greg's Porsche took up his reserved space near the employees' entrance.

Laura climbed the steps to the newsroom.

Overhead, one of the TVs was turned low to a newscast that had preempted regular programming. It showed the president of Egypt, his arm bandaged, waving weakly as he boarded an airplane.

Greg sat alone at the copy chief's desk, punching instructions into the computer. "This is amazing," he said, without looking up.

"None of the leaders seems to know who was holding them, or where." He pressed a button. "What'd you find out?"

Briefly, Laura told him what the police had said about Joe Pickard's mysterious double. "I'll keep checking to see if they've caught the guy."

"Weird," Greg said. "The whole past few weeks have been weird." He stood up. "I'll be in my office, if you need me."

The TV cameras shifted to a close-up of President Whiting, who was saying that today's events in no way modified his determination to avenge the death of President Harkness.

Laura checked the clock as she sat down. Nearly two-thirty. The rest of the Sunday crew wouldn't be in until around four.

It was hard to concentrate. Well, the lead was easy enough. *The body of San Paradiso mayor Joe Pickard, a suspect in the murders of three young women, was found in a shallow grave at his house Friday night, and police said another man may have been posing as him at a prayer meeting.*

Pickard was apparently strangled sometime Thursday. . . ."

The story, the strangest Laura had ever tackled, unrolled from there with an inner momentum. She was surprised to see, when she stopped to answer the phone, that half an hour had passed.

"Laura?" Steve said over the phone. "Why aren't you in the hospital?"

"Somebody has to cover Joe Pickard's murder," she said.

"Yeah, I just heard about that. I wanted to be sure Greg knew," he said. "Well, you sound healthy enough. Listen, I need to interview you as a witness."

"Later," Laura said.

"Do you know anything about a basement room?" Steve said. "Rita hasn't been too coherent, but apparently she said something about it to one of the firemen. The house didn't have a basement."

"Then it must have existed in some other dimension," Laura said.

"Right." He coughed away from the phone. "Damn, that shit in the air must have frosted my lungs. Oh, wait a minute. I'm next door, and the fire marshal's waving at me." He yelled, "What?" so loud it hurt Laura's ear.

After a moment, Steve came back on the line. "Hey, they've found a body, and they think it might belong to the Fillipone guy. I'll get back to you."

Bob? Laura thought, stunned, as she hung up. He'd been a demon all along. His body couldn't be in the house. Could it?

Overhead on TV, a lady giggled as she squeezed a roll of toilet paper. The commercial faded back to a news team from the local station, breaking into the national feed.

"Here in California," said a blond anchorwoman, "Governor Fisher staged a surprise news conference this afternoon to reveal his appointee to the U.S. Senate seat held by the late Cruise Long."

There was no sound in the newsroom but the hum of the TV, no movement but the inhuman blink of the computer screens. The flat overhead lighting tightened into narrow spots that sought out Laura's desk and the row of blown-up color photos along the wall, the framed images of storm-racked piers, spectacular sunsets and children playing in the sand.

The narrow, bony face of Governor Fisher filled the screen. "I've decided to go outside the usual political spectrum for my choice. It was my decision to seek out a man or woman with enough national and international experience to make a successful senator but one who could bring a fresh perspective to our government.

"I'm pleased to announce the appointment to the U.S. Senate of Gregory Evans. Greg, who is currently the editor of the *Paradise Herald,* is a former United World Press reporter who covered China's political struggles during the 1960s and was a war correspondent in Vietnam from 1965 to 1970, when he moved to Washington. . . ."

. . . Washington. Where James died. Greg, who had a drink with Cruise Long right before his death. Greg, who brought Laura to San Paradiso in the first place. . . .

On the wall below the TV, a wide-angle shot of lightning over the ocean began to shift, to swell and distend until it filled the wall. The other pictures, the bulletin board, the entrance to the photo department, disappeared beneath a huge panorama whose backlighted thunderclouds rolled and blew, whose churning air smelled of sea salt and sulfur.

There were faces behind the storm, white-rimmed eyes and taut mouths. They stared at the black, twisted figure of a goat-cloud. No, not at the goat, but beyond him at a thin vertical slit of scarlet reaching from floor to ceiling. The light coming through the door to hell.

CHAPTER THIRTY-SIX

"I had hoped to be able to tell you before now." Greg's voice sounded shockingly normal.

There was nothing in the newsroom anymore except a fiery slit in the textured darkness and the all-too-familiar slim figure taking a seat on the edge of Laura's desk. "We've waited a long time. It wasn't easy, infiltrating key positions around the world without arousing suspicion. I can't tell you how frustrating it is, struggling through that tiny crack, afraid it'll slam shut in your face."

Laura felt no panic, only cold determination. "You can't get through any other way?"

"Oh, there're always a few of us around," he said. "Each human has a match, a spiritual twin, if you will. We can be summoned, if our human counterpart wants to give himself over to evil. But that's a synthesis, not a replacement, and we can't count on getting summoned by anyone important. Although it's been known to happen."

In the black void where the wall and the long-disguised painting had been, the door creaked with an unearthly thin sound. Waves of heat slid across Laura's face.

"Is there really a Devil? Is it you?" She concentrated on relaxing her head and neck against the residual ache. The test was coming.

Greg shrugged. "I'm hardly that important. Oh, Laura, you don't know how long I've worked on you. Bringing you along, letting what was inside you work its way to the surface. I certainly didn't intend to rush things the way I did with your father."

His voice grew flat, with a mechanical ring to it, as he talked about James. About a placid scholar lured subliminally to Madrid, to a miraculous painting that had focused both the known and unknown genius of the great part-demon Goya. Of how James's own alter ego, the inner twin that all half-breeds carried, had guided his hand as he copied it.

And in so doing fixed his own pathway to the netherworld, a clear and simple route in or out, for him and the demons and Laura.

Then, a year later, confronted with the truth, James tried to set fire to the canvas. And Greg had stopped him, forever.

Laura shivered. "Why did my father trust you, of all people?"

"A series of articles I wrote for *Future* magazine," Greg said, only he didn't sound like Greg anymore. "Interviews with theologians, psychics, science-fiction writers, about the concept of the millennium. In fact, the real Greg Evans wrote the first one. I merely carried on his work in my own way until James couldn't help seeing I was the one person in the press who wouldn't think he was mad."

Haloed by red light, Greg's body was becoming a translucent column. How tightly the scales were packed, the snake-tongue licking within the man-mouth through which it had spoken for twenty years.

Trying to save me, my father let this monster in, Laura thought.

The sound of footsteps startled her. Someone was climbing the stairs to the newsroom. Steve? The backshop foreman? If she could warn them . . .

A yellow-gray beam of light picked out the hollow faces as they came in. Joe Pickard. Cruise Long. The anti-Lew; oh, God, that leering smile. A young man in a police sergeant's uniform. Doubles, fakes, demons; followed by the wild-eyed ayatollah she'd seen on TV, and others, glimpsed these past few days—the new Canadian prime minister; Ivan Ivanov of the USSR; René Dubois of France; Colin Edwards of Great Britain. And more—oh God, the king of Jordan, the prime ministers of Israel and India and Japan, the leaders of West Germany and China and Egypt, the seven who'd come ashore at Piraeus. All of them unstable tubes in the wavering light.

"You see, we're strong enough now to gather this way from around the earth." Greg nodded to the arrivals. "We've breathed our own air again. Soon you'll all be breathing it."

The demons chanted softly as they formed a circle around Laura. Urging her to join them. Calling to the beast that stirred inside her.

"Don't fight us," Greg said. "Laura, don't destroy yourself struggling against something that was meant to be."

In his eyes, she could see the earth burning in darkness, blue fires flickering in oily pools. Black towers crumbling, freeway overpasses twisting, the cries of the lost muting into a chant of many tongues, a universal prayer. *Help us, Satan, now in the hour of our need.*

The door swung slowly toward her of its own volition. Around her, the demons reached out with false human hands to draw her forward.

How had Laura ever imagined she could close this portal to hell? Merely to come near it was to pull it open. Now, in this time of hideous ripeness, she had become a magnet.

Things massed on the far side of the door. She smelled a stench like rotting flesh. Things, waiting to come through.

The door inched wider. The light blistered her eyes.

Let it follow her, then. She would pull it shut while she still remembered who and what she was. As Greg grasped her intention and reached to stop her, Laura dodged around him and leaped through the fiery opening.

Scarlet light kindled, blinding her. Heat billowed against her skin, burning away the moisture of the living world. As Laura stumbled forward, she heard from outside the furious howling of the world's demon-leaders, and then a thump as the door lodged against wedged bodies. Not shut. Not shut yet. Yellow earth-light still glimmered in through a crack, playing across humped figures and misshapen eyes.

Slurping noises rippled around her. Things pressed close. In the roiling light, she could make out only random details, a claw padded with leathery skin, a rheumy eye half-hidden by drooping flesh, a pustulating sore eating through matted fur. As she staggered onward, she inhaled the foul breath of a thousand creatures eager to unleash firestorms across the earth.

Oh, God, she knew this place from long-buried nightmares. From a night long ago in Nice, France, when her father had carried her out of the hospital.

Daddy! Daddy! She'd felt herself changing, being pulled apart. Terrified, the little girl had turned to Daddy, only to see that she was in the arms of a monster. And then she'd looked down at her own hands, her own arms, only no longer her own. . . .

A moment so horrible it had stopped her memory of it, and of all that led up to it. Until now.

Now, it was happening again. And there wasn't any Daddy to carry her home.

The thing that lived inside Laura coarsened her skin and thickened her legs as she stumbled clear of the throng. Upward she stamped, lost, blinded, bruising herself against outcroppings.

A saurian eyelid lowered itself from inside her head, and she saw through alien eyes that she stood on a twisting path that glowed with a scarlet sheen. Around her, veined boulders pulsed like living organs, blotting out the sight of anything beyond this narrow passageway.

She had become a monster in a monstrous world, and yet she still thought as Laura. The battle for her self wasn't over.

Something moved behind her. There. A shadow, barely glimpsed, panting like a thirsty dog as it moved among the rocks. Closing in, its emptiness probing toward her.

This was what she'd run from all her life, the inner vacuum that would suck away her soul. Only it didn't lurk inside her anymore; it had split away, and it was coming for her.

Laura launched herself clumsily downward, each jolting step a new lesson in her unfamiliar body. She had run in through the door prepared for oblivion, but not for . . . this. She had to find her way back. Out. She had to get out.

She rounded a bend too fast and stumbled on the rim of a quagmire, a brown boiling slush. Faces stared up from the slime, their mouths working like hooked fish.

Laura stepped backward and heard a soft slither.

It was coming. It was almost here.

A morass in front of her, rocks behind. No, there was an opening in the rocks, faintly iridescent. Laura lumbered toward it, squeezing her reptilian body into the soft muck of a cave. Water dripped onto her neck in the semidarkness. Behind her, she heard a soft rushing noise, like blood in an artery.

There was only a pale, glittering emanation to guide her, and a swaying pinprick of light leading the way far ahead as the tunnel coiled upward through the hill. The cave widened as she climbed. Every now and then it would shift, like the bowel of some great sea monster, sending her scrabbling for purchase on the oozing floor. From behind, the panting noises reverberated.

Ahead, the wavering spot of light clarified into a lantern. She stopped, gorge rising. It was no lantern but a head lighted from within, held aloft by a crumpled figure with a stump for a neck. It swung toward her, points of light streaming through the eyeholes as if in search of something, and then the grotesque figure moved away through a branching cavern.

The weight of the earth pressed against Laura's lungs. With hope dimming, she slogged through the mud to where the headless creature had disappeared, and saw that the side channel opened to a red mouth. A thin draft of air reached her, faintly scented with the newsroom odors of page proofs and cigarette smoke. It meant she must be getting near the door again.

Laura had to escape, whatever the cost. Staying in this abyss was more than her spirit could bear.

She blundered out of the tunnel into a landscape of *noir et rouge,* black oily sumps and spits of flame. Only a few hundred feet ahead, a golden radiance cracked in through the door, the outline of the living world.

Footsteps. Laura twisted around.

A young woman faced her, a shape she had known in mirrors, a brown-haired girl. Madness and triumph shone in its eyes. The demon-spirit had gone into Laura's earthly body, leaving her with this hideous carcass, and her human consciousness.

If I go out, I can have my own body again.

Freedom. It became tangible for the first time, a release from slogging heaviness, from sulfurous air and brown muck. Fingers, wiggling lightly; toes, and slim legs; a head that swiveled easily on its neck. A trace of perfume, a voice that modulated sweet words. A human shape. To claim it, she had only to step through the door and let it swing wide after her. Leaving behind one weightless thing, her soul.

Laura in her monster body looked one more time at the girl. And for an instant, she became a terrified child again, crying, "Daddy! Daddy! Save me!"

But there was no home left, no safety anywhere. Might as well make the unthinkable sacrifice, to live forever sentient in this monster shape and this hell, because in the end there was no choice. Courage had become a simple matter of logic.

I'm coming for you, Laura thought. *It's my turn.*

She was used to this new way of moving. Surprising, how fast she could uncoil across the black rocks, how smoothly her gaping jaws could open. And shut again, on a screaming, cursing wisp of a human body that used to be hers.

Blood spurted out like liquid fire and trickled down her throat. The thing screamed, a high, piercing intrusion that went on and on until it became indistinguishable from silence. Little bones crunched. Skin clung briefly to her teeth, and the hair tickled obscenely as she swallowed it.

It was gone now, the only thing that could tempt her to betrayal.

Inside, the chunks were dissolving. Opening, molecule by molecule. Laura stretched, disconcerted by the pinging sense of fission and then by the sudden hot glow of cells flowing into each other.

Dear God, what was happening to her now?

Juices swirled and mingled through her arteries, and an electric shiver ran along her skin as her monster body began to transform itself.

Scales sloughed off, rolling and bouncing down the rocky slope. Hairs quivered, filtering the stinging fumes from her nose.

Her tongue touched the metallic crown on a molar. Light-headed, Laura flexed her wrists and marveled to be back in her human form, purified and cleansed. One whole being, at last.

A volley of shrieks drew her attention. The door was groaning inward, closing, crushing the demon-bodies that had held it open. Swinging past the threshold, inward, cutting a vacuum into hell.

For one moment, an immense figure blocked the flow of light. The Greg-demon braced himself in the portal, blue light crackling and snapping around him.

From beyond him came a faint sigh. From out in the newsroom, a swirl of rushing air.

Something fluttered past his shoulder, a shred of paper. The wind tightened into a whistle. A folder flew in. A dictionary, its pages riffling. A flock of papers, torn newspaper sheets, spiral notebooks flapping like wounded birds. The Greg-form staggered as something square and heavy thudded into it and splintered into shards of glass.

The whistle rose to a scream. Unable to fight her way out through the wind, Laura huddled behind a boulder as she watched Greg struggle against the blast.

Objects spewed in, computer screens and swivel chairs, a file cabinet, a tripod, a candy vending machine. They spun relentlessly into a vortex, pulling Greg, overwhelming him, sucking away the human frame of the demon. His bare snake face hissed viciously at Laura for one instant before he, too, went tumbling down the black rocks.

A wailing rose up in Laura's ears, echoing to the reaches of darkness. A great blast of moist earth-air sucked into the vacuum a crumpled human shape that blossomed like fungus in a nature film, Ayatollah Al-Hadassi, unfolding his cramped scales from beneath white robes. The king of Jordan, or something that looked like him, was tossed in on the heels of previously little-known party functionary Ivan Ivanov, both of them erupting from their tight human buds. So many faces that the world had come to know slashed in on a torrent of hard, cold rain and thundered away in a burst of warring red and black.

And then came the creature she'd taken for Lew. Not flying past her but to her, its viperish face wrinkled with evil mirth. Heavy arms clutched her, its thick-skinned haunches wriggling obscenely.

"Fuck me," it said. "Bitch. You've wiped out the life I planted in your body; now, we'll start again."

She caught its scaly head and jerked hard, feeling a strange power in her muscles where the beast had fused with her cells.

The Lew-thing roared. Other shapes ploughed toward Laura, dragon-fiends eager to avenge her victory by raping and tying and holding her until a little half-demon screamed into hell from between her thighs.

She shoved the Lew-creature at her pursuers and ran, squelching furiously through the muck. The door was gone, but from off in the distance came a pinprick of light that was her only chance.

More buoyant than her pursuers, and more desperate, she splattered past throbbing scarlet rocks and a river of seething, incandescent mud. Who or what she had become no longer mattered, only that hint of a world beyond this one, fixed ahead of her like a star.

The beasts reached her as she halted beneath the opening, so impossibly far overhead. All useless, her last flight, and now the demons had swelled to the size of titans, great hideous miscreations that could crush her with a whisper.

The Greg-thing led the pack, its saurian face dark with fury. It reached for her, but the Lew-creature thrust it aside, demanding primacy. The two monstrosities snarled and bit at each other.

Laura leaped up the Greg-demon's back, scrambling toward the neck, the head that reached almost to the opening. A crusted hand clutched her legs—the Lew-thing—and then the Greg-beast turned to swipe at its rival, and she was flung upward, grasping for a crevice barely as wide as her shoulders.

She caught the opening with her hands, pulled with all the newfound strength in her arms, and scraped through. A claw raked her leg into scarlet agony, and she collapsed onto hard, rocky soil.

The ground rumbled beneath her, and the fissure slammed shut on a grasping, scaly hand. Something huge slung itself back and forth beneath the earth as Laura lay, spent, terrified that the monster below would tear yet another opening in the fabric of the earth.

Her breath rasped painfully. Only a great rushing sound remained, and then not even that.

Someone was calling her name. Laura tried to lift her head, but it felt impossibly heavy.

Slowly, she opened her eyes to see a square pastel room, to smell disinfectant, to hear a cart rumble by in the hall. On the public-address system, an operator summoned a doctor to the emergency room.

Lew leaned over her. Just behind him, Madeleine sat with hands tightly clasped.

"What . . . ?" It emerged as a croak.

"We came as soon as we heard about Greg's appointment," Lew said. "It looked like some kind of tornado hit the newspaper."

"There was a terrible storm, across the world." Madeleine spoke for the first time. "It was only luck a helicopter spotted you in the oil fields."

"How long . . . ?"

"You were out for a few hours." Lew sat down carefully on the edge of the bed, his body held away from her.

"Were—are—people missing?"

"Many of the world's leaders." Madeleine picked her words carefully. "It's said to be another catastrophe."

Laura sank back into the pillow. Her leg ached.

A nurse came in to take her temperature and blood pressure and to check the bandage. "Good," she said. "The doctor should come by in a few minutes."

Madeleine left with the nurse. "You need to be alone now," she said. "The two of you."

"Rita?" Laura asked when she was gone.

"She'll be discharged tomorrow." Lew met her eyes only for a moment. "She seemed relieved that they found Bob's body."

Relieved. Of course. That her friend and supporter hadn't been a traitor after all.

Dizziness closed in and then receded. "Lew, I don't think that . . . thing . . . will come out of me again. But I'm not like other people. I never will be."

"You never were." He tried to smile.

"Now what?" Laura forced herself to sit up straighter. "Come on, Lew. Let's be honest."

"Damn it," he said. "I've been asking myself how I could love someone who isn't quite human."

"Do you? Love me, I mean?"

He shot her a look that was half exasperation and half appreciation. "The problem is, I can't seem to picture myself living without you."

"Well, that's a relief," she said.

"It's not necessarily the same thing as love."

As he spoke, she took his hands in hers. "You're splitting hairs," Laura said. "Your Honor."

Finally, Lew grinned at her. "I always did like science fiction. I just didn't expect to be living with it."

A pent-up breath sighed out of Laura. "But I would never have children. I don't want there ever to be another monster like I . . . was."

"Neither do I," he said quietly. "But we'll have Kyle and Terri. So who cares?"

She was thinking about kissing him when she fell asleep.

CHAPTER THIRTY-SEVEN

Rita peered into the mirror one last time and dabbed a bit of powder on her nose. "Now I know how Daniel felt."

"Daniel as in lions?" Meg Lowell reached up to flick an almost microscopic piece of lint off Rita's silk suit jacket. "You've met the press before."

"Not as the chief bite-ee." Rita felt as if she ought to spritz on a little perfume, but remembered Meg's advice. Women in politics, she had explained, had to transform themselves into honorary males in order to be taken seriously. It was the sort of insight for which Meg had been hired.

Rita's Cartier watch showed that it was two minutes after eleven. "Ready," she said.

They walked out of the ladies' room, down the hotel corridor, and through a side room that was empty except for a janitor folding chairs. From the ballroom next to it, they could hear the buzz of several hundred people. Meg held the door, and Rita walked through.

Scattered clapping greeted her measured march up to the dais. The ballroom was packed with people and equipment, photographers crouching in front, the chairs filled, the back crammed with lighting equipment and minicams. All those bodies created an energy hum that gave Rita the beginnings of a headache.

She sat down and let Meg take the microphone. "As you know," Rita's new aide said, "Mrs. Long's appointment was only announced yesterday. I hope you'll understand that she hasn't had time yet to prepare any positions on the major issues. We'll be flying to Washington tomorrow, and the senator will be spending the next week in an intensive crash course with the help of her staff. . . ."

My staff. Cruise's staff. With one tragic exception.

Meg had come highly recommended by Mel Kawakami. With Bob gone, Rita had wanted her own person as adviser, not someone left over from Cruise's days, someone to whom Rita was still an interloper. Meg was just right, an experienced campaign manager in her late forties, sharp and professional, with a trace of a Texas accent. The sort of woman who, in less enlightened times, might have been a chaperone at a beauty contest.

If only Bob were here. Oh, God, at least she hadn't been wrong about him.

"Ladies and gentlemen of the press, I give you the junior senator from California, Rita Crane Long."

She stepped to the microphone, smiling to acknowledge the applause. She wished Laura were out there. It was Laura and Lew who'd stood by her side at Bob's funeral, Laura who'd cheered when she learned Rita was going to take the appointment after all. Laura and Lew were the only real friends she had now. That had been a crazy hallucination that night when she thought she saw Laura turning into some kind of—of whatever. It hadn't taken long to realize that someone, maybe that Joe Pickard lookalike who'd never been caught, must have drugged Rita and murdered Bob. No point in dwelling on it, no point in worrying over exactly how or why everything had happened. It was over, and she intended to leave it that way.

The reporters were waiting.

"In a way, I'm as surprised as any of you to find myself up here." Meg had coached her on this point: Take away their thunder. At the same time, let them know that attacking you would be an act of blatant chauvinism. "Like a lot of women, I'm used to working behind the scenes. But sometimes circumstances beyond our control force us to discover new strengths within ourselves, and I hope that will be the case with me."

A few heads nodded. No doubt some smart-ass somewhere would write that Rita Crane Long was merely playing another role. Well, fine. As long as they learned in the next two years that she was a better actress than anyone had thought.

"Questions?" Rita said. Hands shot up. "Yes?" The reporter from *The New York Times* stood up.

"Do you plan to run in the next general election to fill out the final two years of your husband's term?" he said. "And what about after that?"

Meg had seen that one coming. Rita smiled in silent gratitude. "If we're talking lame duckery, don't expect to hear any quacking just yet. There's a good possibility I'll run, yes."

The next question, from a Los Angeles TV anchorman, was also predictable. Why had she changed her mind about accepting the appointment?

"Initially, I felt the job would be better handled by my husband's chief aide, Bob Fillipone," she said. "Now that he's gone, well, I think I'm the next-best person to carry on."

A woman from *Newsweek* asked the toughest question. What had really happened at her house the night Bob died? Could it be related to Cruise's death?"

"That's two questions," Rita said. "As far as who killed Cruise goes, I don't know. I wish I did. There's been some suggestion that Greg Evans had both the opportunity and the motive, but he's not here to defend himself." Heads bent; pens scribbled rapidly. "As for my house, the fire marshal says the problem was a malfunctioning stove. Bob was in the kitchen, making coffee, I believe." Meg had suggested people might wonder why he'd been broiling pork chops; it sounded too intimate. "Laura Bennett, excuse me, Laura Bennett Tarkenton, the former political reporter for the *Herald*, was also with us, and she saved my life. I'd like to thank her and Judge Tarkenton."

There were more questions, mostly about political issues, which Rita dodged. The last question, from the *Christian Science Monitor*, was whether she felt the strange events of last month, including the tornadoes that apparently carried off Greg Evans and a lot of other people whose identities had since been questioned, was a sign of divine intervention.

Behind her, Rita heard Meg's intake of breath. Walk carefully. "I'm no theologian, but I certainly hope so," Rita said. From Meg came a soft "whew."

It was over. Some of the reporters came up to ask final questions, others—mostly women—to wish her luck. With practiced courtesy, Meg hustled Rita away.

Outside, a car waited to take them back to the new condo in Newport, where Ramona would have lunch waiting. For a moment, breathing in the cool September breeze, Rita wondered what the boys from UCI thought about all this. She hadn't heard from them again. She hoped she never would. Not that any of them was likely to risk looking like a fool.

Still, there were shadows on her heart. Always.

Rita slid onto the car seat as gracefully as possible. That was one thing male senators didn't have to contend with, how to keep their skirts from hiking up.

"Now, the new amendments to the tax bill . . ." Meg handed over a folder as the car pulled away from the curb.

"Right," Rita said, and began to read.

• • •

"What's in this box, your anvil?"

"Books." Laura held the door as Lew grunted past her down the steps. "Aren't you glad we're nearly done?"

Her apartment looked weary and abandoned, with only the rented furnishings and a few final cartons of odds and ends. Kyle and Terri lay on their stomachs in the living room, playing with Laura's threadbare stuffed animals.

"Can I take these with me for show-and-tell?" called Terri, who had started kindergarten two weeks before.

"Why not? They're practically antiques," Laura said. She knew she ought to help Lew carry her stuff down to the car, but she couldn't seem to make her muscles move. It was too pleasant, standing here on the landing, watching a seagull drift down through the late-afternoon haze.

Her mind clicked off things to do. Get some groceries. Take her car in for a long-overdue tune-up. Pick up the photos of their Lake Tahoe wedding last weekend, more of an elopement, really, except that they'd taken the children along. Terri had looked so cute with flowers in her hair, and Kyle so grown-up in a junior tuxedo.

And she still needed to run by the *Herald*'s newly remodeled facility and collect a few reference books that, Steve had informed her, turned up in the rubble with her name on them.

She missed it a little, the pressure and excitement and stale air of the newsroom. It wasn't going to be quite the same, free-lancing out of the house she and Lew were buying in Santa Ana. But it meant she could be there when the children got home from school.

"Daydreaming again?" Lew swung up past the apartment that had been Madeleine's before she went back to France. "Or remembering?"

"Thinking about the future," Laura said. As she followed him inside, she added, "Do you ever wish Rita hadn't changed her mind? That you'd gotten the job after all?"

"Hell, no." Lew hefted a carton of bathroom gear. "We need a couple of years just to be a family. Besides, a lot of people think Fisher needs some strong opposition in the next primary."

The committee investigating his campaign funding had brought in its report three days ago, a mere slap on the wrist. The governor had got off, officially, but not in the minds of the public.

"Okay." Laura held out a can of warm Pepsi so he could take a sip. "I think I could handle a campaign."

"So do I," he said.

"And then, one of these days, I may write a book." Catching the look in his eye, she said, "Not *that* book. Nobody would believe it."

"I'm beginning to," Lew said. "All those leaders disappearing at once. There isn't any rational explanation, even to my skeptical mind."

"You'd be surprised," Laura said. Already, the newspapers and magazines were full of conspiracy theories and scientific speculation. For once, the tabloids made just as much sense. She'd particularly enjoyed the story headlined, I SAW A UFO CARRY OFF AYATOLLAH AL-HADASSI.

Laura picked up the last carton, called the children, and went out. At the bottom of the steps, she stopped at the mailboxes and used her key one last time, to check for mail. There was a fat envelope from Aunt Ellen. After collecting it, she dropped the key into the box as she'd arranged with the manager.

The children were buckling themselves into the backseat, and Lew slammed the trunk as soon as Laura tucked her carton inside. "Anything interesting?"

"Just Ellen," she said.

The radio came on as soon as the engine started. It was playing an excerpt from President Whiting's speech this morning at the swearing-in of former Speaker of the House Phillip Smithers as vice president. "I can't think of anyone better qualified to run this office while I'm attending the peace talks next month in Geneva. . . ."

Lew switched off the radio. "I think I've had about enough news for this century," he said.

Inside the envelope, Laura found a note from Ellen. *I'm so looking forward to visiting you as soon as you're settled,* her aunt had written. *And I'm feeling much better now. Maybe it's just as well I couldn't make the wedding. This way, we'll have time for a really nice visit.* A bad summer cold, worsened by inattention, had turned into bronchitis.

Oh, Ellen had written in her round, schoolgirl hand, *here's one last thing I found during my final poke around the attic. I thought it might mean something to you.*

As the car jounced over a railroad track, Laura unfolded a magazine article. It was entitled "Theologians Look at the Millennium," and bylined Gregory Evans. Next to his name, her father had scrawled a phone number and an address.

Something stirred way back in Laura's mind, an edge of red flame, a whiff of sulfur. She tensed. But it was gone, just as suddenly. She was hardly even sure it had been there.

There was *something* in her cells, fused and fixed, a permanent, well-controlled part of herself. Knowing it was there scared her sometimes. Other times, she felt good, remembering that she was strong enough to handle it. As strong as her father had managed to be, in the end.

Ahead, between the tangle of telephone poles and signs on Beach Boulevard, the sky shimmered a clear blue. Through the open window blew the familiar scents of brine and exhaust.

"Can I have an ice cream?" Kyle said from the backseat.

"Me, too!" Terri chimed in.

Lew slowed as they neared a Baskin-Robbins. "Well, we've got a few hours till dinner. What do you think, Mrs. Tarkenton?"

Ice cream wasn't really a nutritious food for growing youngsters. On the other hand, mothers had to be flexible.

"Sure," she said. "Why not?"

Daryl stared down at the files in disgust. Cruise Long, apparently murdered by that newspaper editor who had vanished under suspicious circumstances. Joe Pickard, killed by an unknown suspect, who must, they had concluded, have had plastic surgery to make him look like Joe, and who hadn't been seen hide nor hair of in the past month. Three women dead, one of them with Joe's fingerprints on her purse. There was nothing like unsolved and probably unsolvable cases to leave a bad taste in your mouth.

Daryl rubbed his hand over the back of his head. A little knot remained as a souvenir of his near-demise, but at least it didn't hurt anymore. God, he'd like to catch that bastard.

Will Machado was watching him from the next desk. Damn and double fucking damn, how had he managed to get Guinness to switch assignments? What kind of a fool wanted to be in Traffic when he could be in Detectives? Guinness always had been a pushover.

The phone rang. He stared at it balefully before answering on the third ring.

"Daryl?" Now there was a voice he hadn't heard in a few weeks, Swedish accent and all.

"Hi, Nina." No sense in being rude just because she hadn't given him the time of day after he got out of the hospital.

"Uh, I need to talk to you," she said.

"Fine. Talk."

"Now?"

"It's not tapped."

"Ya, but—" He could almost hear her shrug. "Okay. We have a little problem."

"*We* have a problem?"

"Ya," she said. "I'm—you know—knocked up."

It took him a minute to figure out she wasn't using some obscure Scandinavian slang. "You mean you're"—he lowered his voice quickly—"pregnant?"

"Ya," she said.

Machado was busy on the phone, thank God. "Well, it isn't mine," Daryl said. "I used safes, remember?"

"Except for that one night," Nina said.

Which night? Being thumped over the head had sure fuzzed things up. They'd been together twice, hadn't they? Or was it three times? "I always—I mean, I make a practice of—" Come to think of it, he wasn't absolutely sure he'd remembered every time.

"I haven't been with anyone else since July," Nina said. "And I got my period the beginning of August."

Well, he wasn't the kind of jerk to deny it. "What are you, er, planning to do?" Daryl didn't believe in abortion, but Swedish girls were supposed to be ultraliberal. It wasn't his place to tell her what to do with her life, right?

"Have it," she said promptly. "It's American, you know? It ought to be born here. But my visa runs out next month. I thought maybe you could help."

Daryl didn't like the feeling that came over him, that he was acting like a heel and Nina was being one hell of a good sport. "I didn't mean you should go through something like this alone," he said.

"I don't expect you to marry me." Was that a catch in her voice? "I can take care of myself, you know."

"Hey, it's my kid, too, right?" He couldn't quite picture one of those red-faced babies belonging to him, but he could imagine a little boy about, say, eight or nine, with sandy hair and a cocky grin. Wearing a baseball cap lopsided, and carrying a bat. Freckles, too.

Nina. Not exactly the kind of wife he'd always dreamed about, but there were worse things than getting married to a blond bombshell who liked sex any way she could get it. Maybe she was kind of a mental lightweight, but she ought to be a good mother. Most of the guys he knew, they didn't talk to their wives much, anyway.

Backyard barbecues. Little League. Yeah, he could get into that. Now that he thought about it, maybe that was what he'd been missing. Someplace to unwind when he got off work.

"Daryl?"

"Hey, yeah," he said. "How about if I come over tonight and we talk about the wedding?"

A brief pause. She wasn't going to turn him down, was she? "Really? You're sure?"

"Damn right," he said.

"You know," Nina said, "I'm sure it was that night when we did it ten times. It's kind of nice to think we made a child and it felt so good, too."

"Exactly," Daryl said, and wondered again if she'd been imagining it. Ten times?

Still, he felt kind of proud as he hung up the phone. A kid. Boy, that was a big responsibility. And a privilege, too. Somebody who'd look up to you, and live on after you, and give you grandchildren.

They were what made life special, children were.